CW01654066

# THE MOVE

Also by JP Delaney

*The Girl Before*

*Believe Me*

*The Perfect Wife*

*Playing Nice*

*My Darling Daughter*

*The New Wife*

# THE MOVE

JP DELANEY

QUERCUS

First published in Great Britain in 2026 by Quercus
Part of John Murray Group

1

Copyright © 2026 Shippen Productions Ltd.

The moral right of JP Delaney to be
identified as the author of this work has been
asserted in accordance with the Copyright,
Designs and Patents Act, 1988.

Lines on p. 212 taken from 'A Father's Advice'
by Mark Hanbury Beaufoy (d. 1922).

All rights reserved. No part of this publication
may be reproduced or transmitted in any form
or by any means, electronic or mechanical,
including photocopy, recording, or any
information storage and retrieval system,
without permission in writing from the publisher.

This book is a work of fiction. Names, characters,
businesses, organizations, places and events are
either the product of the author's imagination
or used fictitiously. Any resemblance to
actual persons, living or dead, events or
locales is entirely coincidental.

A CIP catalogue record for this book is available
from the British Library

HB ISBN 978 1 52944 875 7
TPB ISBN 978 1 52944 876 4
EBOOK ISBN 978 1 52944 878 8

Typeset in Swift by CC Book Production

Printed and bound in Great Britain by Clays Ltd, Elcograf S.p.A.

FSC
www.fsc.org
MIX
Paper | Supporting
responsible forestry
FSC® C104740

Papers used by Quercus are from well-managed forests and other responsible sources.

Quercus
Carmelite House
50 Victoria Embankment
London EC4Y 0DZ

John Murray Group
Part of Hodder & Stoughton Limited
An Hachette UK company

The authorised representative in the EEA is Hachette Ireland,
8 Castlecourt Centre, Dublin 15, D15 XTP3, Ireland (email: info@hbgi.ie)

# THE MOVE

*For a moment, she thought nothing was happening, that the scaffolding wasn't going to give, but the savage wind was helping her and she felt movement underfoot. She wrapped her arms round the metal corner bar and got her feet against the wall, putting her back into it, trying to ignore the huge clots of icy snow pelting her face, and with a sudden wrench she felt the scaffolding peel away from the house, ripped off by the wind, the metal poles flying like matchsticks, the wooden planks collapsing under her feet. She saw his look of incredulity and shock, and then they were both falling, in a blur of wood and metal, a cascade of spars and planks and debris, and she mentally braced herself for the impact that was about to come—*

# ONE

As it turned out, the house was lovely. No, Kate thought, more than lovely: it was spectacularly, breathtakingly perfect. She hadn't expected that, to be honest. The agent's particulars – such a quaint word for what was, these days, little more than a two-page printout and a listing on Rightmove – had been almost impossible to make sense of, even with the help of the floor plan. Rooms appeared to open into other rooms almost at random; there were two staircases; the kitchen windows looked out into the sitting room; upright oak beams were stranded in the middle of floors, like the ghosts of long-removed walls. But when they got there and actually saw it, it all made sense. Trade Cottage, it turned out, had originally been not one house but three, a small terrace of knapped flint built as accommodation for the retainers of a nearby estate. The estate had long since shrunk to the other side of the woods that bordered Trade Cottage's garden, though its traces still lay all around: the farm next to the house was very much a working one, its fields dotted with sheep and dung, but the rusted iron fences and guards around the trees hinted at a past grandeur as parkland. Even as they made their way up the dilapidated drive, Kate had been imagining the Mitford sisters hunting their ponies across it.

The agent, Damon, had got there before them, his spotless blue Tesla parked a discreet distance from the house so as not to detract from the wow factor of its façade – the big bay window at one end, the ancient oak porch at the other; the former topped by a wisteria, pendulous with blossom, the latter by the carved crest of the estate and a delicate climbing rose. As Matt parked their Kia alongside the Tesla, Tilly said wonderingly from the back seat, 'Is this really it?', and even Will looked up from the game he was playing on Matt's phone and muttered, 'Cool.'

They got out and walked slowly towards the front door. The outbuildings, about which the particulars had been a bit vague – possibly exhausted by the effort of breathlessly describing the house's interior: *As you ascend the second staircase towards the sumptuous main bedroom, dazzling views past wildflower-strewn woods await . . .* – looked to be substantial structures in their own right. Kate glimpsed a small barn, stables, and an open-fronted thatched shed containing a sit-down mower and a battered old Land Rover. That was good; converting one or two outbuildings into Airbnbs was the only way they could possibly make this work, even with the bonanza from Matt's earn-out and the sale of their house in Dulwich.

Damon must have seen them arrive – the door opened a moment before they could knock. 'Come in, come in,' he said, stepping back and beaming with almost proprietorial pride as they took in the utterly beautiful entrance hall – not large, but lined with manorial oak panelling. Kate tried to guess its age, but couldn't.

'The story is, a sea captain related to the Pelham family retired here in the 1840s – he was the one who had it converted into a single dwelling,' Damon was explaining. 'So some parts are late Georgian, some Victorian – although there's a bit in the middle that may be the remnants of an older building still. Tudor, quite possibly. The seller can tell you more – she's done loads of research on the place. Anyway, it's hardly a cottage, I know, but I guess when your frame of reference is Pelham House . . .'

'And the name?' Matt asked. 'Where did that come from?'

'Ah, yes – Trade Cottage, on Smugglers Lane,' Damon said with relish. 'Short for "Free Trade Cottage" originally, I understand. In the eighteenth century, the government slapped tariffs on imports of brandy and rum to pay for the Napoleonic Wars. Apparently, this was one of the main smuggling routes up from the coast, and the sea captain wasn't above taking a few barrels off his old naval contacts and selling them on. There's even a secret cellar under the dining room.'

'Hear that, Will? A secret cellar,' Kate said encouragingly, hoping their son wasn't being put off by all this talk of Tudors and Georgians. But when she turned to look, she saw he was hanging on Damon's every word.

'Come on through.' Damon opened another door – also oak, and also impossible to date; the latch, she saw, had been hand-hammered in a forge. 'It's a bit of a warren, but that's part of its charm. We'll say hello to the vendors, then I'm generally just letting people wander.'

So there had been other viewings already, Kate noted. It had only come on the market that week – they'd got an alert from the selling platform. Well, the interest wasn't surprising, given how unique it was. But no actual offers yet, or Damon would have told them.

A small passage – oddly misshapen, as if tunnelled round obstacles – led into a lovely light-filled sitting room. This was the room that had perplexing windows opening into it, but, she now saw, that was because it was actually an oak-framed structure that had been added to the rear of the house at a later date. The spaces between the beams were mostly glass; the view was of the large, pretty garden, but also beyond that, to rolling fields of grazing sheep. She was trying not to fall in love with the place – she'd had her hopes dashed so many times when they were looking in Dulwich, four years ago – but, at the thought of having her first coffee of the day in this room, overlooking that valley, her heart melted.

'Hello! Welcome!' a voice boomed. A tall, white-haired man was coming round a sofa towards them. He was using canes to support himself – even so, Kate noticed, both knees were buckling slightly – but was clearly determined to greet them properly. He had to fiddle with the sticks to get a hand free. When Kate took it, he clasped his other hand firmly over hers as well – as much for support, she thought, as out of hospitality: she could feel a slight tremor in his fingers. He had clearly once been handsome, possibly dazzlingly so; even now, a lock of white hair flopped fetchingly over one of his blue eyes as he pumped her hand vigorously.

'Oh, Paul, there's no need . . .' A slight woman jumped up from an armchair – that was the thing Kate noticed straight away, how she almost sprang from the chair, the agile movement of someone far younger than her neatly coiffed grey hair suggested her to be. 'Hello.'

'Nonsense! Guests!' the man – Paul, presumably – said cheerfully. He turned back to Kate. 'Normally I'd have a glass of champagne in your hand as soon as you walked through that door, but I suppose it's a bit early for that.'

Kate wondered if he meant a bit early in the day or a bit early in the process. Probably the latter, she decided. She knew some sellers liked to stick around for viewings, to answer questions or simply to keep an eye on things, but she'd never been called a guest before.

'Rosemary,' the woman said, indicating herself. 'And Paul. Please, make yourselves at home. Would you like a scone while you look round? I baked them this morning.' She turned to the agent. 'Damon?'

'I don't mind if I do,' Damon said happily. 'Particularly if there's some of that raspberry jam . . . ?'

'Masses!' Rosemary smiled at Kate. 'Do you make jam? I'm afraid you'd have to, living here. The fruit cage is far too large – we built it forty years ago, when we were younger and more sprightly – and we always get a glut.'

'Well,' Kate said apologetically, 'we live in London at the moment, so . . .'

'Oh, of course.' Rosemary turned to Will and Tilly. 'And what are *your* names? Any takers for a scone and raspberry jam while you go and choose your bedrooms?'

'It might be a bit soon for—' Kate interjected, but the children were already telling Rosemary their names, and she was pointing them in the direction of 'the back staircase, the one that leads all the way up to the attic, and then why don't you see if you can find the room with a pony in it.'

Kate watched them beetling off, already appearing somehow energised by the house, or perhaps the country air, or perhaps just Paul and Rosemary's effervescent welcome. As for choosing bedrooms – she worried about getting their hopes up, of course she did. They'd debated whether to even bring the children on a whole day of traipsing round viewings, but there was the problem of what to do with them if they didn't – and, besides, she wanted them to want this move too. Leaving London would be a wrench for Tilly and Will, despite the fact they were both, in their different ways, struggling where they were. It would be better if they were committed to it, even if it did take a while to find the right property.

Although, she thought dizzily, perhaps they already had.

As promised, Damon let them wander, while Paul and Rosemary stayed downstairs in the sitting room – Paul levering himself back into a chair with some difficulty, Kate noticed. She was surprised they were so relaxed about letting people just roam around their house. When she and Matt put Liphook Crescent on the market, the estate agent had been under strict instructions not to let viewers out of his sight. But Paul and Rosemary, it seemed, were more trusting.

The listing had called it 'a family home of character and charm', and for once that had been no exaggeration. From the children's heights proudly recorded in black felt-tip on a wall – each one signed and dated, all the way back to the 1980s; from the look of it, 'Jamie' was older than 'Tessa' by about eighteen months, the same age gap as there was between Will and Tilly – to the framed hand-drawn map of the house and garden in the loo, the sense of a childhood lived here to the full was palpable. The map's features were labelled in neat, childish handwriting: *Paul's Pool*, *Christmas-Tree Thicket*, *Jamie's Citadel*, *The Silver Brook*. It was signed *Tessa 1986*. The same feel was there in the enormous boot room – bigger even than the dining room – crammed with the detritus of a dozen outdoor pastimes: fishing rods, croquet mallets held together with electrical tape, ancient tennis racquets, shooting sticks, a plastic ball-thrower with a chewed tennis ball jammed into it, all stuffed into two huge old chimney pots, along with half a dozen walking sticks and a shepherd's crook. The tennis ball, she guessed, was for the grey-snouted black Lab which thumped its thick tail lethargically at her from its bed by the back door.

The kitchen, by way of contrast, was almost comically ugly: small and functional, with two fluorescent strip lights overhead, the countertops made of pale Formica. The only redeeming feature was the cream-coloured Aga, and even that had Dalmatian-like patches where the enamel had flaked off and revealed the black iron beneath. It was oil-powered, the listing had said – surely, therefore, the least climate-friendly cooking device on the planet, but one she instinctively yearned to keep. Could Agas be re-enamelled? Or, indeed, converted to electric? She made a mental note to google it on the way home. And, of course, it wouldn't stay here, in this room; it was the dining room that cried out to be made into a spacious kitchen-diner, while this poky little space would become a utility room . . . She was good at this, she knew, reconfiguring every place they'd ever lived in, from their first flat in grotty Camberwell to the four-bed semi they were selling now. And it was great that Trade Cottage hadn't been touched in decades. Matt, ever practical, might have objected if there'd been some expensive designer kitchen she wanted to rip out, but, as it was, she'd have free rein, their stretched finances permitting.

'Mummy! Mummy, we're going outside.' That was Tilly, still fizzing with excitement, dashing in and immediately out again. Behind her Kate glimpsed Will, also heading for the back door. It was great to see them so upbeat – Will, in particular, was capable of announcing he was bored and slouching back to the car after a few surly glances, but there was absolutely no sign of that here.

'Take Daddy,' she called after them, unsure what dangers might lurk in the garden – one of the photographs had shown a pond, complete with a small island for ducks and a rowing boat for getting to it – but Matt was ahead of her.

'Let's go right to the end and see what's in the field,' she heard him say as he followed them out, and she could tell from his voice that he, too, was excited.

She continued her tour alone. Upstairs, it was very much a house of two halves, with no interconnecting door or passageway between the children's bedrooms, up one staircase, and the main bedroom, up another. Checking out the latter, she couldn't help noticing that one of the nightstands was strewn with pill bottles. Paul's, presumably.

She went to the window to look at the view, which turned out to be even lovelier up here than it was from downstairs. At the end of the garden, beyond a belt of woods, farmland stretched for mile after mile. Off to her right, admittedly, was a huge green cliff of leylandii, but that was OK: it was far enough away not to overshadow the house, and, in any case, it gave them privacy from the property next door. On the other side, to her left, the woods had a faint shimmer of blue in them. *Wildflower-strewn*, indeed.

It was musty in the bedroom, and she longed to throw the window open, to lean out and gulp down that clean country air. But that would have felt discourteous to Paul and Rosemary, whose private space this was. When we own it, we can sleep with the windows open, she thought, and was surprised to note that it already felt like a foregone conclusion.

The bathrooms were as ancient as the kitchen – avocado-green baths that doubled as showers; vinyl shower curtains; sinks with spluttering taps that sported drooping moustaches of discoloration and limescale. It was as if the whole house had been stopped in time, a slumbering giant. But, again, that was all to the good: they could live with it perfectly happily while they renovated.

She realised she hadn't yet found the room with the big bay window she'd seen as they approached. Going back downstairs, she followed her sense of direction down a passage, the floor tiled in a black-and-white geometric pattern, the walls hung with painted oars. One, she saw, commemorated a victory for *Brasenose College 1st Torpid 1961*, whatever that was; among the crew's names was *No. 3 Paul Finch*. On the opposite wall, a similar oar recorded that, in 1994, Jamie Finch had rowed stroke for Balliol.

She walked into a room that turned out not to be the one she was looking for, but a second, smaller sitting room. There was a television, a comfortable mishmash of chairs around a small marble fireplace. And a huge, dappled rocking horse, with scarlet nostrils and real leather tack. Its sides were worn where little feet had kicked it into a gallop.

Going back into the corridor, she got her bearings again and went on. What had looked at first glance like an alcove, a counterpart to one opposite containing a floor-standing oriental vase, was, she now saw, a door, and the room she was looking for lay beyond it. She stepped inside.

The particulars – and the more she explored Trade Cottage's quirky, sprawling interior, the more appropriate that word seemed – had called this 'the study'. She'd scoffed inwardly at that – estate agents' 'studies', she'd generally found, were box rooms at best, cramped work-from-home cubbyholes at worst. But this was neither. Even 'study' undersold what was almost a small library, the walls on two sides lined with oak shelves filled with books. In the middle of the room sat a big pedestal desk, with a wheeled leather chair facing the window. 'Captain's chairs', they were called, she vaguely remembered. So perhaps this was where the sea captain himself had sat in his retirement, and the desk was where he'd spread his maps.

She realised that the bay window, too, had a nautical feel – it jutted out at each side, like the windows that projected over a man-of-war's stern. Yes, this had definitely been his favourite room, she decided, looking around, just as it would be hers. In such a room, with its view over the quiet front garden and drive, she might even be able to carve out a few hours a day to realise her long-held dream of writing something, once the children were settled. *I for this, and this for me* – she'd forgotten where she'd read those words, but it was exactly what she felt now: as if Trade Cottage was somehow choosing her, just as much as she was choosing it.

As she went to the window, she couldn't help glancing down at the sheets of writing paper neatly laid out on the desk. They were thank-you letters, she saw, written with a fountain pen, the signature a shaky but regal *R*. She bent closer to see who or what was being thanked, then jumped back as the door opened and Rosemary herself came in, holding a plate of scones.

'I see you've found Captain Pelham's cabin,' she said, with a smile. 'I always think it's the nicest room in the house.' She gestured at a small portrait Kate hadn't noticed before, hanging beside the door. It showed a short, thickset man in naval uniform. 'I like to imagine that his spirit still watches over the place, though Paul thinks that's sentimental nonsense.'

'The whole house is lovely,' Kate said truthfully. 'But, yes – there's something about this room, in particular.' She hesitated. 'It must be so hard to leave. Where are you going, if you don't mind my asking?'

Rosemary waved the question away. 'It's a wrench, of course it is, but it's time to move on. This house should have children running round it.' She nodded outside, to where Will had discovered a rope hanging from the elm tree that bordered the pond. 'Yours seem to have taken quite a shine to it already.'

'Do you have grandchildren?' It wasn't as intrusive a question as it might have been; all around them were framed photographs, including several of a tall, bearded man – Jamie, presumably – with a blonde woman and two dark-haired children.

Rosemary picked up the nearest one, her eyes softening as she looked at it. 'Yes. Hamish and Flora. But Jamie's something big at the IMF, so he's based in Washington. They come over every year, and of course we Zoom, but . . .' Her voice trailed off. 'The children have American accents now, which feels strange. And Tess never wanted children. She lives in Wales, on a sort of commune.'

There were many more pictures of Jamie and his family, Kate noticed, than of Tessa. And a whole shelf of him as a young man – Jamie in cricket whites, Jamie with a surfboard, Jamie brandishing a football trophy – flanking a single picture of Tessa in her matriculation garb.

'Jamie's a bit cross we're selling, actually,' Rosemary went on. 'But it's him who keeps telling us we have to have a wet room. And Paul will need a wheelchair soon. His Dalek wheels, he calls them – he's already been measured up. Really, a wheelchair in this house would be impossible.'

Kate nodded sympathetically. Trade Cottage was a house of many levels, with a step up or down into almost every room, and both staircases were narrow and steep.

'And the fact is, I'm not getting any younger.' Rosemary sighed. 'I think I'm doing pretty well for eighty-three – ' Here Kate nodded again; Rosemary had so much energy, Kate had assumed she was early seventies at most – 'But my bones are creaky now and I'm getting forgetful. So we're downsizing, to a lovely little bungalow.' She looked around wistfully. 'But I have been excessively fond of my cottage.'

'"There is always so much elegance, so much comfort about them",' Kate agreed.

Rosemary shot her a glance, clearly pleased Kate had picked up the reference. 'Oh, are you a Janeite, too? She's my guilty pleasure.

I take to my bed and reread *Sense and Sensibility* whenever I feel under the weather.'

'I'm like that with *Love in a Cold Climate*,' Kate confessed. 'And some of Dodie Smith. But I like Austen, too.'

Outside, Will was swinging on the rope, out over the duck pond and back in a wide looping spiral, lifting his knees high to avoid getting his feet wet. A part of Kate wanted to run out and stop him – the rope, if it had been there since Jamie and Tessa's day, must be forty years old at least, and the sludge-brown water was presumably full of duck poo – but something held her back. Rosemary was watching Will with an indulgent smile on her face, and the moment felt, somehow, like a kind of test.

When she didn't move, Rosemary's eyes came back to scrutinise her face, a strangely searching look.

'I do hope you buy it,' she said quietly. 'I mean, I'm sure you're looking at lots of other nice places too, but perhaps . . . Damon says, for the money we're asking, most people want something grander. We had someone yesterday who said the first thing he'd do is rename it Monkwood Manor. Can you imagine? Just throw away two hundred years of history, to make himself look posh. Like those awful people who buy themselves a title, or rename pubs so they sound like wine bars. But Damon thinks the right person might walk through the door and fall in love with it, just like we did, forty-odd years ago.'

You were meant to play it cool, Kate knew. Matt always said it was a bad negotiating tactic to appear too keen at a viewing. But something about Rosemary – the fact Kate genuinely liked her, for one thing – made her say, 'Well, I *do* love it. And I can tell that the children adore it. I'll have to talk to Matt, of course, and we'll need to do our sums. But I can see us being very happy here.'

Rosemary beamed, and was about to say something else when a noise in the corridor signalled the approach of the others – Tilly and Will bursting in first, followed after an interval by Matt and Paul. Matt was loitering discreetly by Paul's side, Kate saw, ready to catch him if his canes slipped. The children wanted to tell her excitedly about the lambs they'd seen in the field, and Paul and Matt were discussing irises – 'They're called Purple Knights,' Paul was saying, 'and they like a bit of grit every autumn –' and Matt was making a point of getting out his phone and noting that down, and she could tell from his body language that he liked Paul, and liked Trade Cottage, too.

'Well, darling,' Rosemary remarked, 'I don't know about you, but I'm very much hoping the house has found its rightful heirs.'

She was smiling, but was that the glint of a tear in her eye? It was hard to be sure, and, of course, older eyes like hers were more prone to watering.

'Not heirs, darling. We're not dead yet!' Paul said cheerfully. 'A new chapter, that's all.' He put his arms round her, but with the sticks in his hands he was clumsy; one swung round and hit her lightly on the back. 'How exciting!'

'Yes, of course,' Rosemary said, and Kate saw her discreetly blink the tear away. 'How very, very exciting.'

# TWO

She was still reeling as they went back to the car, intoxicated by the house's loveliness and the possibility it might become theirs. Matt shot her a questioning look, but she was too wrapped up in her thoughts to say anything. It was like when they left a cinema after a really good film, and that interval – the silence before one turned to the other and said, 'What did you think?' – was too precious to break.

Besides, she wanted to drink in Trade Cottage's exterior one more time. It was funny, she thought, turning to look at it again, how regular, even symmetrical it seemed from here, the even spacing of its windows giving no clue to the higgledy-piggledy warren on the inside.

Matt saw her looking, and glanced back too. The smile he gave her told her all she needed to know. But there was still the faff of getting the children into the back of the car and settled before they had a brief moment to themselves.

'Shall I cancel those other viewings?' he said in a low voice.

'No!' There were still too many things that could go wrong – a higher offer, a bad survey, a mortgage withheld for some reason. 'We've come all this way. And besides, we might need a backup.'

As if to underline her words, another car was already coming up the drive – a smart Range Rover, ninety grand's worth of metal if it was a penny. Damon was striding towards it, a welcoming smile on his face. Estate agents deliberately scheduled viewings so they'd overlap, she knew, to give the impression of a queue of eager buyers all ready to put in offers. But, to be fair, she and Matt had spent nearly an hour looking round and chatting to Paul and Rosemary about the village – which sounded lovely: there was a community-owned pub that did wood-fired pizzas, a shop, a thriving book club, an active parish council from which Paul had recently retired as chair – and why should Damon be expected to leave long gaps between his viewings on a weekend?

'I said we'd call him this evening,' Matt said, following her gaze. 'He knows we're interested, but I told him there are a couple of others we might make offers on. Just to keep him on his toes.'

She nodded. Of the two of them, Matt was the one more used to handling negotiations. He'd recently sold his start-up to a giant French gaming company, in a lucrative but incredibly complicated deal that had taken months to broker.

'Don't worry, I won't let us lose it,' he added quietly.

Tilly and Will asked if they were going to buy it almost as soon as they drove off, of course, and of course they had to say, 'Well, possibly; nothing's certain yet.' But it meant every other property they looked at was viewed by the children with grudging suspicion: surely their parents weren't going to be so stupid as to favour this dumb place over Trade Cottage? Will started groaning every time they turned into a new driveway, and even Tilly became quiet and morose.

Some of the other places did have advantages. One was within walking distance of a station, for example. For Matt – required by the terms of his deal to be in the office at least three days a week for the next eighteen months, after which he'd receive another, even larger, lump sum and be free to walk away – that would shave twenty minutes off an arduous commute. Another had a swimming pool; another, a Smallbone kitchen. But none of them came remotely close to Trade Cottage's dilapidated charm, or those incredible views. Matt's mind, like hers, was clearly still running on it; all their conversation, as they slogged along the Hampshire roads to look at other properties, was actually about Trade Cottage. So when she asked, 'How was the garden? I didn't get to see most of it,' he knew immediately she didn't mean the garden of the house they'd just visited.

He pulled a face. 'A bit sad, unfortunately.'

She glanced at him, concerned. 'In what way?'

'It's got out of hand. Paul told me a gardener comes one day a week, but he only does grunt stuff, like mowing and clipping. Some of the borders are turning into jungles.'

'Could it be rescued?'

'Absolutely. Paul's done a beautiful job with the design.'

She smiled at him. 'You liked him, didn't you?'

Matt slowed down to let someone into the traffic. 'Yes. I mean, there's all that jovial hail-fellow-well-met stuff. But he's also sharp as a tack. You know he had his own educational-publishing business? He sold out to a big conglomerate too. I told him about our set-up with the French, and he asked some very astute questions. I bet he was a really effective chair of that parish council.'

'What about the outbuildings? Did you manage to get a look at those?'

Matt nodded. 'Loads of potential. We'd need permission – it's a listed building – but Damon said, if we use the right architect, it shouldn't be a problem to convert a couple. Plenty of other people round there have done something similar.'

'Would you want one? For an office, I mean?' She kept her voice neutral; she was dreading him saying he quite fancied the captain's cabin.

He glanced at her. 'I thought, maybe, the attic room? If that's OK by you. The views up there are to die for, and it's not like we'd be short of bedrooms.'

She smiled at him, relieved. 'Perfect. And I bagsy the study.'

'Incidentally,' he added, 'I don't think we should mention the Airbnb thing to Damon just yet.'

'Why not?'

'Paul told me one of the viewings was "a bloody developer". He sounded quite indignant about it. Admittedly, the guy was talking about hiving off most of the garden for two new houses, but I don't think they like the idea of too much changing.'

'OK. So now there's the million-dollar question: how high do we go?' They'd gone to view Trade Cottage on the understanding it was over their budget, and that, even if they liked it, they'd need to offer under the asking price.

Matt checked on the kids in the mirror. They were both asleep, worn out by the sheer number of viewings.

'I think we give them the full amount,' he said quietly. 'Fuck it. We can't risk letting it slip through our fingers.'

She felt a surge of amazement. 'We can do that?'

'It'll be tight,' he admitted. 'But I can probably leverage some more out of the company. We might have to renovate in stages, though. Maybe do some of the work ourselves.'

'I'd be up for that. Bringing a house like that back to life – it'd be fun.' She'd been feeling guilty about giving up her admittedly rather uninspiring part-time job in HR when they moved out of London, and the Airbnb enterprise was going to take ages to set up.

'Shall I call him now?' Matt indicated the car's phone controls. 'Or do you want to think about it?'

She never made big purchases quickly. Whether it was a holiday, a sofa, or a gadget for the kitchen, she invariably spent days researching the different options, looking at reviews, driving herself half mad trying to work out what the right decision was. Matt used to joke that she'd needed to make a spreadsheet before she said yes to marrying him. But, for some reason, this – probably the biggest purchase they'd ever make – seemed like a no-brainer. She'd fallen for Trade Cottage hook, line and sinker, a coup de foudre quite unlike anything she'd experienced before.

She nodded. 'Go on, then.'

He tapped at the controls. She felt a sudden pang of nerves as the ringing tone filled the car. Then she heard Damon say cheerily, 'Hello, there.'

Matt explained that they were offering the full asking price for Trade Cottage. There was a slight pause before the estate agent responded.

'I was just about to call you, actually. The last viewing has also offered at the asking price. Did it right then and there. The vendors are pleased, naturally, but they specifically asked that I let you know.'

She felt as if she'd fallen off a cliff. Next to her, Matt mouthed a furious, '*Fuck*.'

When they didn't immediately say anything, Damon added, 'In the circumstances, I think the best thing is to go to full and final offers. With a cut-off in the middle of next week, in case any more potential buyers come out of the woodwork.'

'Sealed bids, in other words,' Matt said resignedly.

'Exactly. It's the fairest way, in a situation like this. Everyone submits their maximum, and the vendors make a decision based on that.'

'These other buyers,' Kate interjected, 'have they sold their own house yet?'

'Yes. Like you, they should be able to move pretty quickly.'

*Damn.* 'Have they got a mortgage in place?'

'An in-principle one, yes, also like yourselves. But they have the benefit of being in a smaller chain, and they've already got a solicitor.'

'We'll get on to ours first thing Monday,' Matt said immediately.

'Great. Well, I'll obviously let you know if anything changes—'

'How much would it take,' Matt said desperately, 'to take this whole sealed-bid thing off the table? Some kind of pre-empt?'

When Damon spoke again, it was with a touch of froideur, as if Matt was suggesting doing something faintly improper with his filthy lucre. 'I really don't think that's the best way forward, certainly not as far as the sellers' interests are concerned. And you should know that the other party just asked me the exact same question.'

They drove the rest of the way home gutted. Kate could feel Trade Cottage slipping from her, like a mirage of a life that would now never be lived. If only those other buyers had come down with food poisoning and cancelled, or had a blowout on the way to the viewing, or been in a crash . . . She suddenly realised she'd just wished some perfectly innocent people into a traffic accident, and felt bad about that; but, really, what were the chances?

'We should write a letter,' she said suddenly.

Matt glanced at her. 'Who to?'

'The sellers. Alice and Ted did it. Their house went to sealed bids, and they'd reached their absolute limit, so they added a letter saying how much they loved the place and all the things they could picture themselves doing there, plus how important it was to live close to Ted's elderly parents. And it worked.'

'Really?' Matt was frowning. 'If I had to choose between a nice letter or another ten grand, I know which I'd take.'

'Maybe. But what if the difference was less than ten grand? Besides, Paul and Rosemary are sentimental about that house – they want it to go to a family who'll enjoy it the way theirs did. And, yes,' she said, raising her hand to forestall his objection, 'those other buyers probably have a family too. But I think they really liked us – Paul and Rosemary, I mean. After all, we liked them, and things like that are often mutual, aren't they? "The house has found its rightful heirs" – you can't get plainer than that. And the fact they straight away asked Damon to tell us – I think they *want* us to have it.'

'So much they'd knock a chunk off their old-age savings?' Matt said dubiously. 'I think we just have to bid as much as we can afford.'

'Yes.' Kate nodded. 'As much as we can afford, and then a bit more. But I'll write a letter, too.'

# THREE

The next few days were agony. There was a particular cruelty about sealed bids, she thought to herself more than once, in that you were really bidding against yourself – one minute telling yourself an extra ten thousand would surely do it, the next that it would be crazy to let it get away for less than twenty. In any case, the fact there were two buyers after it proved Trade Cottage had been undervalued, so it was worth offering even more – say, thirty, or even forty . . . All the arguments and counterarguments were in your own head, as were the fantasies of actually living there. And the sums involved were so enormous! When had this become normal for them, she tried to remember – thinking in millions and hundreds of thousands, instead of pounds and pence? But, of course, they'd been lucky: the boom in London property values had boosted their net worth like a tide floating a boat. It wasn't as if they were wealthy people, not really. They still struggled to afford a villa abroad in school holidays, and, as for the schools themselves, even before the addition of VAT, private ones had been out of reach. And their mortgage was already colossal. She shopped at Aldi as well as Waitrose, bought clothes from Joe Browns and M&S as well as Jigsaw and Boden, and, until their move, would continue to work part-time around the children's schedules. In the early days of Dulwich, they'd even put their spare room on Airbnb, which was how she knew she was good at hosting. And Matt had worked incredibly hard for his buyout. They both had – she and the other wives had jokingly called their WhatsApp group 'Tech Widows' because of all the late nights and lost weekends. Parents' evenings, school plays, even pick-ups and drop-offs were all last-minute scrambles. It was one of the reasons she'd suggested this move. Matt had always wanted a proper garden, and she was hoping the lure of a family home in the country would tempt him to a better work–life balance, once the start-up was fully sold.

Now, he did the sums over and over, adjusting numbers in a spreadsheet and wincing at the results. They looked at other houses online – ones that were already sold, this time, researching what they'd gone for. There was no point in offering more for Trade Cottage if the mortgage company rejected it as overpriced. And they tried, desperately, not to become any more emotionally invested than they already were. By unspoken agreement, there was no more discussion of what they might do, what changes or colour schemes they might implement. But, secretly, Kate couldn't resist getting Trade Cottage's listing up again on her phone sometimes, tracing the floor plan with her finger, revisiting the rooms in her head, one by one.

She started writing the letter to Paul and Rosemary on Monday, while Matt was at work and the children were at school. It seemed like the only concrete thing she could do. Besides, she wanted to give herself time to get it right, anticipating doing multiple drafts before the deadline, which had been set at noon on Wednesday.

She began by explaining why they were looking to move, hinting at the children's problems and what living in a place like Trade Cottage might do for them. And then she simply described all the things about the house she'd loved, from the clubby panelling in the entrance hall to the old rocking horse in the playroom. She talked about how, once she was back in London, she'd realised Trade Cottage had felt like a ship, cramped but comfortable, with everything in its place and in proportion, and how connected that made her feel to its original owner. *We even love the fact it isn't particularly grand*, she wrote. *It feels unpretentious, and easy, and welcoming – somewhere a guest would instantly feel at home.* But, most of all, she came back to the children, and how happy they'd be there: how she could imagine them splashing in the Silver Brook, and playing in Paul's Pool, and maybe even discovering and rebuilding Jamie's Citadel, if it was still there in the woods. She explained that she and Matt were offering as much as they possibly could, and maybe even a bit more, and that was the only reason the offer wasn't even bigger.

The words flowed from her fingers, and when she reread it, she couldn't see a single word she'd change.

She showed it to Matt that evening. He read it in silence. She was scared he might pooh-pooh the whole thing, or tell her she was being too emotional about what was, at the end of the day, a financial transaction. But she was ready to fight her corner. She felt deeply, instinctively, that this was the right approach.

He reached the end and thought for a moment. She waited on tenterhooks.

'It's brilliant,' he said at last. 'Don't change a thing.'

As he handed it back, he added, 'You do realise what this is, don't you? You've written a love letter to their house.'

On Wednesday, Matt worked from home, emailing their offer, the letter, proof of funds and their solicitor's details at exactly 11.30 a.m. In the end, they'd offered four per cent above the asking price – a sum considerably larger than Kate earned in a year.

They followed up with a phone call, but Damon was non-committal: he'd speak to the vendors that afternoon, he said, and get back to them when there was news. The only thing he let slip was that there were now three parties interested, one of whom had put in their bid the day before.

And then they just had to wait. Sellers sometimes took days or even weeks to decide, Damon had warned; sometimes they needed to consult family members, or wanted to see further evidence of funds, or even took the house off the market altogether. But in the event, it was less than an hour before Matt's phone rang, and she could tell, simply by the way he looked at the screen, who was calling.

He answered tersely. 'Hi. Yes, great, thanks. What's the news?'

As he listened to the answer, he turned towards her, and she saw he was beaming.

'Hang on, I'm putting you on speaker.'

Damon's voice came on: 'I was just saying to Matt, Kate, it's good news. Your offer's been accepted.'

Kate let out a whoop. Her throat had been so tight, it came out as a strangled cry: a high-pitched ululation of triumph, unintentionally primal and blood-curdling, which Damon was polite enough to ignore.

They briefly talked about next steps, but it was all straightforward: the solicitors could get to work right away.

'All right, mate, tell me,' Matt said as the conversation was winding up. 'How much were we ahead of the other bidders? We're not going to back out, I promise. I'm just curious.'

'Well, that I couldn't tell you,' Damon replied. 'Because, as it happens, you weren't the highest bidder. Not even the second highest, in fact. Congratulations – looks like you played a blinder with that letter.'

# FOUR

After that, they entered a sort of limbo. Their solicitor started doing the searches; he'd also sent the vendors a list of questions, he said, some of which might take a bit of digging to answer. The mortgage company gave their blessing, which was a big relief. Getting the extra money out of Matt's company was trickier, but, in the end, they let him have an advance on the next tranche of buyout as a goodwill gesture. A structural survey came back with a long list of things that would need addressing – unsurprisingly, given that Trade Cottage hadn't been renovated for decades – but nothing that was a deal-breaker. The biggest was some longstanding leaks in the roof that had rotted the timbers underneath. A developer friend who Matt consulted suggested they get a quote for replacing them, then try to get that amount knocked off the sale price. But it was going to be a relatively small sum, and it would have seemed churlish, as the underbidders, to start haggling now.

Most of all, though, it seemed very strange not to be seeing anything of Rosemary and Paul. They'd been such a big part of the magic of the house, Kate realised – Paul's booming hospitality,

Rosemary's warmth and poise. She wondered if they'd keep in touch after they moved to that bungalow they'd mentioned. She hoped so. She had visions of showing Rosemary the new kitchen-diner a year from now, the re-enamelled and electrified Aga at its heart, and seeing the amazement and approval on the other woman's face.

'I'm going to ask Damon if we can go and measure up for curtains,' she told Matt impulsively.

He seemed surprised. 'Isn't it a bit soon for that?'

'Not really. Those old windows will all be non-standard sizes, and made-to-measure curtains can take months. Besides, it'll be good to see Rosemary and Paul again. To thank them properly, I mean.' Damon had already passed on her and Matt's effusive thanks, but it wasn't the same as doing it in person.

'OK,' he said distractedly. He was scrolling on his phone as he spoke, flagging and deleting emails. It was the only way to keep on top of his inbox, she knew, constantly chipping away at it like this, but since the acquisition it felt as if a whole new stream had been added to the deluge – the new owners were demanding their money's worth, sometimes in French. She longed for the time when he'd be fully hers again – hers and the children's.

'D'you want to come too?' she asked.

He shook his head. 'We're in the middle of merging our APIs. Tell them I'm really looking forward to moving in, though.'

She called Damon, who sounded positively cheerful at the prospect of speaking to Rosemary and Paul again. He got back to her within a few hours. Measuring the windows was absolutely no problem, he reported; Rosemary had offered a couple of dates, both a few weeks away. Kate was a little disappointed it wasn't sooner, but took the earliest one, anyway.

When the day came, she drove down to Hampshire with a tape measure on the seat next to her and a song in her heart. It was the first week of July, and the summer, which had taken forever to get going, was finally hotting up. She turned off the air con and opened the windows, enjoying the warm air mussing her hair.

When she reached Trade Cottage, she went up the drive slowly, as much to savour the new thrill of ownership as to avoid the pot-holes. This incredible place was going to be theirs! She wondered if she'd ever get so used to this that she'd take it for granted. Surely not. Surely the reverse would happen, and this sight – the house coming into view from behind the garden wall of speckled flint, matching the building beyond it – would make her spirits soar even more once it was her long-time companion. But, for now, she felt both nervous and excited, almost as if she was about to meet a lover.

She parked where Damon had at the viewing – it would still have felt presumptuous to pull up next to the house. Rosemary was already stepping out of the front door, beaming at her and waving.

It felt natural to give her a hug. 'It's so lovely to see you again. Trade Cottage too, of course.'

'And you,' Rosemary said, equally warmly. She glanced at the car, and a shadow crossed her face. 'Aren't the children with you?'

'No – they don't break up for another two weeks.'

Rosemary looked surprised. 'Oh! Someone told me . . . but perhaps it's different in London. Where are you going to send them, by the way? Townley's still has a good reputation, though I hear it's become more academic since Tess and Jamie were there.'

Kate shook her head. 'Actually, they're going to the local state schools. They've got great Ofsted ratings – not that ratings are everything, of course, but we went to the open days and they seem fantastic.'

It had been one of the things that had first sold them on the area, even before they'd found Trade Cottage. Good primaries were one thing, but the combination of a good primary and a good secondary was as rare as hen's teeth in London, and family homes in those catchments commanded huge premiums. It had been another reason to move out – if they were going to buy somewhere new anyway, she'd argued, and find extra money to do it, why not make a complete change? And she'd felt, instinctively, that schools in the country were going to be friendlier, with less of the terrible knife crime, drugs and rape cultures that seemed to be afflicting so many London academies just now.

'We can't afford private, in any case – we stretched ourselves pretty thin to buy this place,' she added, then mentally kicked herself; she didn't want to sound as if she was complaining. 'Though it's worth every penny, of course. And you were so incredibly generous in accepting our offer. I still can't quite believe we're going to be living here.'

Rosemary beamed again – complimenting Trade Cottage, Kate realised, was always going to be the way to her heart. And if the older woman was disappointed Tilly and Will hadn't been able to come too, she hid it quickly.

'Well, do bring them next time. Matt too, of course – Paul's dying to talk to him about the garden. Now, come round – it's so nice today, we're outside.'

She led Kate round the side of the house to a flagstone terrace. It was a suntrap, but above the stone table a honeysuckle spread its tendrils across an artfully positioned fan of wires, providing partial shade. The sun was bringing out the fragrance; as they approached, Kate caught a gorgeous cascade of sweetness.

Paul was already there, sitting in a wooden garden chair. He started to struggle to his feet, but Kate stopped him, bending down to kiss his cheek.

'Marvellous to see you,' he grunted. He gestured at the table, where a bottle of Pol Roger sat in a cooler, a napkin wrapped neatly around its neck like a scarf. 'Now we *are* celebrating.' He reached for a glass, but his hand shook and he knocked it over. 'Darling, would you?' he asked tersely.

Rosemary took the bottle and filled three of the four glasses. There was a jug of squash, too, and Kate felt a stab of guilt that they'd clearly assumed Matt and the children would be coming too – had probably chosen the date deliberately, in fact: this was the first week of holidays for private schools, which always broke up earlier. Never socially confident, she was afraid her lone self might bore them. Or, worse still, that she might gabble at them non-stop, as she sometimes did when she was nervous.

Trade Cottage, she thought. I must talk about the house, then I'll make an excuse to go and start measuring.

As Rosemary handed her a glass, Kate said, 'The estate agent mentioned you'd done lots of research about the house's history.'

'Well, that's an understatement,' Paul said jocularly. 'She's written a whole book about it.'

'Wow.' Kate was always impressed by anyone who'd written an actual book.

'Oh, nonsense,' Rosemary said, waving the comment away. 'I did some research and made a few notes, that's all. Which I now seem to have mislaid, annoyingly.'

'That's the real reason we're moving,' Paul added. 'So we'll find those bloody notes.'

Rosemary said nothing, but her smile was slightly brittle.

Paul raised his glass. 'To Trade Cottage, and all who sail in her.'

Kate dutifully echoed the toast, then took a sip. She mustn't drink too much on an empty stomach, she reminded herself. But it was very good champagne.

On the table, alongside a plate of home-made cheese straws – unsurprisingly, they turned out to be delicious – was a bowl of papery pods, bright chartreuse green, each one encasing what looked like a seed. 'What are those?' she asked.

'Ah! See if you can guess,' Paul said happily. 'I'll give you a clue. They're edible, and they come from this garden.'

He offered her the bowl. She took one and peeled off the papery skin – it reminded her of those sweets they'd had when she was little, sherbet flying saucers – before cautiously popping the seed into her mouth. It was softer than she'd expected, almost pea-like, and surprisingly sweet, redolent of green leaves and hazelnut. She nodded her approval.

'You can boil them, put them in salads, or eat them raw,' he said proudly. 'Now, what plant do you think they're from?'

She dredged up some long-ago snippet from a nature documentary. 'Are they by any chance from the wych elm?'

'Good Lord!' Paul doffed an imaginary cap at her. '*Chapeau*, my dear Kate, *chapeau*. There's very few of our guests get that one right. Yes, they're called samaras. The tastiest ones come just before the new year's leaves start to grow, but these late ones are still delicious.' There was a tiny pause before he added quietly, 'Strange to think this'll be our last ever lot.'

'But extra points,' Rosemary added, 'for spotting that it's a wych elm.'

Paul pointed his cane at his wife. 'Before Kate goes, darling, you must show her where the wild garlic grows.' He turned to Kate. 'It'll be over now, of course, but there's a terrific spot just inside the wood. Rosemary makes a famous pesto with it. Wild garlic leaves, olive oil, salt and a few walnuts, all whizzed up in a blender. Pop it in the freezer, and you've got the taste of spring all year long.'

'It makes a lovely cheat's dip at parties,' Rosemary added. 'Mix it with Hellmann's and some grated parmesan. Then just open a box of breadsticks and let people tuck in.'

On they went, back and forth, eager to impart every scrap of their knowledge about Trade Cottage and its surroundings. For Kate's part, she was just as eager to receive it. She imagined having a party here herself one day, serving wild garlic pesto in this very spot, while their friends drank gin and tonics and their kids ran free in the vast garden.

'And you must tell Kate about the covenant we're imposing,' Paul added.

'Covenant?' she echoed, suddenly alarmed. It had been one of the things the solicitor had warned them he'd need to check – whether previous owners had imposed any legal restrictions on the property.

'Yes. Anyone who lives here has to abide by the house rule.' He tapped his glass. 'At least one bottle of champers in the fridge at all times!'

'Oh,' she said, relieved. 'Well, we'll try. We're not really massive drinkers, but . . .'

Rosemary got to her feet – again, Kate was amazed by how lithely she moved for her age. 'Why don't we go down to the wood now, and I'll show you where Paul meant?'

'I should probably get on with measuring up,' Kate said reluctantly, glancing up at the house. She would have loved to have walked down to the wood – she still hadn't explored the whole length of the garden – but the curtains really did need to be measured, and Trade Cottage must have had a dozen windows on this side alone.

'Well, about that.' Rosemary sat down again. 'We've been thinking. It just seems ridiculous to take the curtains with us. After all, it's not as if we're going to use them – the bungalow has electric blinds. Why don't you have them, and then there won't be any rush to get new ones made before you move in?'

'Really? That's extraordinarily generous of you,' Kate said, taken aback.

Rosemary shrugged. 'And there are a few other bits and pieces that, when we thought about them, really seemed to belong here, at Tray. You mentioned the way the vase sits in that alcove, for example.'

Kate thought back. It had been when they were in the captain's study that time, chatting. She'd glanced through the open door and commented on the fact they'd found a floor-standing vase exactly the same shape as the alcove behind it. It had been a chance remark, nothing more, a compliment on the subtle elegance with which Rosemary and Paul had furnished their home. 'God, I hope you didn't think—'

'No, no, of course not.' Rosemary waved the remark away. 'The thing is, you're right – wherever we put that vase, it's never going to fit as well as it does here. And we'll think that every time we look at it, which is a bit sad – completely the wrong attitude to be taking to our next adventure. It's not like it's even worth much – we had it valued for insurance once and were rather disappointed.' She glanced at Paul. 'What did the man say it was, darling? I can never remember.'

'Meiji period,' Paul said. 'Roughly Edwardian. They knocked them out by the dozen, apparently.'

Rosemary nodded. 'So there you are. That's yours too, if you'd like it, and there are probably a few other things we can think of, as well.'

'Well, if you're absolutely sure,' Kate said anxiously. 'We should give you something for it—' But both Paul and Rosemary were already making vigorous noises of disagreement.

'It's incredibly generous of you,' she repeated, rather feebly.

'Nonsense. Just being practical.' Rosemary stood up. 'Now, shall we take that walk?'

# FIVE

Kate drove back to London feeling very different, her nervy apprehension replaced by a sated, drowsy bliss. All her senses felt fulfilled, the way they sometimes did after sex or a really good massage. She wondered if that feeling, too, would wear off once she actually lived at Trade Cottage. But perhaps – again, like sex – familiarity would bring its own sense of contentment.

She was aware that she was anthropomorphising the house – romanticising it, even. But it had so much presence, somehow, so much charisma, that it was impossible to think of it as simply an arrangement of building materials. And Rosemary, she'd noticed, had talked about it in a similar way. As they'd walked down the garden, the older woman had paused and looked back wistfully. From there – the wych elm on one side, that big wall of leylandii on the other – it looked particularly beautiful, a picture-perfect cottage framed by its surroundings.

'Is it awful, to love a block of stone as much as one loves a person?' She gave a slight laugh. 'Paul always used to say he needn't worry about me having affairs – I was far too besotted with our house.'

Kate wasn't quite sure how to respond to such frankness, though she felt honoured by the intimacy it implied. 'Well, I promise we'll look after it for you.'

Rosemary nodded. 'I know you will.' Turning to look up at the house again, she said thoughtfully, 'Paul calls it "she" – like a ship, I suppose. But I've always felt Tray's male.' She glanced at Kate, a little shamefacedly. 'The children caught me kissing it once. A proper smacker, on one of the outside walls. They made such fun of me. I told them they were too young to understand what it's like to love a place – *really* love it, I mean. I think it's something you need to grow into.'

'Well, I *do* understand,' Kate said. 'And I swear I'll snog Trade Cottage whenever it – he – feels the need.'

Rosemary laughed, and they continued on towards the trees at the bottom of the garden.

'Do you actually own this wood?' Kate asked. 'The solicitor sent the Land Registry plans over with the other papers, and it looked as if you don't. Has he got that wrong?'

'Oh – no, it belongs to Pelham Park. It runs with Gordon's tenancy – that's the farmer. But he's not bothered, not unless there's pheasants in there, which is only around Christmas. Besides, he's a sweetheart. Give him a bottle of Bells every year and you can basically do what you like. Will's not too old for dens, is he?'

'I'm not sure,' Kate said doubtfully. 'I hope not. A den sounds much healthier than a Nintendo Switch.'

'Jamie was still making dens at fourteen. Except by then they were called forts and they had trenches and fortifications – he and his pals used to arm themselves with BB guns and stage mock battles for them. The trenches might still be there, if Will looks. What about Tilly? Is she into ponies?'

'Well, again – it would have been difficult in London . . .'

'Put her up on Auriel.' Seeing Kate's look of incomprehension, Rosemary added, 'The rocking horse. She can learn to hold the reins before she sits on the real thing. Or if you don't want the hassle of a pony of your own, get Gordon to shove a couple of ewes in the paddock, to keep the grass down. Oh, and see if he'll let the children help with lambing. He'll probably say yes, if you ask nicely and they're sensible. It means a few late nights, but it's something they never forget.'

Dens, ponies, lambing . . . It was such a blur of lovely things that it was only as she reached the M25 that Kate realised Rosemary must be giving them the rocking horse, too. Such generosity – but, of course, Auriel would be out of place in a bungalow, and from the sound of it, it wasn't the kind of thing Jamie or Tessa would have any use for, given how old Jamie's children were now.

She felt a sudden stab of anxiety. What if they couldn't live up to all this? Will might shun the woods in favour of video games and mooching around; Tilly might decide horses were boring and lambing gross; Kate herself might never master parmesan straws or wild garlic pesto.

But at least they'd have the opportunity, she thought.

There'd been another curious moment as she and Rosemary walked back up to the house. The famous wild garlic spot had turned out to be just a rather ordinary patch of earth beneath some beech trees – 'You can't miss it, in any case,' Rosemary said dismissively. 'Just come into the woods when the first bluebells appear and follow your nose. I don't know why Paul was making such a fuss.' Kate realised with a shiver of pleasure that Rosemary had agreed to show her mainly because she wanted some time with Kate on her own. We really are almost becoming friends, she'd thought. Or, at least, Rosemary has taken a shine to me. The realisation had given her a little jolt of confidence.

They'd gone back up by a slightly different route. Off to the side, where it didn't impede the view, was a whole area of garden Kate had barely realised was there: a small orchard, the branches of the trees already festooned with fruit; an overflowing compost heap; a small greenhouse with several broken panes. And, not far from the leylandii, a palisade of wood and chicken wire. That must be the fruit cage Rosemary had mentioned. Kate glimpsed raspberry canes, some bushes she couldn't identify, some strange-looking upturned pots that she dimly thought might be rhubarb forcers.

'How about your parents, Kate?' Rosemary had said, pausing for a moment – perhaps for a rest; the incline wasn't steep, but they'd been walking for a good fifteen minutes, and in all that time she hadn't slowed up once, or showed any other signs of age. 'Where are they in the picture?'

It was such a direct question, so guilelessly asked, that for a moment Kate was almost tempted to confide in her. It would have been a relief to talk about it, and she was already certain Rosemary would be a good listener. And it would, to some extent, have reciprocated the intimacy Rosemary had been bestowing on her.

But she'd only met Rosemary twice – would it be a faux pas to overshare so soon? Kate's woes about her mother would surely seem insignificant to someone whose husband had a degenerative illness and who was having to move out of her beloved house to care for him. People of that generation believed in stiff upper lips and getting on with things. The last thing Kate wanted was to come across as some bleating snowflake.

So she only said, 'My parents divorced when I was twelve. I don't see much of either of them now. And Matt's parents are lovely, but they're up in Northumberland. He's the youngest, and his siblings all live nearer, so it's their kids who see more of them. But I'm sure they'll come and visit. It'll be lovely to have enough room.'

Rosemary nodded, and for a moment Kate thought she was going to say something else. But then a shaggy old tennis ball landed at their feet and the fat Labrador came lolloping round the corner after it.

'Oh – Biddy, come here.' Rosemary bent down and retrieved the now rather soggy ball from the dog's mouth. 'I keep telling Paul not to use the thrower – it's bad for their hips – but he says it's better than no exercise at all. And I don't have the time, what with everything else that's been going on. Poor old Biddy hasn't had a proper walk in ages.' She suddenly took a breath, as if hit by a twinge of pain, and looked up at the house, and with a flash of insight Kate realised that walking the dog had been Paul's thing, and that Biddy hadn't always been fat and under-exercised, and that what she'd just witnessed was a well-concealed moment of grief – grief for Paul, for Biddy, for the house, for this whole idyll of life at Trade Cottage that Rosemary was so selflessly parcelling up and handing on to Kate – and she was even more glad she hadn't said anything about her own, relatively minor, family issues.

They reached the terrace, where Paul was still sitting in his chair, waving the ball thrower like a conductor's baton. He made Kate describe all the things she'd seen, commenting enthusiastically on each one, then pressed her to have another glass of champagne. Reluctantly, she'd said no and taken her leave, but not before she and Rosemary had exchanged contact details and she'd promised to come again before the move.

When she reached the end of Trade Cottage's drive, she had to take a left and then another one to get back to the main road. At the junction was a big modern gate, the sort you couldn't see through, between two brick pillars. One of the pillars had an intercom on it. That must be Trade Cottage's neighbour, she realised, the house whose garden backed on to that great wall of leylandii, although from here the building itself wasn't visible. Still basking in the warm glow of her afternoon with Rosemary and Paul, she thought it would be polite to go and introduce herself. She pulled over and went up to the intercom – it was a Ring video doorbell, she noticed, the distinctive blue circle glowing bright; one of their neighbours in Dulwich had one, so he could buzz delivery drivers in with his phone. She pushed the button and waited, but there was no reply. She'd try again the next time she was here, she decided.

# SIX

But, in the event, there wasn't a next time – at least, not until after they moved in. The conveyancing, which had been crawling along so slowly, suddenly shifted up a gear. A series of complicated questions about Trade Cottage's oil tank were resolved to both solicitors' satisfaction. Contracts were exchanged, a date fixed for completion. They would be in by the beginning of August, which was perfect – the children would have a full month to get settled before starting their new schools. And, in the meantime, Kate and Matt were kept busy saying their goodbyes. It seemed as if everyone they knew wanted to get them round one last time, 'before you move to your mansion in the country,' as Kate's friend Jude jokingly put it. No matter how many times Kate pointed out that they were only going to Hampshire, and that it barely took any longer to get there from Dulwich than it did to struggle across London to Willesden, say, there was a sense they were crossing some kind of Rubicon, emigrating to a completely new life. She made all their friends promise to come and stay, once the bedrooms were sorted, but she didn't press them to come too soon. She wanted Trade Cottage to herself for a little while, so they could get to know each other.

In the meantime, she and Rosemary emailed. No, that was the wrong word, Kate thought: they *corresponded*. The older woman wrote her lovely long missives – letters, really – that started with a formal *Dear Kate*, and ended, *With my very best wishes, R.* They began as follow-ups to her visit – there was a set of curtains that Rosemary discovered had moth damage, so those she was chucking; would they like the big chest freezer in the outbuilding, and, if so, should it be left on? What about the ride-on mower? But they quickly segued into more personal matters. Paul's motorised wheelchair had arrived, Rosemary wrote, but it was really only useable on the terrace; it slipped if he went on the steepest parts of the garden, and it was too wide to navigate inside the house.

> So at least he's impatient for this move, which helps me stay positive. But it will still be a wrench. There's a mythical plant, the mandrake, which is said to scream and bleed when it is pulled up. I shall do my level best not to shriek when we leave this house for the last time, but I fear I may not entirely succeed. It is such a comfort to know we are passing it on to a young family who will enjoy it as much as ours did. Jamie continues to rumble and cuss from Washington, but he didn't even manage to bring his children over for one last summer hols – they have to go to 'camp', he tells me, though I told him they could perfectly well camp in Trade Cottage's garden. That reminds me: you will find a small treehouse – just a wooden platform, really – in the largest apple tree. We used to spend at least one night there every summer, sleeping under the stars . . .

Kate replied to these emails equally warmly, if not quite so frankly. She felt it was her responsibility, as Rosemary's successor, to make her leave-taking as painless as possible. So she promised they would sleep in the treehouse, and treat the cesspit with the respect it deserved, and never plug in two heaters at opposite ends of the house at once, and everything else Rosemary asked of her.

'This is like that movie,' Matt said to her once, when she relayed some particularly arcane piece of domestic instruction.

'Which one?'

'You know – where the older woman makes friends with a younger one and gives her their house in the country. The family burn the letter of wishes, but she ends up getting it anyway. Anthony Hopkins was in it. And Emma Thompson.'

'Oh – *Howards End*.' Matt was right, she realised. How could she not have made that connection herself? She loved houses in fiction – Alconleigh in *The Pursuit of Love*, the gatehouse in *I Capture the Castle*, Manderley, Top Withens Farm, San Salvatore in *The Enchanted April* . . . As a child, books had been her escape, and there was no better escape from a succession of homes where all was chaos and shouting than a house described in words, comfortingly immutable. *Howards End* had been one of her absolute favourites – the book, even more than the film; she loved Forster's conversational, almost laconic waspishness. That, and the fact the Schlegel sisters had no mother.

On moving day, they had to be out of Dulwich by noon. After breakfast, Matt stayed behind to supervise the removals and give the keys to the estate agent, while Kate crammed the children and the most essential boxes into the car and drove down to Hampshire. Paul and Rosemary, she knew, had moved out a few days before, as their bungalow wasn't part of the chain, so it didn't matter what time she arrived. She picked up a few groceries on the way and reached Trade Cottage before lunchtime.

For the first time, she allowed herself to park next to the house. We belong to each other now, she thought with a surge of excitement as she bent to retrieve the keys from under the mat where Rosemary had left them. Damon was too busy to come and hand them over in person, he'd said; when she'd asked anxiously about security, he'd laughed, telling her that Rosemary and Paul usually didn't even lock the place. The key itself was suitably ancient, like something you'd use to unlock a church. As she put it in the equally ancient keyhole, another book came to mind – *Through the Looking Glass*, Alice trying the golden key. But there was no time to enjoy that thought, because the children were clamouring at her to 'hurry up, Mummy, let us in.' No sooner had she got the door open than they were racing inside, hollering with excitement.

She paused on the doorstep. It felt momentous, to be stepping over this threshold as owner for the first time. Brides used to be carried into their new homes by their husbands, she recalled. She wondered how many had been carried into this one.

To her surprise, the panelled entrance hall still contained the same ancient console table as on her last visit, complete with the same silver bowl for keys. She went through to the sitting room. The sofas and chairs were gone, but the oak side tables were still there.

Puzzled, she did a quick tour of the other rooms. The dining table and chairs had been left behind, as had the massive old sideboard. The painted oars had been removed from the corridor, but in the study, although the bookshelves had been cleared, the captain's chair and desk remained where they'd always been.

She recalled Rosemary saying there were a few things that she and Paul felt belonged with the house. This was way more than a few, though. In every room, she found vases, paintings, an old chest, rugs . . . In some rooms it looked as if they'd barely moved out. Much of what had been left was beautiful, if a little battered or threadbare.

A sudden thought occurred to her. Where would the removal men put all Matt and Kate's furniture now? She called Matt as she went upstairs. He was on the road, in a hired van, but he picked up straight away.

'We'll just have to use a couple of bedrooms as storage,' he said when she'd explained. 'That's assuming they've taken the beds?'

'Checking now.' She went into the main bedroom. 'This one's gone, at least.'

'Phew.'

'Hang on.' Just because she could, she went to the window, to throw it open. She looked out, drinking in that glorious view, then glanced to her right and gasped.

'What's up?' Matt asked.

She said breathlessly, 'Someone's cut down the leylandii.' At the further end of the great green cliff, almost a quarter had gone, ruthlessly trimmed from about thirty feet high to about six. It had clearly been done very recently – from where she was standing, she could see the trunks' innards, almost white, surrounded by brown branches. It made the hedge look dead and hollow, a series of empty eye sockets. Beyond, where it had previously been completely hidden, she could just make out the edge of a modern house with big glass windows.

'The cheeky bastards!' she exclaimed. 'They've waited until Rosemary and Paul left, then opened up their view. They can see right down the end of our garden. Are they allowed to do that?'

'I guess it depends on who owns the hedge,' Matt said uneasily. 'I'll check with the solicitor.'

'Even if it's us, it's too bloody late now.'

'Hardly a nice way to kick off relations with your new neighbours,' Matt agreed grimly. 'Maybe I should go round and have a word. But I'll check the legal position first.'

She was still fuming as she went downstairs and into the garden. You couldn't see the chainsawed trunks so much from here, but there were several places where you could now see the other house over the lowered hedge, its stark modern lines a jarring contrast to Trade Cottage's ancient flint walls. It took the shine off what should have been an ecstatic day.

She wasn't even cheered up by the bottle of Pol Roger she found in the kitchen, along with a card in which a shaky hand had written, *Time for a wonderful new chapter at T.C.! Just remember the house rule!* Beneath that, a different hand had added, *I forgot to say, don't poison the mice. There's an owl nesting in the barn and you will kill him too.* That must be Rosemary, though she'd already told Kate about the owl several times.

The same hand, she discovered, had left more notes scattered around the house. *Careful – loose step,* warned one on the stairs. *Window is broken!* was tucked behind one of the latches in a bedroom. And in the ancient downstairs loo, with its thunderbox seat and clanking overhead cistern, *If you flush ANYTHING but toilet paper down here, it WILL block.*

Matt called back a little later. 'Anwar says it's a party boundary, so they shouldn't have done anything without Paul and Rosemary's agreement. But he also said there are specific regulations about leylandii hedges – if the neighbours asked for it to be cut down to two metres, for example, they wouldn't have been able to say no.'

'I'll go and see how high it is.' She walked outside, the phone still to her ear, then stopped. 'There's a gate.'

'What?'

'A wooden door. In the hedge.' From the amount of weathering, the gate looked as if it had been there since the hedge was planted; the leylandii had simply been allowed to grow around it, which was why she hadn't noticed it before. 'It must go into their garden.'

'Even bloody cheekier. Is it locked?'

'I'll see.'

Ringing off, she tried the handle. It turned, but the wood of the door had swollen against the frame and she had to put her shoulder to it. She fell through it in a rush.

She was on a kind of narrow terrace, looking up a grassy incline towards the house – a long, low, modern construction that dominated the small space around it. The windows reached from floor to ceiling, so she could see right in. In the corner nearest her was a stubby telescope on a tripod, which made her bristle – it overlooked the bottom half of Trade Cottage's garden. Then she saw an electric wheelchair gliding towards the window. There were reflections on the glass, and for a moment she couldn't see clearly who was in the wheelchair, or make out the other, much slighter figure walking alongside. The wheelchair stopped, but the second figure came right up to the glass, and it was only when it waved enthusiastically at her that she saw it was Rosemary.

# SEVEN

'So it turns out that bit of land used to be Trade Cottage's tennis court,' she said. 'When they decided to hive it off to build their modest bungalow, as they still insist on calling it, they deliberately went with an ultra-modern architect because Tessa had told them about passive houses – you know, built to need very little heating – and they've both been feeling the draughts at Trade Cottage. And they wanted something completely different, anyway, so they wouldn't constantly be comparing the two.'

'And the hedge?' Matt asked sceptically, eyeing it from where they were sitting on the terrace.

'They've been trying to get it trimmed for ages, Paul said, but the tree surgeon was always booked up.'

Matt snorted. 'So nothing to do with selling Trade Cottage first and then moving the goalposts. What did *you* say?'

Kate spread her hands helplessly. 'What *could* I say? They were so pleased to see me, and kept asking if I was OK with them leaving so much stuff, and about the kids, and how they must come round to look through the telescope—'

'Ah, yes,' Matt said. 'The telescope. What did they have to say about that?'

It felt, Kate thought a little mutinously, as if she was a junior teacher having to report back to the headmaster – a headmaster, moreover, who clearly felt she hadn't been assertive enough. 'Apparently, Gordon asked Paul to keep a lookout for foxes taking his lambs – which Rosemary has encouraged, because it's something he can do from his wheelchair.'

'And they thought they'd just help themselves to our views while they were at it. Well, I'm glad we didn't pay any more than we did. They've probably just lopped fifty grand off Trade Cottage's value. And added about the same to theirs, of course.'

She couldn't disagree, though how much of Matt's grumpiness was really about the hedge and how much was the result of the exhausting day he'd had, she wasn't sure. The truth was, once she'd got over her own surprise at discovering Rosemary and Paul had only moved next door, not only had her crossness over the hedge evaporated, but she'd found herself feeling rather pleased. Her friendship with Rosemary felt integral, somehow, to the Arcadia she envisaged for her family at Trade Cottage.

'They showed me round, actually,' she said. 'It's stunning – like something on *Grand Designs*. It's been Paul's present to himself, Rosemary said, ever since his MND diagnosis. He's bubbling over with excitement about it – what she's like with Trade Cottage, he's like with The Old Tennis Court.'

'That's what they've called it?' Matt said, frowning. 'Interesting how even the name relates to our house.'

It gave her a little jolt of unfamiliarity and amazement when he said 'our house' so casually like that. She nodded. 'And in fact they've been quite considerate about the hedge, when you see it from their side. It's still mostly leylandii between us and them – they've taken down just enough at the end to open up the view to the fields, but left the rest.'

'Well, it sounds like we just have to lump it, anyway.' He shot her a look. 'Did you tell them we wouldn't want their hideous dining table even if we had room for it?'

'Not in so many words,' she admitted. 'I just said we already had one.' That had the virtue of being true, although theirs was an extending kitchen table, nothing like the massive mahogany edifice Paul and Rosemary had bequeathed them. But she wanted the new kitchen-diner to be a light, airy space, a complete contrast to Trade Cottage's manorial oak-panelled entrance hall and the clubby captain's study. 'They said, in that case, give it to a charity shop or something.'

'More work for us. We may even have to pay someone to collect it.' Matt yawned. 'I think, now we're in, we should keep our distance a bit. For a while, anyway. Like it says in the Bible – good fences make good neighbours.'

She didn't say anything. She would only sound like a bookish smart alec if she pointed out that he was, in fact, quoting a poem by Robert Frost.

'Do we have anything for supper?' he added. 'I didn't have any lunch.'

'I thought maybe we could check out those takeaway pizzas at the pub?'

He brightened. 'Great idea. And I'll stick that bottle they left us in the fridge.'

He got to his feet, then stiffened. 'What the hell?'

She followed his gaze. Rosemary was walking up the slope towards them. In her arms was something small and square, wrapped in what looked like an old sheet.

'She must have come through that gate,' he said darkly. 'I think it's time something was said.'

But in the event, it was Rosemary who spoke first, when she was still a good ten yards away. 'I'm so sorry to intrude,' she called. 'But I come bearing gifts. And an apology.'

She handed Matt an envelope. He took out a card, which he read, frowning, as she went on: 'When I thought about it, I realised you must be furious about that hedge, and rightly so, really. It was all a mix-up: I thought Damon was going to explain things, but I suppose he didn't want to put you off. Anyway, by way of saying sorry, I've brought the sea captain back. He looked so uncomfortable on our wall – I felt his eyes were always resting on Trade Cottage, as if he was trying to tell me that was where he'd rather be. So he's come home again.'

As she spoke, she was unwrapping the object in her arms. It was the naval portrait that used to hang on the study wall.

'Rosemary, we can't possibly—' Kate began, but the other woman was already forestalling her.

'No, really, my conscience won't be clear unless you accept it. Besides, the captain's very determined. When he gives an order, he expects it carried out – and in this case, it was "Abandon ship!"' She smiled at them.

Kate didn't know what to say. Matt was looking at her, but the fact was, she was torn – it was way, way too generous a gift, but, equally, she longed to hang the picture back in its rightful place by the study door.

When she didn't say anything, Rosemary gave a quick nod. 'You feel it too, don't you? Trade Cottage is where he belongs. And that's why you're going to be such lovely people to have as neighbours. That, and your wonderful children. Now, I'm not going to stay and inconvenience you any further. I'd better go back and explain to Paul, before he spots the captain's missing and calls the police.' She gave a little laugh. 'He might be a bit surprised at first. But I know he'll agree it's the right thing to do. Getting on with neighbours is absolutely the most important thing to him.'

She handed the picture to Kate and turned, striding down the hill with her customary energy.

Matt was already squinting at the portrait's signature and pulling out his phone. A few moments later, he gave a low whistle.

'Well, I think that probably compensates us for any drop in value.'

He showed her what he'd found. It was an auction listing from a few years back, another portrait by the same artist. The estimate was followed by a long series of zeroes.

'She's either completely mad,' he added, 'or she really, really wants us all to get along.'

The children were busy with their bedrooms, arranging their possessions exactly as they'd had them in Dulwich. Neither wanted to be dragged out to collect pizzas, so Kate and Matt decided that, so long as they absolutely promised to stay inside the house, they could be left. Or rather, Matt did. Kate was by nature a worrier, a just-to-be-on-the-safe-sider. Garment care instructions, best-before dates, recipes, traffic regulations – she couldn't help but follow all of them to the letter. She wouldn't even put crockery that wasn't categorically labelled 'dishwasher safe' into the dishwasher, even when all the evidence – i.e. the fact Matt had put the same item through half a dozen times already – proved her caution unnecessary. She knew there was no legal age at which children were considered too young to be left on their own – she'd checked on her phone, the first time Matt had suggested it, back in London, and had been shocked to discover something so fundamental was left up to parents – but, really, when would Tilly and Will ever be old enough that she wouldn't worry about them? But she trusted Matt's judgement. It was one of the reasons their partnership worked: some of his self-confidence rubbed off on her.

They took the car and drove the short distance to the village. The Pelham Arms turned out to be just as lovely as everything else about the area – unpretentious, pretty without being twee. In the beer garden, there was a small wooden shack with a steel chimney emitting smoke that carried the unmistakeable aroma of pizza.

As they walked through the pub's open front door, a man about their age looked up from the pint he was pulling and gave them a friendly smile. 'Hi. What can I get you?'

They ordered four pizzas to take away. 'Might as well get a drink too, while we're waiting,' Matt said, eyeing the selection of local beers.

'Visiting the area?' the man asked as he served them.

'We moved into Trade Cottage today,' Matt replied, with just a trace of pride.

'Ah!' The other man's eyes lit up. 'You must be Matt. And –' he turned to Kate – 'Kath, was it?'

'Kate,' she corrected him.

'Of course! Matt and Kate. I'm Jason.' He pushed away the card reader and handed them their drinks. 'First two are on the house. The pizzas, too. Don't worry, I'll make it back in the years to come. Particularly if your tastes are as expensive as Paul and Rosemary's.'

He indicated the glass-fronted fridge behind the bar, where, Kate saw, three shelves were stocked with Pol Roger.

'Not that I take Paul's money,' he added. 'If it wasn't for him, I probably wouldn't still be in business.'

The pub, it transpired, had been put up for sale by the brewery a few years back, and was already being eyed by property developers when Paul had organised a group to purchase it, with almost everyone in the village now a shareholder.

'I have a tenancy, same as any other pub,' Jason explained. 'But anything that benefits the village, like the pizza oven, they chip in for. And Paul runs his eye over the accounts for me every now and then, to make sure the business is going in the right direction.' He was silent a moment. 'I've been taking the books to him, since he's been less mobile. It'll be strange not dropping into Trade Cottage anymore for a glass of Pol and a chat.'

They ate the pizzas on Trade Cottage's terrace, washed down with champagne and followed by some plums Kate had found in the orchard, watching the sun sink slowly over the rolling fields. The only sound was some muted birdsong from the woods and the bleating of distant sheep. Will and Tilly were doing cartwheels up and down the lawn, revelling in all that space. There was still masses of unpacking to do, but the beds were made up. Everything else could wait. For Kate's part, she felt dizzyingly happy. No, she thought, analysing her emotion more carefully: it wasn't just happiness she felt, but an overwhelming sense of achievement. Storms might crash on distant oceans, but here, in their little harbour, they were safe. When she thought of her own childhood – its rootlessness and chaos – the fact she'd ended up somewhere like this seemed almost miraculous. But she had. She felt a rush of gratitude to the man beside her, who'd made all this possible. She reached for his hand and squeezed it.

For almost a minute, they stayed like that, savouring the moment.

'Grass needs cutting,' Matt said at last. 'I'll get on to it tomorrow.'

She nodded, then gasped. 'Look!'

Nearby, a head had appeared from behind a bush – small and demonic, with two stubby horns. It looked exactly like the bust of a satyr she'd seen once in a museum. It was followed by a glimpse of another, smaller satyr; then two tiny deer, barely bigger than foxes, emerged and pattered across the grass.

'Muntjac,' Matt said. 'They must live in the wood.'

She held her breath, certain she'd startle them. Then Matt put his glass down, inadvertently making a clink. But although the muntjac swung their heads in his direction, they were completely fearless, going on their way unconcerned.

Dusk fell. Matt took the children inside to get them to bed – they were so tired, they barely protested. Kate could tell that, secretly, they were looking forward to sleeping in their new bedrooms. But she stayed outside, basking in the simple fact of being where she was.

Above her, there was a hoarse rasp, almost a screech. She looked up to see a huge pale owl swooping over her head, floating down towards the wood on silent outstretched wings. She wondered if Paul and Rosemary, sitting behind their big plate-glass windows, had seen it too. She made a mental note to tell Rosemary about it, the next time she saw her.

# EIGHT

She woke the next morning with a strange sense of dislocation. Daylight was streaming through the open window. But it was so quiet! It was like the silence when a noisy machine you've become used to was suddenly switched off. The frenetic background roar of South London at night, the sirens and car alarms, the hum of the South Circular, the honking of Ubers and the buzzing of Deliveroo mopeds – all were gone, replaced by distant baaing and the occasional rattling bark of a magpie.

Beside her, Matt was still asleep – a rarity; usually he was up long before her, running or on the rowing machine. The rest of the house was silent as well.

She got up without waking him and walked barefoot around the garden, enjoying the coolness of the dew on her feet as she picked another bowl of plums. She loved the way these orchard plums were so much less perfect than supermarket ones, studded with tiny crystals of dried sap. You had to split them open with your nail before you put them in your mouth, though; occasionally, tiny weevils were to be found feasting on the insides.

By the time she came back in, the others were up and eating breakfast.

'Will has a request,' Matt told her. 'He thinks the first thing we should do is . . .' He cocked his head at Will.

'Find the secret cellar!' Will finished.

'Oh – definitely.' It was crazy to think there was a whole room they hadn't even discovered yet. But Damon hadn't offered to show them and it hadn't been marked on the floor plans. 'Damon thought it was under the dining room, didn't he? Maybe we need to move the table.'

Matt shook his head. 'I've looked at the floorboards. There's nothing that could be an opening.'

They abandoned breakfast, all eager to solve the mystery. 'Perhaps it'll be full of rum,' Tilly said breathlessly. 'You know, that the captain was going to sell to his friends.' It was what Kate would have imagined at her age, although now – perhaps because she was a mother – her mind jumped instead to all the things she wouldn't want her children to find, even though she couldn't quite picture what those might be.

They looked in all the obvious places, opening cupboards, lifting rugs, tapping the panelling for concealed doors. Kate was just about to say she'd call Rosemary and ask, when Matt, who'd gone to check the cupboard under the stairs for a second time, said triumphantly, 'Found it!'

They all went to see. The floor of the cupboard, it turned out, was actually a hinged piece of wood that could be lifted at the front, then latched to the underside of the staircase, directly above. And the switch inside the cupboard door turned on not just the bare lightbulb next to it, but more bulbs below ground, dimly illuminating some ancient-looking stone steps that led down into the void. There was no handrail. Kate instinctively put her arms around the children – they'd pushed in front of her, eager to see. She couldn't help but imagine them tumbling down, bashing their heads against those unforgiving stones.

'I'll go first,' Matt said, reading her mind. 'Kids, wait till I say it's safe.'

He went down a few steps, keeping one hand on the wall to steady himself. 'They're uneven,' he reported, 'but completely sound.'

He reached the bottom, then turned to look back up. 'OK. One at a time.'

Kate went last. The cellar, she saw as she reached the bottom, was a bit larger than the dining room above. As well as the electric bulbs, there was a grimy window giving on to a kind of lightwell at the front of the house. It was overgrown by a shrub, which was why they hadn't spotted it from the outside. The ceiling of the cellar was particularly beautiful, almost like a crypt, vaulted with ancient bricks. This must be the Tudor part of the house that Damon had mentioned, she thought.

It looked as if the cellar had mainly been used for storage. Where she was, near the steps, were several crates of empty champagne bottles. Further in were piles of cardboard boxes; a desk; an old sofa, black with mould; a vintage stereo, complete with turntable and radio receiver; and a shop mannequin wearing a Trilby hat, with an electric guitar slung round its neck. A sign, grimy with dirt, spelled out *Disco Club*. It appeared to be plugged into a lightbulb holder, though the bulbs inside it were clearly long defunct.

Matt took a look in one of the boxes. 'School books,' he reported. He pulled one out and read the inscription aloud: '*Jamie Finch, Bogle's, 1991.*' As he put it back, the cardboard disintegrated, spilling more books on to the floor. Kate saw an atlas, *Roget's Thesaurus*, a Latin primer. And, beneath those, some dog-eared magazines with scantily clad women on the covers. Deftly, Matt reached down and slid them out of sight before the children spotted them.

'No rum?' Tilly said, disappointed.

'They should have cleared all this before they left,' Matt said, looking around. 'Guess they couldn't be bothered.'

'Or they forgot it was down here,' Kate said, in Rosemary's defence.

'Either way, it's our problem now. I'll order an extra skip.'

After the excitement of the secret cellar, neither she nor Matt felt much like unpacking. She did a bit in the kitchen anyway, putting crockery away in cupboards, then heard an engine roaring to life outside and went to see what it was.

Matt had started the ride-on lawnmower Rosemary and Paul had left them. It sounded massively powerful – a meaty rumble coming from what was almost a small tractor, nothing like the tiny electric mower they'd had in Dulwich. But, of course, the lawn there had been minuscule compared to this.

Will was running towards his father, eager for a ride. Matt let him balance in front of him, then set off with a jerk that jolted them both backwards. Gleefully, he opened up the throttle, sweeping round the lawn, hollering with delight, just as Will was. They looked so alike sometimes, Kate thought, two peas in a pod. Then she saw Matt's exultation turn to concern, and then panic, and she realised something was wrong. He couldn't stop, couldn't even steer – the mower was spinning round in an ever-tighter circle, as if the steering had locked. She saw Will fly off, going sprawling on the ground. And already the mower was coming round again, towards where he lay. Recognising the danger, he was trying to scoot backwards, out of the way, but too slow—

She opened her mouth to shout, but quick-thinking Matt had already leaned sideways out of the mower, toppling it on to its side. Getting to his feet, he went and cut the engine.

'Oh my God,' she said breathlessly. 'Are you all right?'

'All good,' he said calmly. 'Will?'

'That was cool!' Will said. 'Let's do it again!'

'I think we'll wait to find out why the steering stopped working first,' Matt said. He looked at Kate and mouthed, '*Sorry.*'

Impulsively, she went over and hugged Will. He bore it for a moment, then wriggled free. 'Don't be weird, Mum. It wasn't like I was in any danger.'

'Of course not,' she said. 'I just like hugging you.' He was almost at that age, she thought, when physical contact would start to become awkward. She made a mental note to enjoy her hugs with him while she still could.

The afternoon was spent getting organised. A local builder was coming the next day to quote for minor renovations, but they already knew they'd have to do a lot themselves. The plan was for Kate to strip wallpaper and repaint, while the builder moved the Aga and redid the bathrooms. The garden, Matt would tackle at weekends. The conversion of the outbuildings, which would require listed building consent, would be designed and overseen by a specialist architect.

It was about four o'clock when she looked out of the window and saw Paul's black Labrador trotting purposefully up the garden. She called to Matt, in the next room.

He came to see. 'He must have pushed through the hedge. I'll tell him to go home.'

Biddy, though, had other ideas. He positioned himself by the back door, sat as if in response to an unspoken command, and thumped his tail enthusiastically. A glistening stalactite of drool hung from one lip.

'I think he's expecting to be fed,' Kate said.

'Home!' Matt said firmly. 'Go home!' The dog took absolutely no notice.

'I'll take him.' But although Biddy let Kate steer him by the collar towards the gate in the hedge, the moment she let go, he turned and trotted back to Trade Cottage.

She heard Rosemary's voice on the other side of the leylandii, calling him, and shouted, 'He's over here.'

'I'm so sorry.' Rosemary came through the gate, holding a lead. 'I don't think he's quite understood that we've moved. And he usually has his tea and a walk around this time. Well, not so much the walk anymore, but . . .' She shrugged. 'I've been trying to cut his rations, now he's getting less exercise, but it just makes him even greedier.'

Biddy had already returned to his station by the back door. As she retrieved him, Rosemary waved at Will, who was swinging on the rope over the pond at the side of the house. He waved back eagerly, almost falling off in the process.

'I don't suppose . . .' she said thoughtfully.

'What?' Kate asked.

'Might Will and Tilly like to earn some pocket money walking him?' Rosemary gestured at the woods. 'There's a footpath on the other side that goes through Pelham Park towards the village – they wouldn't need to go on any roads.'

'I think they'd love that,' said Matt, always keen on the children earning money for chores – as a boy, he'd done the same. He called to Will, 'How'd you fancy walking Biddy for money, Will?'

'For money?' Will ran over eagerly. 'I'd love to walk Biddy. But you don't need to pay me.'

Kate was rather proud he'd said that. But Rosemary said, no, she'd definitely pay him, and then Tilly ran up too and was instantly jealous that Will had been asked and not her, so it was arranged they'd take turns.

'Incidentally, Rosemary, since you're here.' Matt gestured at the mower. 'We had a problem with the steering on that thing. Are we doing something wrong?'

Rosemary looked blank. 'I've no idea. But Robert will be here tomorrow. I'm sure he'll know.'

'Robert . . . ?' Matt asked.

'The gardener.' She saw Matt's surprise. 'Oh dear – should I have stood him down? I never thought . . .'

There was a slightly awkward silence before Matt said, 'I'm afraid we can't afford a gardener. But it's good he's coming tomorrow – he can show me how it works before he goes.'

'He's very handy round the house, as well,' Rosemary added. 'He's been doing all sorts of odd jobs for us.'

Matt said nothing. He'd already commented to Kate how botched the most recent repairs had been.

To cover the pause, Kate said, 'We found some things in the cellar, by the way – they look like they're Jamie's, from his schooldays. We're assuming you don't want them?'

'Oh!' Rosemary said. 'Yes, he used to have parties down there, before he and his friends were old enough for the pub. Feel free to give it all to a charity shop or something.' She hesitated. 'I don't suppose you've come across my notes anywhere, though, have you? They wouldn't have been in the cellar, but I can't for the life of me think where I did put them. A box of papers, about this big.' She indicated several inches with her hands, and glanced wistfully at the house, as if she might go and search for it one more time.

'Not so far,' Matt said. 'But if anything turns up, we'll be sure to tell you.' His manner was polite but firm, as if telling a drunken guest they weren't allowed back into the party.

Kate said quickly, 'I've been eating the plums, Rosemary. So delicious. Would you like some to take back with you?'

Rosemary beamed. 'That would be lovely. And perhaps a few gooseberries, too, since I know you've got so many. You must be dying to get rid of them.'

It was easier with just the two of them. As they walked down to the orchard, armed with the wooden baskets that had also been left at

Trade Cottage – 'trugs', Rosemary called them – the older woman said thoughtfully, 'He's just being territorial, poor old thing. He'll get over it.' For one awful moment, Kate thought she meant Matt, then realised she was gesturing at Biddy, now padding happily alongside them.

The gooseberry bushes were in the fruit cage. It really was huge, she realised, as she clambered through the little door – the size of Trade Cottage's sitting room. And if the captain's study felt like the house's inner sanctum, this felt like the garden's secret heart. Once past the green, frothy raspberry bushes – already dotted with pale fruits – the two of them were completely hidden from the outside world.

Rosemary had insisted they bring gloves, for which Kate was soon grateful. The gooseberry bushes were covered with spikes, and although her hands were protected, her arms were soon dotted with pinpricks. 'Ouch,' she said involuntarily, as yet another thorn pierced the inside of her elbow – a tiny currant of blood fattening on her skin, then bursting under its own weight. She pulled off her glove to smooth it away with her thumb. Rosemary, she noticed, didn't seem to get pricked at all, even though her basket was filling up at twice the speed of Kate's.

'There, that's masses,' Rosemary said after a minute or two.

'Really?' Kate looked at the laden bushes. 'I don't know what we're going to do with the rest.'

'I usually do a gooseberry fool – it's lovely on these hot summer days. And jam, of course, and chutney. And gooseberry gin is rather fun.'

'I don't know how to make any of those,' Kate confessed.

'Would you like me to show you?'

'Oh – goodness. Yes – I'd love that.' Then, because she suspected Matt would want to prioritise sorting out the house, she added, 'Perhaps when Matt's gone back to work. He's only taken this week off.'

'Of course.' Rosemary smiled at her. 'To be honest, I'm rattling around a bit up there with Paul. It'll be something to look forward to.'

# NINE

Kate was fast asleep that night when a sound permeated her consciousness. Somehow, she identified it as a scream, even before her brain told her that meant she had to wake up. Panicked, she jolted her head off the pillow to listen. It *was* screaming, and it seemed to be coming from the garden. Then she recognised Tilly's voice and panicked even more – what was she doing outside? – before realising that the sound was coming from Tilly's bedroom, at the other end of the house, but was reaching their room through the open windows. These internal walls must be thicker than they'd realised, she thought as she jumped out of bed. 'I'm coming!' she yelled, then dashed for the stairs, Matt a few feet behind her.

They had to go all the way downstairs, along the corridor and then up the other staircase. It seemed to take forever, though it was probably only forty seconds or so. When they got there, Tilly was sitting on the top step, crying.

'Darling, what is it?' Kate gasped. 'What's wrong?'

'There's someone in my room,' Tilly said.

'There can't be,' Matt said reassuringly. 'The house is all locked up.'

Kate knew he was only trying to calm Tilly down, but she felt instinctively that the first thing their daughter needed was to be believed. So when Tilly retorted tearfully, 'There *is* someone. I felt them,' she said, 'OK, no worries. Let's go in together and see who it is.'

She took Tilly's hand and led her to the bedroom door. Her daughter hung back. 'I think it's the witch,' she said fearfully.

For the same reason, Kate didn't say, *Of course there isn't a witch.* Instead, she said, 'What witch is that?'

'The one who lives in the tree.'

'OK,' Kate said. 'Let's see.' She switched on the light.

'Well, if there *was* a witch, she's not here now,' she began, just as a tiny flickering shape hurtled through the open window at them. Tilly screamed again, and even Matt flinched and raised an arm.

The shape jinked and fluttered around their heads. Kate felt the air move as it came within inches of her head. Then it was gone, as fast as it had come, zipping out again through the window.

'It's a bat,' she said. 'Just a bat, looking for some nice insects to eat.'

'Could that have been what you felt, Tills?' Matt asked. 'A bat coming close to your face?'

After a moment, Tilly nodded.

'I expect it didn't know there was anyone in here,' Kate said encouragingly. 'It knows now, though. But shall we close the window anyway, just for tonight?'

A little reluctantly, Tilly allowed herself to be persuaded back to bed. Matt went downstairs to make her a hot drink, while Kate stayed to help her get settled.

'What made you think it was a witch?' she asked gently. 'And why does the witch live in the tree?'

'*You* said it did,' Tilly said accusingly.

'Oh!' Realisation dawned. 'The wych elm. That's a different sort of witch. Though they *were* meant to be magical – I read a story once where there was a wych elm that could cure toothache.'

Tilly considered. 'Is Rosemary a witch?'

Kate laughed. 'I doubt it!' Then, because she was curious, she couldn't help asking, 'Do you like her?'

Tilly nodded. 'And Paul. And Biddy. And when I took Biddy home today, Rosemary said she's going to look for a pony to live in our paddock, to eat the grass. She says I might be able to ride it.'

That was news to Kate. 'Well – either that, or Daddy could mow it.'

'I love it here. We won't ever have to leave, will we?' Tilly asked anxiously, and of course Kate reassured her that no, they were definitely there for good.

# TEN

The next few weeks passed in a kind of beautiful blur. Will disappeared for hours at a time into the woods, where he was renovating Jamie's abandoned forts. Matt, making the most of the warm weather, used his weekends to clear fallen trees from the little stream that Paul last cleared when he and Rosemary arrived, almost half a century ago. Robert the gardener – who turned out to be a strikingly well-muscled young man of few words – came, showed Matt how to work the ride-on mower, hit it off with him and was kept on, 'just while we get on top of things'; watching him zip around the lawn, wearing nothing but a pair of shorts and some trainers, was Kate's guilty pleasure. Tilly was introduced to riding at a nearby livery yard, and within days could talk of nothing else. It turned out Rosemary had kept all Tessa's old riding gear, although Kate did insist on buying a new hat.

Kate and Rosemary, meanwhile, spent hours making jam. Kate could never have imagined how enjoyable it would be. Jam-making, she'd assumed, was like knitting, or darning, or making stock from leftovers: something her grandparents' generation did, and even then, only out of a sense of duty. But with Rosemary, it was fun.

There was picking the fruit, to begin with. They filled the wooden trugs with gooseberries warmed by the sun, each berry translucent, glowing like a pale green marble that had somehow been lit from within. Their plump tautness reminded Kate of her belly when she was pregnant – those striated veins, the tiny navel-like calyx. One bush had berries that were hairy, almost spiny, like tiny blown-up puffer fish. Another's were soft and almost overripe, popping in her fingers with a slimy squirt of seeds – those, she ate straight away, sucking up the burst fruit and pulp from her palm. The ones that split were always the sweetest.

'My father used to say, "Never trust fruit that doesn't have a bruise",' Rosemary told her as they picked. 'Because a bruise means the tree knows it's ripe and has let it go. Whereas no bruises means it's been pulled off by someone.' She slid her eyes at Kate. 'It's a bit like children, isn't it? No bruises means no adventures.'

They talked as they picked, and in the kitchen too, while they stirred Rosemary's enormous jam-making pan on the Aga. Rosemary, somewhat surprisingly, was a keen karaoke singer, and could perform a word-perfect rendition of Bob Marley's 'Jamming', using a wooden spoon as a microphone. 'I had such a crush on him in the seventies,' she confessed. 'There's something about beautiful black men, isn't there?' Kate winced inwardly, but said nothing.

For her part, she started talking to Rosemary about her family – about Tilly, who in London had been bullied by some other girls and had started dreading school, while Will, who had dyslexia and ADHD, seemed only to make friends online, and then only when he played video games. She and Matt had set a limit of no more than ninety minutes' screen time a day, but enforcing it was a constant battle – even here, with the woods to distract him.

Gradually, she also talked more about herself – about the miscarriages she'd suffered between Will and Tilly, and how she'd been convinced they'd never have another child. And, finally, about her mother. She didn't know why she found it so hard to tell people about her, but she did – there was still the shame, somehow, and the years of ingrained secrecy.

'She was an alcoholic,' she said simply. 'Not a mummy-likes-an-extra-glass-of-wine-at-supper alcoholic: a proper, full-blown, vodka-for-breakfast alcoholic. I used to take the bottles from the bottom of the laundry basket where she'd hidden them and empty some down the sink, to try to limit her. But she'd just stagger out while I was at school and get more.'

Rosemary was a good listener, never passing judgement or offering advice, just quietly empathising. Emboldened, Kate told her more: how the alcoholism, and her mother's consequent inability to hold down a job, had meant they were endlessly uprooted – moving almost every year, the houses ever smaller, the walls shrinking in on Kate as if she were growing at five times the normal rate. The housing estates in which they were situated became progressively rougher, too, although her mother tried to pretend the opposite, clinging to middle-class gentility even as she increasingly came to resemble the local crackheads herself. If it hadn't been for a few pivotal teachers, Kate would never have escaped. And then, at uni, she'd met Matt, confident and caring, and her life had changed almost overnight. Not that she'd known back then they were going to be well off, of course; when, a few years later, he'd first mooted leaving his relatively well-paid tech job and setting up his own company, she'd been the one counselling caution.

'I guess that's one reason I love this place so much,' she said, looking around. 'Having been rootless . . . It's not just that Trade Cottage is our forever home – though it definitely is. It's the fact *you* were here for so long, too. That sense of permanence.'

'And the Linwoods – the people before us – were here thirty years, I think.' Rosemary also looked around wistfully. 'You're right – Tray's a hard place to leave.'

Rosemary talked about her family, too: Jamie the golden boy, good at everything, with an extraordinarily well-paid job in Washington, one that made a real difference to the world; his beautiful wife Courtney, who, Rosemary confessed, she was rather scared of, so frighteningly competent was she; Tessa, who had been 'troubled' in her twenties – Kate got the impression drugs and toxic boyfriends had been involved – and had never quite got over an eating disorder she'd had at school. But Rosemary didn't talk, Kate noticed, about Paul, or her feelings about becoming the carer of someone with a terminal illness. There was just the occasional crumb of information – that they were selling Paul's beloved old Land Rover, for example, and getting a car that could accommodate a powered wheelchair. 'Paul calls it the Popemobile. I think he secretly rather likes the idea of me having to drive him around. Says he's going to get me a chauffeur's hat.'

For a brief time in mid-August there was a glut of peaches, too, but those were too precious to make jam from. When Paul and Rosemary first came to Trade Cottage, they'd deliberately planted two varieties you couldn't get in the shops: white peaches and *pêche de vigne*. The white peaches were coarse-skinned, hairy as velvet, but the pale flesh inside was slippery with juice, almost oily, coating Kate's fingers and tongue with floral, muscaty flavours. And the *pêche de vigne* were misshapen and smooth-skinned, but revealed, when you opened them – Rosemary showed Kate how to do that without using a knife, just a sharp twist of the hands – yolk-coloured flesh streaked with red, like a sunset.

'Blood peaches,' she said proudly. 'Even today, you don't see them often.'

Kate took a picture of the blood peach for her Instagram. She was trying not to post too many shots of Trade Cottage – she didn't want to be an Instabragger – but the fruit-picking and jam-making was another matter: she felt she was earning those.

After the peaches came the raspberries, the long green tunnel of canes now dotted with crimson everywhere she looked, little bobble-hats of pulp that trembled between her fingers as they slid off their white cones. She had to pick carefully to avoid crushing them, but she noticed that, even so, she was starting to catch Rosemary up, her trug no longer still half-empty when Rosemary's was full.

One evening, she had to go up to London to join Matt at a work dinner, and it was no surprise when Rosemary and Paul offered to mind the children. Kate suggested pizzas from the pub and a bedtime of nine p.m. When she and Matt got back, sometime after midnight, she was startled to discover Tilly and Will both still up, finishing off an epic game of Risk, and an empty lasagne dish soaking in the sink. It had been, the children told her, the funnest evening ever. Privately, Kate – whose own evening had been long and exhausting; Matt's techy co-founders were not the easiest conversationalists – wished she could have been with them.

'I hope you don't mind,' Rosemary said to her quietly as they left, Paul navigating his way out with some difficulty. 'But it's the hollibobs, and they were all three of them having such a lovely time.' She glanced at Paul's departing back. 'He adores them, you know. And it's so good for his morale . . . If we can do any more sitting, you will say, won't you?'

Kate did try to protest when Will came back from The Old Tennis Court a few days later with a knife – a fearsome-looking dagger in a leather sheath that Paul had given him. But Jamie had had one just like it when he was a full year younger, Rosemary said, and, anyway, part of the gift was that Paul would teach Will how to use it safely.

So Will started going round to The Old Tennis Court every afternoon for whittling lessons, his knife proudly strapped to his belt. After a few sessions, he brought back an animal he'd carved. 'It's Biddy,' he told Kate, and it did indeed look very like the Labrador.

'It's for you,' he added. 'A present.' Touched, she kept it in pride of place beside her bed, so he could see how much it meant to her.

It was while she and Rosemary were making raspberry gin that the older woman had the idea of a party.

'A sort of joint housewarming,' she exclaimed. 'You could get a few friends down from London, and I'll get some people up from the village. There are so many you really must meet. Gordon, of course, and Jake who runs the pub, and Liv who does the book club, and Mary Snow who I happen to know has a pony that nobody's riding.'

'We've met Jason from the pub, actually,' Kate said. Rosemary did this occasionally, she'd noticed – mixed up names, or couldn't remember if they'd added sugar to the gin. It was one of the few reminders she was almost twice Kate's age. 'But being introduced to those others would be great.'

'There's a woman in the village who helps with catering, so it needn't be too much of a chore. How about the last bank holiday of August, when everyone's back from their hols and needs cheering up? We always used to have a do then. And if it starts early enough, we can invite some people with children the same age as Will and Tilly, so they'll make friends before school starts.'

'That sounds perfect,' Kate said. And so the party went in the calendar.

# ELEVEN

There were still eight days left before the bank holiday, and they were filled with activity. Skips arrived amid a great clanking of chains, and were soon lined up like three yellow panzers on the gravel in front of the house. 'Good Lord,' Rosemary said faintly, the first time she saw them. 'Three? Whatever will you put in them?' The builders started work, ripping out the first of the avocado-coloured bathrooms, the whole house reverberating with the thump of their sledgehammers. Rosemary, peering over the skip's edge, saw her old bath sitting atop a small mountain of smashed-up tiles, like a dinghy marooned on a sandbank, and said only, 'Ah,' a touch sadly, Kate thought. An architect, Nikolas, was chosen, briefed, and went away to draw up plans for the outbuilding conversions. The stair carpets, which were old and threadbare, joined the bathroom suite in the skip – 'I hadn't realised they'd got so tatty,' Rosemary said with a sigh. 'They're Axminster, you know' – as did Jamie's boxes of junk from the cellar, carried up by Kate, trip after trip, until her arms were aching, leaving only the two-man jobs – the desk and sofa – for another time. Matt, meanwhile, towed fallen trees up from the woods for a firepit,

Rosemary showing him the exact spot where, years previously, the last one had been lit.

'God, we used to throw some parties here,' she said, looking around. 'It's wonderful you're taking on the mantle.'

It was unfortunate that the moving of the Aga had to take place just before the bank holiday. But the builders were on a schedule, and the last thing Kate and Matt wanted was to give them an excuse to go and start another job elsewhere. So it was turned off, dismantled, and carried by grunting, sweating workmen into what had been the dining room. The kitchen now looked rather bare for the first visit of their friends from London, but Kate was confident they'd be amazed all the same.

Four families came down in the end, which, including children, meant twelve people to feed and find beds for. They arrived around lunchtime, but luckily Rosemary had baked quiches and tarts to go with some salads Kate had made.

'Oh my God, she's amazing,' her friend Lucy exclaimed, as Rosemary, refusing Kate's offers of help – 'You stay here and chat, you haven't seen your friends for ages' – went back to The Old Tennis Court for more. 'It's like having your very own Mary Berry next door, waiting on you hand and foot.'

'Camilla Parker-Bowles,' Jude said. 'I bet she likes a G&T.'

'Helen Mirren,' someone else suggested. 'Rosemary's a glamorous granny if ever I saw one.'

'We've become really good friends, actually,' Kate said proudly. 'And they're like grandparents to Tilly and Will.'

The afternoon wore on in a pleasant daze of drinks and chat. This is what I dreamt of, Kate thought happily: having people round, sipping drinks under the honeysuckle, while the children run free.

Her friend Kashvi came over. 'Jai says Will wants to show him the woods. I'll go with them.'

Kate stretched. 'You don't need to, honestly. It's perfectly safe.'

Comparing herself with her friends, she realised how much these few brief weeks at Trade Cottage had already changed her. That London hypervigilance and anxiety, that constant helicoptering, had floated away from her, like a snake sloughing its old skin as it grew.

She murmured, 'Rosemary's husband says, if your child hasn't broken at least one bone by the time they're eighteen, you've probably failed as a parent,' and saw her friend's expression turn almost comically to alarm.

'I'll go and see what they're up to, anyway,' Kashvi said, slipping away.

It was still hot enough for T-shirts and sunglasses, even at four o'clock, when the first guests from the village arrived. Leaving Matt to host, Kate went upstairs to shower and get ready – they had a big walk-in rain shower now, where the avocado bath had been. Afterwards, as she dressed, she glimpsed Paul, coming up the grass in his powered wheelchair, Rosemary walking slowly alongside. 'Welcome!' she heard him shout to the people on the terrace. 'Let's get this damn party started!'

She put on some make-up and went downstairs. Rosemary was introducing herself to their friends. 'Lovely to meet you,' she said to Kashvi, then turned to Kate. 'And who are you?'

'Rosemary!' Kate said. 'It's me, Kate!'

'Oh, of course it is!' Rosemary laughed, but for a moment, Kate thought, she'd looked alarmed. 'You've done something different to your . . .' She made a twiddling motion in front of her own face.

'Mascara. And I'm wearing my hair down. Gosh, I suppose you've never seen me with make-up before.'

'How hilarious!' Rosemary exclaimed. 'Now, let me introduce you to Gordon before I get even older and dottier.'

Gordon was the tenant farmer, older and posher than Kate had expected, wearing red corduroy trousers and a twill check shirt, his thick hand curled under a glass of champagne. She stammered her thanks for letting them use the wood, which he waved away.

'Just tell the children to keep Biddy on a lead when the shooting season starts.' He lowered his voice so Rosemary, who was regaling Kate's friends with a story about Trade Cottage, wouldn't hear. 'It's good you're all getting on so well. Some of us thought she'd find it impossible to leave this place. But you seem to have made it bearable. And they clearly adore your children.'

'It's mutual,' Kate said truthfully. 'We're so lucky to have them just next door.'

She went over to see how Matt was getting on, accepting another drink as she did so – the waiting staff were barely more than children, but they were very efficient about getting the drinks out. She arrived in time to hear the man Matt was talking to ask, 'Will you be doing much to the place?'

Matt nodded non-committally. 'Well, it needs a bit of a spruce-up. Lick of paint and so on.'

'Not going to be doing Airbnb in the barns, then?'

Matt managed to hide his surprise. 'I suppose that could be an option. Haven't made any big decisions yet.'

She changed course so as not to be drawn into the conversation. Had one of their friends said something? Either way, she was glad Rosemary or Paul hadn't heard. She and Matt really must find a way to bring up their plans sometime, she thought, before the application went in.

She went round with a bottle, topping up glasses, as a good way of introducing herself to people. A tall, sandy-haired man a little older than her nodded politely as she filled his glass. 'Guy Pemb,' he drawled. 'Pleased to meet you.'

He must be a villager. 'Have you lived here long?'

'A fair while,' he said vaguely. 'I was at prep school with Jamie. Used to go on holiday to Polzeath with this lot.' He nodded over at Rosemary. 'Had a bit of a crush on his mum, actually.'

Kate chatted for a bit and moved on. When she reached Rosemary, the older woman said, 'I see you met Guy Pelham.'

'Pelham?' Kate stared at her. 'As in Pelham Park?'

'Yes. Known him since he was a kid. He used to have fort battles with Jamie in the woods.'

'Oh my God,' Kate said, aghast. 'I misheard his name. I just asked him if he'd lived in Pelham long.'

Rosemary hooted with laughter. 'His family's only been here about three hundred years. Don't worry. Guy's lovely – he'll think that's hilarious.'

Around eight, as the sun set over the woods, the firepit was lit. Kate had expected things to get more chilled after that, but in fact the opposite was true. The villagers sat round the fire in a circle and belted out drinking songs, most of which seemed to be about deflowering fair maidens. And they drank. My God, did they drink! Jason had brought a keg of beer from the pub, and she'd made jugs of gooseberry gin fizz, and there'd been three cases of champagne, but by nine o'clock all were running low. The only thing that wasn't in short supply was the non-alcoholic elderberry cordial she'd spent hours making. She remembered Rosemary saying something about *better too much than too little* when she told her how much booze they were ordering. She realised now that had been the other woman's tactful way of suggesting they lay in more. But, actually, she didn't mind that they were running short. She wanted to relax with her London friends now; hopefully, the villagers would take the lack of top-ups as a hint to be on their way.

She went inside to get a glass of water. Rosemary was standing in the empty kitchen, staring disconsolately at the space where the Aga used to be.

'We haven't got rid of it,' Kate said quickly. 'It's being re-enamelled and converted to electric. But we're going to make the old dining room into the kitchen, so it's in there for now.'

'That sounds clever.' Rosemary gave her a quick smile and hurried past her, but not before Kate saw she'd been crying.

She went outside again. Paul, his wheelchair crammed into the circle of people around the fire, was using his empty glass to conduct what he announced was 'the house song'. From the lusty way they all roared the lyrics – something about always having champers in the fridge – it felt like it might be the singing's climax. She rather hoped so. She was tired now.

'Right!' Paul yelled as the song ended, propelling his wheelchair backwards. 'Back to ours!'

He trundled off down the slope. The others streamed past him, making war-cry sounds. Kate spotted mild, quiet Liv who organised the book club, who'd been so sweetly excited earlier to get a new recruit, picking up her skirts so she could pelt even faster down the hill.

After they'd gone, it was very quiet.

'Blimey,' Matt said. 'That went with a bang.'

'What a bunch of characters,' Ed agreed. 'And what a place.'

From the other side of the leylandii, there was the sound of a window sliding open. The heavy throb of a reggae beat heralded Bob Marley singing 'Get Up, Stand Up'.

'It's like when we lived in Brixton,' Kashvi said, laughing. 'Only with posher accents.'

'And more weed,' Ed said. 'I think I even saw the vicar having a toke.'

But, behind the banter, Kate could hear the envy in their voices and, although she knew it was an ignoble response, she couldn't help lapping it up.

# TWELVE

The next day, they all slept late, even the children. One by one, their friends came downstairs, got cups of coffee and glasses of juice, and straggled out to the terrace, where they sat around discussing the party and asking Kate about the house. Without the Aga, she couldn't cook them breakfast, but there were croissants and her own home-made jam, and fresh fruit from the orchard – as well as the plums, the first greengages were ripening, and there were still a few peaches left, which she cut and put in bowls with the last of the raspberries. A plan to walk to the pub for lunch was slowly emerging, but no one was in a hurry to move.

'There's your lovely neighbour,' Lucy said, pointing down the garden.

Kate looked. Sure enough, Rosemary was walking up the lawn towards them.

'We should really put an intercom on that gate,' Matt muttered.

Ignoring him, Kate waved. Rosemary, she saw, was carrying a bunch of flowers.

'How are you all?' Rosemary called as she reached them. 'There are a few delicate heads at The Old Tennis Court this morning, I can tell you. Naming no names, but some people didn't make it back to their own beds.' She held the flowers out to Kate. 'For you. To say we're so terribly sorry about the racket. I didn't even realise our windows were open until someone fell out of one.' She nodded at the flowers. 'I thought you might put them in the oriel window, so they'll catch the light.'

'Oh – it was fine, really,' Kate said as she took the flowers. 'But thank you.'

It hadn't actually been fine at all. Somehow, The Old Tennis Court had acted like a huge loudspeaker, pumping out bass so deep she'd felt it in the pit of her stomach, while the vocals echoed back from the woods like a shriek bouncing off a cliff. Even with the windows closed, which made her and Matt sticky and overheated, it had been hard to get to sleep.

'And I'm the bearer of good news,' Rosemary said, beaming. 'I spoke to Mary Snow last night, and she's just texted an invite for Tilly and Will to go and sit on Fresco this morning. She's going to take them both out on a leading rein, to see what they think of him.'

'Actually,' Matt said, 'I think we're all going to the pub.'

Rosemary frowned briefly, then her expression cleared. 'That's all right. I can take them over in the Popemobile.'

'They don't often get to see their friends from London,' Matt explained, just a fraction more firmly than Kate would have liked. 'Sorry, but we'd better rearrange your thing. Presumably Fresco isn't going anywhere anytime soon.'

'Well, why don't we ask Tilly and Will which they'd rather do?' Rosemary said reasonably. 'I'd rather not say no to Mary, not when I've worked so hard to get her to offer.'

'I know which they'd choose,' Matt said tersely. 'That isn't the point, Rosemary – we want to keep them with us today.'

Rosemary didn't reply, but just for a moment Kate thought she saw a flash of irritation cross her face.

Will ran up, slightly out of breath. 'What's going on?'

'Nothing,' Matt said. 'Rosemary's passed on a really kind offer for you and Tilly to go and ride someone's pony, which we'll definitely take her up on sometime. Now, go and round up the others – we're making a move to the pub.'

'Pizza!' Will yelled enthusiastically, running off again.

'Is that all right?' Matt said to Rosemary, his tone friendlier now he'd got his way.

'Of course!' she exclaimed. 'I'll text Mary and say they're busy. I'm sure she'll be happy to rearrange.'

# THIRTEEN

Somehow, though, a new date to go and sit on Fresco didn't materialise, and Kate felt it would be rude to push for it when they'd been the ones to postpone. In any case, they were busy now. Tilly and Will had started at their new schools – Kate was on tenterhooks all that first week, dreading some tearful homecoming and the accusation, however unfair, that she'd been the one to drag them out of London against their will. But none came. All their chatter was about nice teachers, friendly classmates, sociable school buses, breaktimes that sounded refreshingly free of fights and bullying and knives.

Liv, who ran the book club, followed up after the party with a lovely handwritten thank-you note and a PS that said, *By the way, it's sort of a tradition that the new member chooses a personal favourite as our next read. So we can get to know you through books, as it were!* It was a perfectly reasonable, even kind, thing to ask, but at the same time terrifying. Was Kate best represented by something relatively recent, like Sarah Waters's *The Little Stranger*? Or a classic, like *The Tenant of Wildfell Hall*? She should definitely avoid anything show-offy or ponderous. But, equally, the lighter books she loved – the

Jilly Coopers and the Freya Norths – might be too much the other extreme. And it would be stupid to choose something they'd all have read before, like *The Secret History*, or *Rebecca*, or *The Remains of the Day* – great books, all of them, but dull choices.

In the end, she plumped for *Brother of the More Famous Jack* – it was amazing how many people still hadn't read it, and almost everyone she'd pushed it on had thanked her afterwards for the recommendation. She sent an email to the address Liv had included on the card, and was gratified to get a reply that said, *Ooh! Don't know that one! Intriguing! PS: Just to warn you, we spend as much time on village gossip and character assassination as we do on literature!*

The builders began work on the new utility room, ripping out Rosemary's Formica-topped kitchen units and replacing them with a washing machine and a butler sink. Then they moved on to what would now become the kitchen, which Kate had designed with the help of a local kitchen company. They were putting in underfloor heating, but, with the cellar immediately below, something time-consuming had to be done with insulation. It was a couple of weeks before Steve's team were ready to plumb in the new island and wire up the newly electric Aga, but she knew, the moment they'd finished, that she'd made the right decision moving the kitchen here. It was exactly what she'd wanted – spacious, light-filled, welcoming, the warm centre of the house. She knew, too, that a huge beech-wood island with a breakfast bar and a row of pendant lights above it was a bit of a cliché, but it was also the kitchen she'd dreamt of, back in London: sleek and contemporary, but with subtle nods to the house's age, such as the rack of gleaming copper pans hanging above the Aga.

Meanwhile, she was painting. Windows, walls, ceilings, shelves – there was the whole house to do, and several of the rooms had rather twee wallpaper that needed to be stripped off first. She tried not to let Rosemary see any of this work in progress. It would be kinder, she felt, to show her only the final, beautiful product, Trade Cottage gleaming with fresh new colours, but not the process of getting there, during which – even she had to admit – some of the rooms looked a bit battered.

'You've worked so hard at this,' Matt said appreciatively one evening, when she showed him what she'd done that day. There was a technique that was big on Instagram just then called 'colour drenching', where you painted the ceiling, window frames, sills and even doors the same colour as the walls. She'd tried it in the downstairs loo, using the colour of the moment, a rich cocoa-brown with a silky eggshell finish, and was amazed at how much larger and more stylish the room looked as a result.

'I'm enjoying it,' she said. It was true: the slow, sensual rhythm of putting paint on Trade Cottage's walls was bringing her even closer to the house, like one of those hermit crabs that gradually becomes fused with its borrowed shell. It had been less than two months since they'd moved in, but already everything before that seemed a kind of distant dream. Sometimes it felt as if she'd been at Trade Cottage forever, that she was a reincarnation of the sea captain's maidservant, say, or the Mrs Linwood who Rosemary had said lived here before her and Paul . . . Painting, she'd found, did that to her – gave her all sorts of vague, mystical fantasies, which flitted idly through her head even as her hands moved methodically, almost ritually, over the centuries-old walls. Perhaps I will live all my life here, and die in this very room, she found herself thinking as she applied another brushstroke, and the thought gave her a serene, meditative sense of calm.

It was Steve, the builder, who popped his head round the door one day and said, 'I think there may be a bricked-up cavity beside that fireplace.'

They'd already decided to replace the fire surround in the small sitting room. It was one of the house's few jarring features: an elegant but incongruous Wedgewood-style confection, a marble mantelpiece beneath which Grecian nymphs cavorted in white relief.

'I've just run the laser measure over the walls,' he added. 'Either they're really, really thick, or there was some kind of passage there that got blocked up when the first conversion was done. I think there might be an older fireplace behind that one, too – maybe the original inglenook.'

'You mean, one of those big old fireplaces with a seat in it?' she asked, immediately intrigued.

He nodded. 'Want us to take a look? It'll mean knocking a few holes, but we can go through that big cupboard, where they won't show.'

She agreed enthusiastically, and the sledgehammers started up again.

It wasn't long before Steve came back, smiling. 'You're going to want to see this.'

She followed him to the sitting room. Inside the floor-to-ceiling cupboard, a work lamp illuminated a space they'd uncovered at the back. To one side, there was a domed alcove – an old bread oven, perhaps. Beyond that, there appeared to be a small wooden door, some kind of hatch or recess – it was hard to make out.

She stepped forward, and the work light's harsh glare was lessened. Even so, it took her a moment to realise that what she was looking at was an ancient wooden barrel.

It was empty, unfortunately. But it still smelled dankly of alcohol, evaporated by the centuries.

'The back of the cupboard was brick,' Steve explained. 'But it hadn't been mortared at the edges, only plastered. It could easily have been pushed aside, if you knew where.'

So the cellar was only a decoy, she realised. Finding it empty, the customs men would have moved on, never thinking to unbrick the cupboard by the fire.

Tilly was going to be overjoyed. But first, she knew, she had to share this news with Rosemary.

She and Paul came straight away, in the Popemobile. Leaving his wheelchair at the front door, Paul levered himself slowly into the house on sticks, Rosemary hovering by one arm to steady him.

Eventually, they got there, and Kate showed them the cupboard. Paul peered through the cupboard door, but didn't venture in. Rosemary darted inside, ran her finger round the rim of the barrel and touched it to her lips.

'Brandy,' she reported. 'All gone now.'

'The angels have drunk deep,' Paul announced. Turning to Kate, he explained, 'When spirits evaporate from a cask, it's called "the angels' portion". The more the angels drink, the smoother what's left becomes. Shame it's all gone. A hundred-and-fifty-year-old brandy would be quite something.'

'You should brick it up again,' Rosemary said. 'So there'll still be a secret for future generations to find.'

'I had the same thought,' Kate confessed.

'I don't understand that at all,' Paul said, shaking his head. 'How will they even know it's there?'

The two women smiled at each other, enjoying the fact that they were both on the same wavelength.

While Rosemary was here, Kate decided impulsively, she'd show her the new kitchen, too. 'I'm dying for you to see your old dining room. I think you'll be amazed how the re-enamelling turned out—'

'What's going on here?' Rosemary interrupted. She was pointing at the fireplace, where Steve's men had been chipping away at the cement. They'd spread an old dust sheet on the floor, on which they'd left their tools – chisels, hammers, a couple of crowbars.

'Well, that's another of Steve's discoveries,' Kate began. 'He guessed there was an older fireplace behind this one, so they're going to—'

'They've broken it!' Rosemary was pointing to the bottom left corner, where the marble had indeed got cracked.

'We're not actually going to keep it. Even if there isn't an older one behind, we'll probably . . .'

Her voice trailed off. Rosemary was staring at her, red with fury. 'That fireplace cost over a thousand pounds!' she snapped. Bending down, she picked up a chisel and hurled it across the room. 'We put it in because the old one smoked. As we could have told you if you'd only asked, instead of just arrogantly tearing Trade Cottage to pieces like fucking *barbarians*!'

Kate was too shocked to respond. It was as much the fact that Rosemary had sworn, as the suddenness of her fury. She stared back, willing herself not to cry.

There was a long moment where nobody spoke. Then Paul said gently, 'Come on, old girl. Let's get you home.'

Rosemary rounded on him. 'I *am* home. This is where I ought to live, you stupid old *cripple*.'

# FOURTEEN

'What was really odd was how Paul didn't even seem surprised. He just said something about needing to get back and put the kettle on. And she went with him like nothing had happened, saying things like "Mind that step" in a perfectly normal voice.'

'Could she have the beginnings of dementia, maybe?' Matt suggested.

They were standing at the new kitchen island with pre-supper G&Ts. At least, pre-supper for him – she'd eaten with the children. He got home so late, now he was commuting. And her drink was more G than T. She was still shaken up by Rosemary's reaction.

'I suppose it's possible,' she said doubtfully. 'She does forget things occasionally, but most old people do that, don't they? And she didn't seem confused, like Jude's mum used to be.' Her first thought, when Rosemary was still staring at her in wordless fury, was that the other woman had been drinking. It was one of the reasons she'd been so upset – just for a moment, she'd been thirteen again, being shouted at by her mother. But Rosemary's speech hadn't been slurred, and she'd walked out of the house without a stumble.

Matt shrugged. 'There are other kinds of dementia besides Alzheimer's, though. I think, with some of them, you do get these dramatic mood swings.'

'Or perhaps she really does think we're fucking barbarians.' Kate looked around the kitchen – the gleaming white cupboards, the granite countertops, the rack of copper pans. 'I was so looking forward to showing her this. Now, I can't help wondering . . . Is it *bling*? Are we just London yuppies making Trade Cottage look exactly like every other London yuppie would?' She gestured at the pendant lamps. 'I mean, a hundred years from now, archaeologists are definitely going to wonder what this obsession with having fancy filaments in our lightbulbs was all about.'

'We can always change the bulbs,' Matt said reassuringly. 'Though, actually, I really like them. And you've done an amazing job on this room. Don't let it get to you.'

But it had got to her. After Paul and Rosemary had gone, she'd succumbed to the urge to cry, locking herself in her new bathroom so the builders wouldn't hear. She'd felt so good before, basking in the warmth of Rosemary's approval. To have that suddenly torn away was almost too much to bear. *Fucking barbarians.* She thought back to all the other times Rosemary might have had the same thought, but hadn't voiced it – when she'd seen her Axminster stair carpet in the skip, for example, or the colour drenching in the downstairs loo. Kate had naively assumed she might appreciate seeing Trade Cottage rejuvenated, but had it actually been torture to see the things she'd done forty years ago torn out and tossed aside, as if to imply that the life she'd lived there wasn't good enough for its new owners? That wasn't what Kate thought at all, of course it wasn't, but she considered how she'd feel if she had to watch someone rip out what she and Matt had done, and felt awful. She didn't see how it could have been avoided – the house had to be renovated – but perhaps she could have been more considerate of Rosemary's feelings along the way.

She was dreading the book club now. She knew Rosemary usually went, and the prospect of having to pretend in front of a roomful of strangers that nothing had happened was unbearable. But she couldn't not go, not when it was her inaugural book choice they were discussing. She'd always promised herself she'd never drink for self-medication, but on the night it took place, she had a few therapeutic gins beforehand to steady her nerves.

In the event, though, it was Rosemary who didn't show up. That meant there were six of them: as well as her and Liv, there was Gordon's wife, Sally; Elizabeth, who waitressed in the pub; and Helen and Ellie, who both worked in a nearby care home. Liv, who was hosting, had provided wine and nibbles. At least everyone swooned over *Brother of the More Famous Jack*. Normally, Kate would have revelled in that – she felt a kind of vicarious pride when other people liked books she'd recommended. It was such a personal thing, after all. Matt was almost the opposite – if someone didn't like a beer he'd suggested, or a pub, he'd just shrug, as if it was their taste that was probably defective, rather than his.

Afterwards, she stayed to help Liv clear up. As they stacked the dishwasher, she said casually, 'No Rosemary tonight?'

Liv gave her a concerned glance. 'I was going to ask you if she's all right, actually. She's usually the most reliable of all of us.'

'I haven't seen her for a few days.' And then, both because she was curious and because, if Rosemary did say something, she wanted to establish a possible context for it, she said, 'Liv . . . Have there ever been any signs of Rosemary having dementia?'

'Dementia!' Liv looked startled. 'Not that I know of. She's usually sharp as a pin.' She put her head on one side and thought. 'Though she did turn up to a book club once that had been cancelled. And last month she mixed up Doris Lessing with Muriel Spark. But that's normal, isn't it? Particularly at her age.'

Kate agreed that it was. In any case, at least it seemed Rosemary hadn't said anything to Liv about her and Matt being barbarians.

She was painting a bedroom the next day when she heard tyres on the gravel outside. Going to the window, she saw the Popemobile. Rosemary got out, then reached back in for something – a book, it looked like. A few moments later, there was a knock on Trade Cottage's front door.

'Oh, God,' Kate said out loud. Turning off the radio, she went downstairs.

'Hello, Rosemary,' she said as she opened the door, in what she hoped was a neutral but not unfriendly voice.

Rosemary didn't speak for a moment, and Kate braced herself for another diatribe. Then Rosemary said helplessly, 'Oh, Kate, I'm such a blithering idiot. I don't know why I got so cross – Jamie always used to say, if Trade Cottage was his, ripping out that stupid fireplace was the first thing he'd do. And I know it was out of keeping – Paul's parents were awfully grand, and they went on about there not being a drawing room, so in the end we agreed we'd posh it up a bit, just in that one room. But the other day, something just snapped – I think I was just so, *so* jealous that you'd found that barrel and I never did, even though the difference in the room sizes had been literally staring me in the face. And now I've ruined everything, haven't I? Your lovely children are going to hate me, and your nice husband, and you probably think I'm a horrible wife as well as a horrible person.' She was crying now, ignoring the tears spilling on to her weathered cheeks. 'Anyway, I've brought you a gift. When I heard you'd chosen it, I was so thrilled – it's been my favourite book forever, literally yonks. This might even be a first edition.'

She held out *Brother of the More Famous Jack*. It was, Kate saw, the original hardback, the one with the pincushion cover.

'It's a signed copy,' Rosemary added. 'I went to a thing she did in Blackwells.'

As Kate took it, automatically opening it to look at the signature, Rosemary turned as if to leave.

'Where are you going?' Kate gasped, noticing. 'For goodness' sake, don't go now.'

The other woman hesitated, long enough for Kate to step out and give her the most enormous hug.

They sat at the kitchen island, drinking tea. 'You've made it so nice in here,' Rosemary said, looking around appreciatively. 'I love these lights.'

'Not too fucking barbaric?' Kate ventured.

Rosemary groaned. 'Don't. I am never, ever going to live that down, am I? Paul says I was absolutely *monstrous*.'

'You were magnificent, actually. The captain would have been proud of you – chucking the marlinspike across the deck like that.'

For a moment, Rosemary looked wistful. 'I don't suppose your clever builder has come across my notes?'

Kate shook her head.

'Anyway,' Rosemary said, 'from what I recall, you're right – the captain was actually rather a bloodthirsty brute. He once repelled an attack by cutting off a boarder's head with a single blow from his sword. And he was awarded the . . . the . . . Ach, it's gone.' She was silent a moment. 'That's the thing about getting old. When you're young and you forget something, you just think, Never mind, it'll come back to me. But when you're old, you're always asking yourself if it's the beginning of something more sinister.'

'Is that something that worries you?' Kate asked. 'That you might get dementia, I mean?'

Rosemary nodded. 'To lose who you are like that . . . And, if I was in a home, who'd look after Paul? But none of us knows what's coming down the line, do we?'

Impulsively, Kate reached out and squeezed her hand. 'I think you're amazing. And it must have been so hard, to watch a new family come in and make changes to your beautiful home. Really, you've been so good about it.'

'Thank you. And you're right, it hasn't always been easy. But we're so lucky. We couldn't have hoped for better neighbours.' Rosemary paused. 'Incidentally, do you know what you'll be doing at Christmas?'

'Christmas?' It was so far away, Kate hadn't given it any thought. 'Why?'

'Jamie's invited us to go to them, in Washington. We're just not sure . . . We think the journey might be a bit much for Paul, now. So we're going to say no.'

Kate wondered at the selfishness of a son who wasn't prepared to fly his family over for what might well be, surely, one of the last Christmases they'd get with their grandfather. But it was none of her business to say so.

As if reading her mind, Rosemary added, 'He came last year, so strictly speaking, it's the other grandparents' turn. And it's not as if we'd all fit into The Old Tennis Court, anyway.'

'Well, we're here,' Kate said, 'and we don't have any plans. We'd absolutely love to have you over on Christmas Day.'

Rosemary beamed. 'That's very kind.'

'Not at all. The children will be delighted.' She added, 'By the way, Rosemary, I've been meaning to tell you. We're thinking of doing up a couple of the outbuildings and putting them on Airbnb. I just wanted to check that you and Paul would be all right with that?'

'Of course,' Rosemary said. 'Why wouldn't we be? And that reminds me – I must chase Mary Snow about that pony.'

When they'd finished their tea, Kate walked Rosemary to her car. It was only as the other woman opened the driver's door that she glanced at the pond and said, 'Oh – one of your ducks is injured.'

Kate followed her gaze and gasped. One of the half-dozen ducks who usually lived on the little island was fluttering at the pond's edge, helplessly thrashing around in circles.

'Something's had its wing,' Rosemary added. 'Fox, most likely.'

'Should I take it to a vet?' Kate said, aghast. She didn't even know where the nearest vet's surgery was.

'Oh, God, no. They'll charge you hundreds of pounds to bandage it up, and, even if it heals, it won't survive long with a handicap like that. I'm afraid the only option is to put the poor thing out of its misery.'

Kate stared at her, suddenly terrified that Rosemary was going to drive off and leave her to do it. She'd never killed anything in her life.

'D'you have a coat I can throw over it?' Rosemary asked. 'Or an old towel or something?'

'Um – I'll have a look.' Flustered, she went into the house and located an old raincoat of Matt's. But by the time she got back, Rosemary already had the duck in her hands.

'Really, it's just something you get used to.' She moved her hands up to the duck's neck. 'Twist and pull – firmly, like you're pulling a cork out of a champagne bottle. There.' The duck's head hung limply. Its legs thrashed briefly, as if it were trying to paddle away. Then it was still.

Rosemary turned it over. 'One of the drakes. Poor old chap.' Before Kate realised what she was doing, she'd tossed the carcass into the nearest skip. 'It happens to them all, in the end.'

# FIFTEEN

The weather turned that week. Summer, which had looked as if it might linger as long as half term, suddenly collapsed like a soufflé toppling under its own weight, storms and rain piling in from the Atlantic. Sitting on Fresco had been rearranged for the weekend, but when the day came it was lashing down hard enough to put Will off, so Tilly went on her own. Predictably, she fell in love with Fresco at first sight, and arrangements were made to transfer him to Trade Cottage on loan. Kate, who knew nothing about horses, felt completely overwhelmed by the prospect of being responsible for one, but Rosemary assured her she'd be on hand to answer any questions, as well as to supervise Tilly's riding practice. 'She'll be doing little jumps in no time. And it's safe as houses – Fresco's completely bomb-proof.

'Oh, and by the way,' she added, 'we were thinking – well, Paul was – that Will might be feeling a bit left out, now Tilly's got a pony. So he wondered if Will would like to learn to shoot.'

'Oh,' Kate said, surprised. She instinctively wasn't a fan of shooting, though she suspected Will, with his love of video games, might be. But she didn't see how someone with MND could possibly supervise a loaded gun safely.

'Not here, of course,' Rosemary said, noticing Kate's hesitation. 'There's a gun club over at Four Marks. He can start off with Paul's .410 – it's lighter than a full-size shotgun, so there's hardly any recoil. Paul would watch and give him tips.'

Kate said she'd ask Will, but in fact she spoke to Matt first, that evening. Was learning to shoot normalising violence? But, as Matt pointed out, Will was already gunning down various monsters and baddies on a screen, and shooting clay discs might teach him that weapons had real-world consequences.

'I'm quite jealous, actually,' he added. 'It sounds fun.'

Will, as expected, also leapt at the idea. 'That'd be really cool.'

So, on Saturday mornings, Tilly had riding lessons on Fresco, trotting round and round the paddock on a lunge rein under Rosemary's watchful eye, and in the afternoons Will went with Paul and Rosemary in the Popemobile to the gun club. He came back from his first lesson bubbling with excitement. He'd hit over sixty per cent of his clays, he told Kate proudly; the man who ran the club said he had an eye for it.

'If I can get to eighty per cent, I can apply to join the under-fourteens team,' he added. 'Paul thinks playing *Metroid Prime* must have given me fast reactions.'

The weeks went by without the weather improving. But both children still went out in the rain to practise – Tilly in her hand-me-down riding gear, Will decked out in wax jackets and flat caps from The Old Tennis Court.

'Paul says there's no such thing as bad weather,' he reported solemnly to Kate. 'Only bad clothing.'

'Our children are becoming countrified,' Matt commented, watching Will climb into the Popemobile one day, while the heavens opened overhead.

She glanced at him. 'You don't mind, do you?'

He shook his head. 'They're making the most of their opportunities. It's great.'

It became too muddy to walk Biddy, but the children still went round to The Old Tennis Court to play with him. On one occasion, they were gone over three hours. Kate worried they might have overstayed their welcome, so she went round to collect them. She found Tilly and Rosemary doing a jigsaw, and Paul and Will at the telescope with a book on wildlife identification. It was really no trouble, Rosemary told her as Kate coaxed them away. Quite the opposite, in fact: Paul looked forward to Will's visits immensely, and she and Tilly got on like a house on fire.

Eventually, the storms blew through and the rain stopped. Kate realised she hadn't been to the orchard since the bad weather began. Taking a bowl, she headed down the slope.

The ground was littered with fallen figs, mushy from all that rain, but there were a few russet apples that yielded to her experimental twisting of their stalks. She'd picked half a bowlful when she happened to glance across at the fruit cage. It was full of leaves, she noticed; autumn was coming faster than she'd thought, and the leaves were turning in the breeze . . . And then, with a shock that rippled right through her, making her jump backwards, she realised they weren't leaves at all, but rats. Half a dozen rats, the size of rabbits, feasting on the fallen fruit.

Matt was at work, and her phone was back in the house, charging. She had to speak to someone right away – she'd always loathed rats, and her disgust and shock needed an immediate outlet. She hurried through the gate in the hedge, up to The Old Tennis Court. When Rosemary opened the door, she gabbled at her – rats in the fruit cage, and, as she'd dropped the bowl, she'd seen more under the fig tree—

'You'd better come in,' Rosemary interrupted. 'It's only rats – they'll have made a hole in the wire. That must have been what had a go at that duck, too. You can call someone out to deal with them.'

Shocked into silence by the other woman's uncharacteristically unsympathetic tone, Kate followed her inside.

'We're through here.' Rosemary led her to the room at the back, the one with the huge windows that overlooked Trade Cottage's garden. Paul was already there, gazing at the view. As he swung his wheelchair around, using the joystick, she saw he had a glass of champagne in his other hand.

'Ah! Kate, my dear!' he cried. 'We were just talking about you!'

'Why's that?' she asked.

'Glass of champagne? We're having a little celebration, actually. Fetch the bottle, will you, old thing?' he called to Rosemary.

'No, I don't . . .' Kate said quickly, but Rosemary had already disappeared into the kitchen. She turned back to Paul. 'What are you celebrating?'

'Rosemary said you'd very kindly offered to host us at Christmas,' he said. 'Incredibly good of you, but as it turns out, Jamie's going to be over with his family.'

'Oh, that's terrific,' she said, relieved that Rosemary's awkwardness was simply because she was worried about offending Kate over the Christmas arrangements. As Rosemary came back with the bottle, Kate smiled at her. 'No, thank you, but I'm so pleased for you about Jamie. How long are they over for?'

'Well, that's the amazing thing. He's relocating – they all are.' Paul was bubbling over with excitement. 'He's going to look for a job in the UK.'

'How wonderful!' Kate glanced at Rosemary, whose face was still oddly blank.

'It's what we've always wanted,' Paul agreed. 'Though we'd almost given up hope. Hamish turns thirteen in two weeks!'

'I think you need to spit it out,' Rosemary said to him fiercely. 'There is absolutely no point in beating around the bush like this.'

'Indeed,' Paul said. He sat back in his wheelchair and smiled at Kate. 'We'd like to buy back Trade Cottage.'

# SIXTEEN

It was like an explosion going off – the same sense of disorientation, of ringing ears, of not being able to follow what was being said. Paul was still talking, but she was only picking up the occasional word. '. . . haven't agreed with everything you've done, but that's by the by – Jamie will probably want to make some changes too. We'll stay here, in our little dower house.' He gestured at the hedge. 'Get rid of the rest of this bloody thing, so we can see them running around—'

'No!' she said. 'Of course we're not selling. It's our home!'

'You only moved in – what? Twelve weeks ago?' Paul said reasonably. 'Admittedly, Tray's a bit special, but you'll find somewhere else.'

She struggled to think of something, anything – some tangible reason to close down this madness. 'But it doesn't work like that. What about all the stamp duty we paid? It was over a hundred grand, just for that.'

'Of course, of course. That's why we'll pay you a very hefty premium.' Paul held out a piece of paper in one quavering hand. 'The full market value – which, just to remind you, was rather more than you paid for it – plus the stamp duty, plus a bit more to compensate you for the inconvenience of moving. Can't say fairer than that.'

For one terrible moment, she thought he was offering her a cheque, and that, if she took it, the deal would be done, like some awful childish game, or a contract in a fairy tale. She didn't move, and he gave the paper a bigger shake.

'The offer,' he said impatiently. 'We've put it all in writing, so you can chew it over with Matt.'

Reluctantly, she took it.

'That includes the chattels, by the way,' he added. 'The George Hayter portrait and so on. No going and flogging everything on eBay.'

She felt calmer now. She said carefully, 'Of course I'll tell Matt about this. But I don't want you to be under any illusions. The answer's no, and frankly I'm rather hurt you've even asked.'

Rosemary gave a little tut, though whether that was annoyance at Kate's answer or at the way her husband was handling this, she couldn't tell.

'Kate,' Paul said quietly. 'How long do you suppose I've got left to live? Care to guess? No? Well, the docs can't give me an exact time frame, but it's unlikely to be more than a few years. It rather focuses the mind, knowing your time's almost up. You start to think, What's really important? You and Matt seem like nice people, and Tilly and Will are lovely kids. But they're no substitute for our real grandchildren.'

'They were never meant to be,' Kate said, appalled. 'That was never the deal.' But, in a sudden flash of understanding, she realised that, as far as Rosemary and Paul were concerned, it *had* been the deal: that, in the absence of Jamie's children, hers had been a kind of stopgap, a second-best, a way to fill the woods once again with dens and shouts, and the paddock with a pony – and that was the only reason they'd accepted that below-market offer from her and Matt.

'Rosemary, too.' Paul indicated his wife. 'Age cannot wither her, nor custom stale, but the old girl's eighty-three. She can't go on forever. If you won't do it for the money, do it for a dying man and his soon-to-be-dying wife.'

Kate looked at Rosemary, willing her to put a stop to this awful emotional blackmail. But she seemed to take Kate's glance as a request for confirmation.

'It's true,' she said, nodding. 'The doctors think he's got three or four years at the most.'

Kate took a deep breath. 'All right – let's say you're right about that. If so, I am truly sorry, but it means, in just a few years' time, the whole purpose of this sale would be gone. In four years, Tilly will only be thirteen! We intend to spend *decades* here. It would be crazy for us to make a decision based on the next three or four years.'

'Unfortunately,' Paul said, 'it's my entire lifetime.'

She didn't know how to reply to that.

He indicated the paper in her hand. 'Look,' he said, his voice hardening, 'if you want to be selfish about it, fine, that's your prerogative. Go away, talk to your husband, and make as selfish a counterproposal as you feel inclined to. The truth is, you've got us over a barrel, and we'll pay you whatever we have to.'

# SEVENTEEN

'What was so crazy was that they acted like *I* was being the unreasonable one,' she exclaimed to Matt on the phone.

'Maybe they just got carried away by the news that Jamie's coming back. And you said Paul had been drinking.'

'He had a glass of champagne in his hand. And, yes, his speech was slurred, but it's always like that now – I don't think he was drunk. And Rosemary – she was just completely matter-of-fact about the whole thing. Like I was that duck whose neck needed wringing – unfortunate, but it had to be done.'

'Well, I'm glad you were firm with them,' Matt said. 'In my experience, people who say "name your price" immediately start haggling if you do. If Paul and Rosemary want to come back with a better offer, that's up to them, but I think otherwise we simply don't respond.'

'You wouldn't ever do it, though, would you?' she said anxiously. 'You wouldn't sell Trade Cottage?'

'Well – never say never and all that—'

She interrupted him. 'I do say it. I mean it, Matt. I'm not leaving here. They'll have to carry me out feet first.'

*

After he'd rung off, she went outside, to the terrace. The pale autumn sunshine was warming the stone table where, only three months before, she'd sat and eaten samaras with Rosemary and Paul, and they'd made that extraordinarily generous offer of the house's contents. But, in hindsight, had that been, perhaps, the first sign they weren't really relinquishing Trade Cottage at all – that, on some level at least, they'd still expected to be in control of who lived in it, and how?

Below her, the woods were just starting to turn golden, the first hues of autumn. But the fields beyond were still green, and the sheep contentedly grazing them as white as ever. Behind her, Trade Cottage's flint façade glimmered in the sun, a wonderful mosaic of greys and browns.

Perhaps it was the request to buy Trade Cottage back, or perhaps it was those awful rats, or both, but she felt, for the first time here, under threat – the same stomach-churning sense of homesickness and vertigo as when her mother announced they had to move somewhere cheaper.

She placed her hand on the flint wall, feeling its reassuring solidity, its centuries-old permanence. *Don't worry, we're not selling*, she told it in her head. *We're here forever.* Without thinking, she leaned forward and kissed the shining, glossy centre of one of the flints. The gesture was answered immediately by a strange surge of ecstasy, almost as if the house was embracing her in return. She recalled Rosemary telling her that her children had caught her once doing the same thing, and that she'd told them they were too young to understand. But Kate did understand what it was to love a place, and, unlike Rosemary, she had no intention of relinquishing it.

'Don't respond,' Matt had said, and she could see the logic in that. But, as the day wore on, she realised she couldn't just leave it. Not when she and Rosemary had been, such a short time before, so incredibly close. And surely that couldn't only have been because Paul and Rosemary wanted children next door they could pretend to grandparent. Rosemary had genuinely become her friend.

This all started with a letter. It had been perfect – everyone had said so. It had persuaded Rosemary and Paul that she and Matt were the right people to live in Trade Cottage. She just had to convince them – well, convince Rosemary; she didn't really care about Paul – for a second time, and perhaps they'd come to their senses.

She sat down at the captain's desk and wrote. She remembered the first time she'd been in this room, the neat piles of cards and envelopes. She didn't have proper stationery like that, just her laptop and a printer, so those would have to do. She wrote quickly, the words flowing out of her again. She completely understood Paul and Rosemary's situation, she explained, and that, in their shoes, she might well have asked the same question, in case anything had changed. But she reminded them why they'd chosen her and Matt to buy Trade Cottage in the first place: it was because they'd fallen in love with it, just as Rosemary and Paul had, forty-odd years before. And it was precisely because she and Matt loved it so much that they couldn't possibly contemplate selling, not even for Jamie. She wrote:

*I know this may put a strain on our friendship, and that's the very worst thing about it. But you should know that another reason I couldn't sell is because, wherever we lived, I'd never find such a special neighbour. I very much hope that, when the dust has settled, we'll go back to being friends again.*

*All my love, Kate.*

She drove the long way round to The Old Tennis Court. The big electric gate was closed. Next to it, the Ring doorbell glowed, the tiny lens staring at her like the beady eye of an old teddy bear. She almost pressed the button, but it would have seemed odd to summon Rosemary to the door only to hand her a letter. She folded her sheet of A4 and pushed it into the letter box's yawning mouth.

# EIGHTEEN

That night, as Matt slept beside her, she lay in bed, listening to the house. It was windy, and Trade Cottage was responding with a series of moans and reverberations, shaking whenever it was buffeted by a particularly strong gust. The soughing of the leylandii outside the window was like the crashing of distant surf, and the house felt like a ship under full sail, ploughing on through choppy waters.

Her reaction to Paul and Rosemary's offer had been atavistic, she knew – as visceral as her disgust at the rats. Matt couldn't quite get his head around it. As far as he was concerned, they'd made a slightly ridiculous suggestion, and she'd pooh-poohed it, and that was that.

He'd even said he felt sorry for Paul. 'I didn't realise he had so little time left. I should take him to the pub for a drink. It must be so frustrating for him, being stuck in that wheelchair all day.'

'Well, don't ask him until this is over,' she'd said. 'Or he'll think you want a man-to-man chat about the price.'

For her, it wasn't just Paul's gall in trying to buy back a house he'd only just sold them that was so upsetting. It felt like a massive betrayal, after he and Rosemary had been so welcoming. And that, she realised, was something she was particularly vulnerable to, in a way Matt wasn't.

When her mother first started drinking, blaming it on the stress of the divorce, Kate had tried to go and live with her father. Discovering that he and his new partner didn't actually want her while they focused on their own baby had undermined her self-confidence just when she needed it most. Good-looking, charming men like Paul or her father, she'd learnt, always withdrew their favour in the end.

And if Rosemary had been drawn to Tilly and Will in part because they'd filled a gap left by her own absent grandchildren, something similar might also have been true for her, she realised. Perhaps she and Rosemary weren't friends despite the age gap, but because of it. Perhaps Rosemary had become the mother figure that, on some level, Kate had been looking for ever since she was twelve.

Which made her and Jamie siblings of a kind, she thought drowsily. Rosemary's real child, returning to take his rightful place, not just in Trade Cottage, but in his mother's affections.

*Well, you can fuck right off,* she found herself thinking. *You're not having any of it. Or her.*

# NINETEEN

The pest controller came the next morning. Kate took him down to the fruit cage and left him to it. Just thinking about the rats gave her a horrible, creepy feeling of being invaded.

He came back to the house twenty minutes later. 'You need to get rid of their food source,' he told her. 'Rotting fruit and veg are a rodent's favourite meal. Once that's done, I can put out bait boxes. But you've still got the problem of where they're living.'

'Which is where?' she asked with a shudder.

'Your cesspit,' he said succinctly. 'At some point, someone likely shoved a crowbar down there and made a few holes in it – they used to do that, in the old days, to make a septic tank behave more like a soakaway. But the rats have got in, and now they're living in your drains.'

She stared at him, appalled. 'In the *house*'s drains? You mean, they could come inside?'

He nodded. 'Until the infestation's cleared, you'd best keep all the toilet lids closed.'

'Ugh,' she said, horrified. 'That is *gross*.'

So Matt went out and bought a huge rat-proof composter,

which he and Robert assembled near the fruit cage and filled with wheelbarrow-loads of rotting fruit.

'We need to reduce the number of fruit trees, too,' Matt said when he came in. 'There are way too many.'

Next, a drainage contractor came to take a closer look at the cesspit. His news wasn't good, either. It would have to be replaced.

'Septic-tank regulations have all changed now,' he explained. 'You'll need a completely new set-up, with a soakaway and a drainage field to deal with the run-off.' He gestured at Trade Cottage's lawns. 'Basically, we'll have to dig all that up and install porous pipes under it.'

It was unfortunate in terms of their budget. But she felt slightly better now she knew they were getting on top of it. Rosemary and Paul couldn't have managed this, she told herself. This is the proof Trade Cottage needed younger, more energetic owners.

She hadn't seen or spoken to Rosemary since she and Paul made their offer, so she hadn't told her about the cesspit yet. But when she, Matt and the contractor were pacing out the lawn, deciding where the new drainage ditches would go, she caught a flash of light in the corner of her eye and saw the telescope in the window of The Old Tennis Court, dipping in their direction.

Days went by, and there was still no reply to her letter. She waited in a state of nervous agitation – Rosemary had apologised so swiftly about the leylandii, and then again after the upset over the fireplace, that a part of Kate was certain she'd see the Popemobile pulling up to the house any moment, a repentant Rosemary at the door, bearing a card perhaps, or flowers, along with fulsome apologies.

But she didn't.

Finally, five days after Kate had written to her, she found a thick cream envelope on her mat, bearing Rosemary's handwriting. She opened it.

*Dear Kate,*

*Like you, I would very much like to stay friends. I also hope you and Matt will reconsider our offer, which we believe is already very generous, if only for the sake of that friendship.*

*R*

*P.S. Just a reminder to the children not to walk through the wood on Saturday. The beaters will probably come through TC's garden about noon, unless you've any objection. Would Will and/or Tilly like to join them?*

Saturday? What was Saturday? Then she realised. It must be the first day of the shoot.

Of course, it was good that her letter had been at least partially successful, and Rosemary hadn't completely withdrawn the hem of her garment. But she couldn't help feeling disappointed. The tone of the reply was cordial, but chilly – the very opposite of Kate's letter to her, and indeed of the intimate, informal emails they'd exchanged earlier that year. But perhaps this was how it was going to be from now on.

She told the children about the invitation to go beating as they ate tea. Tilly was predictably horrified at the idea of living creatures being blasted out of the sky – rightly, in Kate's view – but Will instantly said, 'Yeah, I'll go.'

Matt came home with a crumb of good news. The plans for the outbuilding conversions, on which their architect had been working since mid-August, were ready to be submitted. They debated whether to delay the application because of Rosemary and Paul's offer – or rather, Kate wondered aloud if it might be a bit tactless, rubbing salt in the wound of ownership as it were, and Matt pointed out that, if anything, it proved how committed they were to being at Trade Cottage for the long term; besides, it wasn't as if Rosemary and Paul didn't know what they intended to do. So they gave Nikolas the go-ahead to upload them, which felt like another milestone, putting their own stamp on the place.

'We should celebrate,' Matt said, when the architect emailed confirmation it was done. 'Do we have any champagne?'

'No.' She'd gone off champagne since Paul had tried to push a glass on her along with his unwelcome proposal.

Matt gave her a glance. 'Not following the house rule, then?'

'We make the rules here, now,' she said shortly. 'I'll open some beer.'

# TWENTY

On Saturday, the day of the shoot, it rained again. Will appeared, looking like some bizarre countryside app had Photoshopped him into a mini-squire – flat cap, check breeches, waxed jacket: his shooting gear, all cast-offs from The Old Tennis Court. A little later, she heard vehicles. Two Land Rovers pulled up and disgorged a dozen or so people dressed similarly to Will, some with dogs. Kate recognised Gordon and a couple of others. They greeted her politely but quietly, then went round the side of the house into the garden, Will eagerly tagging along.

At the bottom, they silently spread out in a line – almost like a police search party, Kate thought. They seemed to be waiting for a signal. Some put whistles in their mouths.

A voice – it sounded like Gordon's – gave a shout, and the line erupted into noise: yelling, whistling, bashing the bushes in front of them with sticks. The dogs, immediately excited, began barking. Already, alarmed pheasants were clattering into the air. The line of people moved forward, hollering and yelping. Ahead of them, out of sight beyond the trees, the guns started up, the barrage of bangs adding to the din. For a moment she thought, What have I done? I've literally sent my son into the line of fire. But then she told herself not to be so fearful – if people got injured doing this, it wouldn't be allowed, and, in any case, the pheasants were flying upwards, over the trees, well above the beaters' heads.

After about twenty minutes, the woods fell silent again. Two beaters returned, hurrying up the garden.

She intercepted them. 'Where's Will?'

'Park Farm,' one of them said, gesturing vaguely. 'There'll be two more drives, then the shoot tea. Don't worry, we'll make sure he gets a lift home.' With that, they climbed into the Land Rovers, clearly impatient to rendezvous with the others.

Will didn't get back until after six. His face was covered in mud, and he was exhausted but exhilarated. 'That was the best day ever. Andy from my class at school was there too. He's getting a shotgun for his birthday. How cool is that?'

'I doubt you can get a shotgun licence at twelve,' Matt said. 'Maybe Andy's exaggerating?'

'He said there's no minimum age. And his dad's one of the guns, so I think he'd know,' Will said scornfully.

Matt pulled out his phone and did a quick search. 'Blimey. Looks like Andy's right. But I'm afraid there's no way you're getting a shotgun for your birthday.'

To change the subject, Kate said, 'How did you get mud on your face?'

'It's not mud,' Will said. 'They blooded me, because it was my first. It was brilliant.'

There was a strange postscript to the shoot. On Monday, Kate was painting a bedroom when she heard a vehicle pull up outside.

She put down her brush and went to see who it was. But, when she opened the front door, a Land Rover was already speeding off.

The door felt unusually heavy. She pulled it all the way open, then jumped back with a cry of disgust. Someone had hung two dead pheasants on it – they were tied together at the neck with a piece of baler twine, looped over the door knocker, so the necks hung limply to each side. You could see where one of the birds had been shot – its elaborate feathers were matted with blood. The other appeared to be unscathed, its dappled plumage startlingly beautiful, its neck the same iridescent blue as a peacock's. Their long tail feathers almost touched the ground.

Her first thought was that it must be some kind of protest, that animal-rights activists had targeted them for allowing beaters through their garden. But she was sure the vehicle she'd just seen was one that had parked there on Saturday. So was it more personal than that? Had she and Matt offended someone, and this was the rural equivalent of waking up with a horse's head in your bed? Could it even be connected to ignoring Paul and Rosemary's offer?

She pushed the door shut, feeling the heavy clunk of the carcasses swinging against it as she did so. Should she call the police? Use the village Facebook page to warn her neighbours? Rosemary might know what to do, but she was still feeling a bit reticent about Rosemary. She pulled out her phone and messaged Liv: *Do you have a minute? Something weird was just left on my door.* She hesitated, then went outside and added a picture of the dead birds, leaving their heads and most of their bodies out of the picture because they were just too gruesome.

Liv called her back almost immediately. 'Did you do the shoot a favour?'

'Well – some of them walked through the garden. And Will helped with the beating.' At the thought of someone targeting her son, her stomach churned.

'The gamekeeper's left you a brace as a thank-you,' Liv said calmly. 'He'll have loads of them to deliver, which is why he won't have stopped to chat.'

'You mean, to eat?' Kate said slowly, realisation dawning.

'Exactly. You should hang them for a week or so, until the flesh starts to get a bit whiffy. You'll need to gut them and pluck them, of course, but you do that after you hang them, not before. Leave them outside, somewhere the foxes can't get them, like over a beam.'

'Oh my God,' Kate said, relieved. 'I thought it was something awful. I was about to post a warning on the village Facebook page.'

Liv hooted with laughter. 'Just as well you called me first. You'd never have lived that down.'

Kate didn't want to look at the dead birds, let alone move them. But she definitely couldn't leave them for Will or, more pertinently, Tilly to find on their return from school. Going outside, she hooked a finger gingerly through the loop of twine and carried them over to the barn. They were surprisingly heavy, the fat bodies bumping against each other with each stride, the twine tight against her finger, the sharp beaks occasionally pecking her ribs. The heads were hanging limply like that because their necks had been wrung, she realised with a shudder. Welcome to the countryside. She threw the pheasants over a beam and left them, quite literally, to rot.

# TWENTY-ONE

To her surprise, Matt and Will greeted the news that there were two dead pheasants in the barn with glee. They looked up gutting videos on Matt's phone, watching intently with their heads pressed together. At one point, she heard Will say, 'I should pull the organs out, because I've got smaller hands,' and felt slightly nauseous. Even Tilly, who was always going on about becoming vegan one day, talked approvingly about zero food miles and eating what you killed. And, miracle of miracles, Matt and Will were even googling recipes now, determined to cook the birds themselves. Coq au vin – or, more accurately, faisane au vin – was decided on, not least because Will was rather excited by the idea of flambéing mushrooms in cognac and then adding a whole bottle of wine.

On Sunday, they left the pheasants slow-cooking in the Aga and strolled to the pub for a drink. This is the life I dreamt of, Kate thought to herself as they walked through the village. My family together, happy, doing something on a Sunday morning that doesn't involve getting in a car and struggling across London. Yes, there had been challenges – she thought of how close she'd come to warning the whole village about a gamekeeper handing out pheasants – but they were meeting them, and getting on top of the renovations, and managing to navigate a tricky patch with their neighbours to boot.

As they walked into the pub, she saw the log fire burning, the locals sitting round in twos and threes, families tucking into Sunday roasts, and felt utterly contented. Matt ordered a pint of Bowman's and she had Guinness. The pub did amazing olives that they marinated themselves in big jars behind the bar, so they had a bowl of those too, and crisps and Coke for the children.

'Hi, Jason,' Matt called over to the landlord. 'How's things?'

'Hi,' Jason said blankly. He turned away.

'Odd,' Matt said. 'He's usually quite chatty. Maybe they're having a bad day in the kitchen.'

Kate recognised the woman who'd been at book club as she passed them with some empty plates. 'Hey, Elizabeth, how are you?' she said. There was no reply or answering smile, just the briefest of nods.

Kate felt the first stirrings of consternation. 'Have we done something to offend the pub?'

Two men walked past, pints in hand. They were clearly villagers – both were wearing check shirts, one with the sleeveless gilet a lot of locals favoured. 'I've got nothing against tourism,' the first man was saying, 'but it's not as if the rooms in this place are ever full, except maybe in wedding season. He's right: there has to be some kind of control.' The other man was nodding his agreement.

'Oh, God,' she said suddenly to Matt. 'I wonder if this could be about our application.' They'd had to specify that the conversions would be used for short-term lets, which these days required additional planning permission.

'The outbuildings?' he said, puzzled. 'Why?'

'They have rooms here, in the pub.'

He pulled a face. 'Totally different markets, though, surely? I'll have a word with Jason, make sure he's not heard something on the grapevine and taken offence.'

He started to get up, but she stopped him. 'Wait—'

At the other end of the bar, the man in the gilet was calling across to someone, 'Signed the petition yet, Mike? It's by the beer taps, so you won't see it unless you buy a round.' There was laughter, and some banter in return.

As if in a dream, Kate got up and walked towards the taps. On the bar was a clipboard, a biro attached to it with string and tape. She turned it towards her so she could read it.

*We, the undersigned, call on our Parish and District Councils to designate Pelham Village a short-let-free zone, and furthermore to refuse planning consent to all new short-let accommodation.*

Below were the words *Pelham Preservation Committee* and some names she didn't recognise.

Except for the one that jumped out at her.

*Paul Finch (chair)*

# TWENTY-TWO

It wasn't just the committee who'd signed it. Underneath were blank rows for other people to add their names. Jason's was there, and Elizabeth's, and page after page of others she didn't recognise. Most of them couldn't possibly know what this was about, she thought in disbelief. They could even just be visitors, popping in for a drink – signing, perhaps, in the time it took a pint of Guinness to settle. But there could be absolutely no doubt: this entire petition was aimed squarely at her and Matt. She flicked through the pages, feeling sick. On the next-to-last page, she spotted Liv's signature.

Jason came over to pull a pint. She gestured at the petition. 'What's this?'

'You're entitled to make your application,' he said neutrally. 'And we're entitled to object.'

'You didn't think to ask us about it first?' she said incredulously.

'We would have done, if that was how you'd wanted to play it. But the first we heard about it was when someone warned us.'

'Paul,' she said with resignation.

Jason nodded. 'It's good of him to give his time on the committee.

Shows how much he cares about this village.' He carried the pint away without another word.

She gestured at Matt, who came over and took in the petition with one swift glance. He looked at Jason, who was twisting a corkscrew into a bottle of wine at the other end of the bar, and opened his mouth to say something. She put her hand on his arm to stop him. The pub was full of locals, and, if she wasn't mistaken, the man in the gilet was watching them with a slightly amused expression.

'Not here,' she said. 'Everyone's watching.'

By unspoken agreement, they didn't tell the children. Back at home, Kate had to feign raptures over the pheasant – she'd completely lost her appetite, which was a shame, because it was in fact delicious. As well as the mushrooms and red wine, Will and Matt had added shallots, smoked lardons and lots of thyme. It was extraordinary how the slow cooking left the wine not tasting of alcohol at all, just oniony, herby meatiness. But there was no way she could enjoy it now, not when she felt this besieged. That sense of everyone turning against her – it was like being back at school, people talking behind her back, ganging up.

Matt was more sanguine. 'It's only some names on a petition,' he said reassuringly as they stacked the dishwasher. 'It doesn't mean we won't get it.'

'It means people will hate us if we do.'

'Does it, though?' he said gently. 'Most of the people who signed will have given it about ten seconds' thought.'

She knew he was right, but she still felt miserable. 'I can't believe Rosemary and Paul could be so two-faced as to try to turn the village against us.'

'Well, we know what their motivation is.' He caught her puzzled look. 'They must be hoping that, if we don't get it, we'll agree to sell up.'

'Oh. Of course.' She hadn't thought of it that way. 'It won't work though, will it? Could we survive without the Airbnbs, if we had to?'

'Maybe,' he said uneasily. 'But it's already pretty tight.' He nodded towards the garden. 'That drainage field's going to cost a fortune. This kitchen wasn't cheap. And I guess we're going to need a planning consultant now, too.'

In some ways, it was easier for Matt – on Monday, he got up early to commute to the office. He'd spend the day in a different world: chairing meetings, untangling issues, solving problems. Trade Cottage was all Kate had, and now it felt under attack.

To take her mind off it, she went for a walk. She'd never been the whole way through the woods before, only as far as Will's forts and the little stream Matt had been clearing of fallen trees. There was a narrow bridge, effectively just a six-foot plank, which she crossed, pressing onwards.

The further she went, the more tangled the woods became. Trees that had fallen lay rotting on the ground, shaggy with moss, or leaned precariously against other trees. The path she was following had been made by animals less tall than her – deer, presumably – and she often had to duck under trailing briars or low branches. Occasionally, pheasants rocketed away from her, making her jump.

Eventually, she reached a muddy track. Turning left, she knew, would take her to Gordon's farm. Turning right would take her through Pelham Park into the village, so she went that way.

As she walked, she wondered if she should write another letter to Rosemary. If the other woman only understood how hurtful this campaign against the two of them was, might she get Paul to back off? She tried to compose something in her head, but everything she came up with seemed either self-pitying or aggressively formal. And, of course, Jason was right: people were entitled to object if they wanted to. It just seemed so utterly unfair.

At the edge of the village, she reached the church – a pretty building also made of speckled flint. The path led through the churchyard, and as she passed the graves, she glanced down at the names: *Theophilius Scott . . . Cassandra Mount . . . Beloved Anne Stevens . . .* There was a section of newer headstones, too. Her eye was caught by one much smaller than the others. It was quite weathered, the inscription already fading, but, when she leaned down, she could just make out the name.

*Andrew Christopher Finch.*

She felt the skin at the nape of her neck prickle. *Finch.* It was the same family – it must be, there was no one else in the village with that name. She tried to work out the dates. Andrew Finch had been just eleven months old when he died. And – she did a rough calculation in her head – he must have been Rosemary's third child, a younger sibling to Jamie and Tessa.

She felt stunned. She thought back to the times she'd talked to Rosemary about her own miscarriages. How was it even possible the other woman hadn't said something about this? Of course, she had a perfect right not to, but those conversations had seemed so intimate, so self-exposing, that to discover Rosemary hadn't been reciprocating felt doubly wounding. Had she been quietly judging Kate all along, dismissing her experiences as being so trivial by comparison that she wouldn't even mention her own bereavement? Or did she think it bad taste, perhaps, even to talk about grief?

Either way, Kate thought, it was a reminder that you didn't always know people as well as you thought. She walked back towards Trade Cottage miserably and a little fearfully, eyeing the houses on either side with trepidation. Like an armada of ships bearing down on them, she thought, a frozen flotilla bent on their destruction.

# TWENTY-THREE

Walking up the drive, she saw there was a car outside the house. A dark-haired woman was standing at the front door, knocking. As Kate watched, she crossed to the nearest skip and peered inside, as if to see if there was anything in it she wanted. Well, good luck with that, Kate thought – the skip contained only an avocado bathroom suite and some Formica-topped kitchen units.

'Can I help you?' she asked as she approached, and was gratified to see the other woman jump slightly.

'Ah,' she said, a little breathlessly. 'I'm looking for Mrs Crowther.'

'Well, I'm not in there,' Kate said, indicating the skip. She smiled to show she was joking. 'I'm Kate Crowther.'

'Excellent,' the woman said. 'I was hoping I'd catch you. Annie Thwaites, the council's conservation officer. Could I take a look at your barns?'

Kate walked her round the side of the house to the outbuildings, slightly regretting that joke about the skip now. The conservation officer, she knew from Nikolas, would be crucial in deciding whether or not their designs were judged to be in keeping with the rest of Trade Cottage. If Annie Thwaites decided they weren't, the planners would almost certainly refuse Kate and Matt's application.

Annie had a printout of the plans, which she compared to the actual thing, nodding and making notes. Eventually, Kate could bear it no longer. 'Is there a problem?'

'We always try to do a site visit when it's somewhere as sensitive in conservation terms as this is,' Annie said reassuringly.

Which was not, Kate thought, actually an answer to her question.

'We've received quite a high volume of correspondence about this application, too,' Annie added. 'So I thought I'd come and see for myself.'

Kate did what she could. 'As you can see, we've tried to follow all the guidance – leaving the exterior as unchanged as possible, keeping the distinction between old and new, reusing traditional materials and so on.'

Annie nodded. 'Yes, your architect's clearly experienced at working with heritage buildings.'

That was a relief. Perhaps Matt was right, Kate thought, and the planning officials wouldn't be swayed by all the flak and noise from the Pelham Preservation Committee. They must be used to it, after all: rising above Nimbyism was part of their job.

'Would you like a coffee while you're looking?' she asked.

Annie smiled. 'I'd love one. But actually, I'm done out here. Shall we go inside, and you can talk me through the plans in more detail?'

In the kitchen, while Kate made the coffees, Annie glanced around. 'This is nice. Was it the same architect?'

'Thank you,' Kate said, pleased at the compliment. It could only help, she felt, that Annie had seen for herself that she and Matt were people of taste who were going to be respectful of Trade Cottage's past. 'No, Nikolas is only doing the outbuildings. I designed this myself, with a local kitchen company. It was the dining room before we came.'

Annie took a mouthful of coffee and nodded appreciatively. 'Have you done much else?'

'Just upgraded the bathrooms – they didn't even have showers before. And we took out a modern fireplace. Other than that, it's only boring stuff like the cesspit – we need a drainage field under the garden, apparently. And I've been stripping wallpaper and painting.' Then, because she realised Annie's question might have been a loaded one, she added, 'Obviously, with it being a listed building, we wouldn't do anything structural. Or anything that would affect the exterior.'

'Yes,' Annie said. She put her coffee down. 'The thing is, as the custodian of a listed building, you're not actually allowed to do anything at all. Even to the interior. Whether it's structural or not.'

Kate looked at her, puzzled. 'But surely painting's all right?'

'Not unless you're exactly replacing like for like. I take it this wasn't?'

'Well . . .' Kate said, astounded. 'No. But—'

'Did you use specialist heritage paints?'

Chastened, Kate shook her head.

'There are specific environmental permissions you'll need for the drainage field,' Annie went on. 'But as it's in the curtilage of a listed building – its grounds, in other words – you'll need listed building consent as well. And you'll need to apply for retrospective consent for everything you've done so far.'

Kate stared at her. 'But what happens if we don't get it?'

Annie gave a tight smile. 'Potentially, you'll be made to put everything back the way it was.'

'But it was just tat from forty years ago!' Kate cried. 'Formica countertops and avocado loos. And that fireplace was totally out of keeping.'

'Actually, preserving evidence of a house's evolution through time is all part of its heritage,' Annie said mildly. 'What you call "tat" might be considered a period feature in another twenty years.'

At the thought of being forced to rip out her beautiful new kitchen, Kate was speechless.

There was a loud banging upstairs. 'Are those builders I can hear?' Annie asked.

Kate nodded. No point in denying it; it was written on their van, parked next to the skips. 'They're putting in a shower.'

'You need to tell them to stop. Until you have consent, you're committing an offence under Section 9 of the Planning Act 1990.' Annie's tone was still mild, but there was steel in it too. Kate half-expected her to announce that she had the right to remain silent, but anything she did say might be given in evidence.

The conservation officer stood up. 'Hopefully, it'll all get sorted out,' she said, more encouragingly. 'I'll write a note to the complainants saying we've had this conversation, and that you'll be following the proper process from now on. You may get a visit from an enforcement officer, to check no more work's been done, but that's standard practice.'

'Hang on.' Kate stood up too. 'So there's been a complaint? About what we've done inside the house?'

Annie nodded. 'Unlike planning objections, we don't make listed building complaints public, so I can't say who it came from.'

'It's all right,' Kate said bitterly. 'I know exactly who it was.'

# TWENTY-FOUR

She phoned Matt, but it went to voicemail. She sent him a text – *Call me asap* – and typed 'Do I need listed building consent for minor alterations/painting' into her laptop's web browser. She didn't expect Annie to have been wrong, but perhaps other people would know how to deal with this nightmare.

According to the forums she found, it varied from council to council. But the internet was awash with horror stories about homeowners forced to restore breeze-block porches and old linoleum floors. And, for every person wailing that they'd been made to keep a colour scheme they didn't like, or spend a fortune matching new to old, there were half a dozen smug wankers telling them that, if they didn't like the rules, they shouldn't have bought an old building in the first place.

Something else struck her. Annie had said listed building complaints were confidential, unlike planning objections. That suggested she could view the planning objections online.

She went to the council's planning portal and typed in her postcode. Two applications came up – Rosemary and Paul's for The Old Tennis Court, two years ago, and Kate and Matt's. Below that were the names and addresses of people who'd commented – over thirty already.

She clicked on the parish council's response. It was headed *PC Decision: OBJECTION*. Underneath was a long list of reasons. *Short term lets associated with rowdy behaviour . . . Taking business away from the Pelham Arms, jeopardising the survival of an important Community Asset . . . Increase in traffic . . . Increased potential for noisy parties . . .* She snorted with disbelief at that, remembering the sleepless night of reggae. *Extra refuse collection capacity required . . . Creeping development within the Conservation Area . . .*

The one that brought her up short, though, was the final one.

*Trade Cottage has already seen part of its curtilage developed into a substantial new dwelling, The Old Tennis Court. Any further development would constitute over-density of this important heritage site.*

That was unbelievable – using the fact they'd already built something to try to stop her and Matt doing the same!

She went back to Rosemary and Paul's application from two years ago. That had sailed through with no objections, of course.

She clicked on some of the other objectors' comments. They'd clearly been copied from a template – they all made exactly the same points. But the sheer number was depressing. Once again, she had that stomach-churning feeling of being ganged up on.

On the village Facebook page, it was a similar theme – the petition was being circulated there as well, and people were being encouraged to 'make their feelings known'. Did the village really have nothing better to do? she thought incredulously. Did none of them stop to consider how disproportionate this was to a couple of small outbuilding conversions that would host, at most, four people at a time?

But, of course, for most of them it was nothing to do with the actual merits of the application. It was about supporting two popular longstanding residents in their battle against some unknown newcomers.

Matt finally called her back. She vented about the horrible objections online, as well as the conservation officer's visit.

'I'm kicking myself we didn't think to check with Nikolas about what we're allowed to do,' she added. 'But ripping out a couple of avocado baths just seemed like a no-brainer.'

There was silence on Matt's end of the line.

'What?' she asked.

'He did mention something,' Matt admitted. 'But he said most people don't bother for really tiny alterations – you're so unlikely to get caught, and once you start to engage with conservation officers, they might pick up on all sorts of issues you'd never even thought about. Like you say – it just seemed a no-brainer.'

She was silent. If she'd known, she'd have followed the rules and put in an application. Their attitudes to risk were fundamentally different – he'd had the balls to start his own company, after all, while she was naturally more cautious. They only had Trade Cottage in the first place because of his entrepreneurial nature, but having got it, she didn't want to take any risks with it.

'Look, let's not panic prematurely,' he said at last. 'I'll speak to Nikolas. He might know what to do.'

He called again a short while later. 'Nikolas knows that conservation officer. He says she's got a reputation as being one of the tougher ones, but he's always found her pretty fair. For an extra fee, he'll draw up retrospective applications for everything we've done so far. But he advises not to get the skips emptied in the meantime, in case we have to put something back.'

'But everything's smashed up!'

'Yes, but at least, if we've got it, we can match it.' Matt paused. 'He also thinks the application for the outbuildings will go to a full planning committee hearing, now the parish council's objected. Each side will be able to address the meeting for three minutes. I think you should do it.'

'Why me?' She hated speaking in public.

'Let's face it, it'll be Paul for the antis. A dying man in a wheelchair, who until recently was chair of the parish council and who helped to save the village pub from closure? Next to him, I'll just come across as a heartless incomer who spends most of his time in London. Of the two of us, you've got by far the better chance.'

After he rang off, she sat there, thinking. She'd do it, of course she would. Anything to protect Trade Cottage from those who wanted to wrest it from her.

She looked around at the gleaming, beautiful kitchen. It still felt utterly right to her. Annie Thwaites had talked about preserving a house's evolution through time, but surely that was the whole point – houses *should* evolve. Trade Cottage was a living, breathing organism; it shouldn't be fossilised at some arbitrary moment forty years ago.

The conservation officer had used the word 'custodian', too. Yes, Kate thought. That's exactly what I am – the house's guardian. And that's why I know what's best for Trade Cottage, more than any paper-pushing council official.

# TWENTY-FIVE

She went to say goodbye to the builders. Since Annie hadn't actually seen how much they'd done, Steve had offered to spend a couple of hours making everything functional before they left. So at least Tilly and Will had a working shower, loo and sink, even if the pipework was exposed and the walls were a mixture of broken tiles and chipped plaster.

'By the way,' Steve said, 'we found this under the bath.'

He handed her a cardboard box stuffed with papers. 'It was behind the inspection hatch,' he added, 'so it looks like someone put it there deliberately. Maybe the previous owners?'

She knew immediately what it was, even before she saw the old title deeds and other dog-eared documents on top. She pulled a page out at random. *Pelham then trained at Dartmouth before joining HMS Curlew as a midshipman* . . . Yes – Rosemary's famous notes. Her handwriting hadn't always been as spidery as it was now: here, it was clear and beautiful, an elegant sloping italic from an era when schoolgirls were taught such things.

'If they put it there for safekeeping, it might be important,' the builder added. 'You should probably let them know.'

'Yes,' Kate said, 'I should.' She gave him a smile. 'Leave it with me.'

It was very quiet without Steve and his men there. She took the box to the study and sat in the captain's chair, under the gaze of the man himself, to look through it.

She quickly realised that Rosemary hadn't been wrong when she'd described the manuscript as being mostly notes. There were a couple of finished chapters describing the captain's early life, and one about the history of the house before his arrival, but everything else was just a jumble of scribblings, maps, newspaper cuttings and some completely unrelated material – recipes, lists of dinner-party guests and what dishes they'd been served, even Jamie and Tessa's old school reports and photographs. Everything that had seemed too important to throw away from a lifetime at Trade Cottage.

She should give it back, she knew. It might even thaw some of this terrible frost between them. But she wasn't feeling very generous towards Rosemary at the moment. And besides, another thought had crept unbidden into her brain, beguiling her with its wickedness.

What if she wrote the history of Trade Cottage herself, using Rosemary's material? What if this was the spur she'd needed to kickstart her writing? It would serve Rosemary right for everything she and Paul were putting them through.

She was still considering that when there was a loud knocking at the front door. She jumped – she hadn't heard a car. Going to the oriel window, she saw a battered old Land Rover, similar to the one Rosemary and Paul used to have. On the doorstep she glimpsed a waxed jacket and a mop of sandy-coloured hair, and recognised Guy Pelham.

'Hello again,' he said when she opened the door. 'Got a minute?'

She led him into the kitchen. He glanced around thoughtfully, but only said, 'I wanted a word about this Rosemary-and-Paul situation.'

'Sure.' She assumed he was going to say they must have taken leave of their senses.

Instead, he said, 'My understanding is, they've made you a pretty decent offer. I just wondered what your thinking was about that.'

'We're not selling,' she said flatly.

'Ah.' He stroked his chin. 'You see, my worry is, if Jamie doesn't get this place back, they might all decamp somewhere else entirely.'

She refrained from saying, *Hooray.* 'What would be so bad about that?'

He looked surprised she'd even asked. 'We might lose them from the village completely. And – well, it may be hard for you to grasp, not having lived here all that long, but they're the absolute mainstay of this community. Paul's given me some very useful pointers about the business side of Pelham Park, for example. And Rosemary is . . . well, Rosemary. It would be devastating for us if they went.'

Annoyed, she shrugged. 'You'll just have to persuade them not to.'

'Paul wants to spend some time with his son and grandchildren before he dies,' Guy said quietly. 'That's not so unreasonable.'

'It was his choice to put this place on the market!' she snapped.

Then, softening her tone – she didn't want it getting about that she was a heartless cow, on top of everything else – she said, 'Obviously, I'm desperately sorry about his condition. But Rosemary told me he was diagnosed two years ago. Jamie knew the timescale, presumably – if he'd wanted to move his family back sooner, he could have done.'

Guy Pelham said flatly, 'So, basically, nothing I say will persuade you.'

She shook her head firmly. 'And no amount of money. My children love it here and they're my number-one priority.'

He nodded. 'Right, then. I'll see myself out.'

And, later, going over the encounter in her head, she realised there was something in his tone as he said those last words that hadn't been the least bit pleasant.

# TWENTY-SIX

She relayed the whole infuriating encounter to Matt when he got home.

'It was like he expected me to tug my forelock and say we'd be out by the end of the week. I can't believe they've got the whole place in their pockets like this.'

'Maddening,' Matt agreed. But he seemed distracted.

'Is something wrong?' she asked.

'Oh . . .' He rubbed his face wearily. 'The French are being more demanding than I expected. They're happy to ignore the terms of the deal when it suits them, but if our profits slip by even one quarter . . .' He shrugged.

She felt a pang of anxiety. 'But it's all OK, yes? There's nothing which could affect the loan?'

'No, of course not,' he said quickly. 'Everything's fine. And we've got a couple of big pitches coming up that should see us sorted.' He gave her a tired smile.

But those last two statements, she realised, were actually contradictory. Things must be worse than he was letting on.

She felt bad he couldn't talk to her properly, when he was so clearly worried. But this had always been the pattern of their relationship: he didn't tell her things that might worry her, even though one of her worries was that he wasn't telling her things.

She squeezed his arm. 'Love you. And we *will* get through this. We'll sort it all out.'

'Yes,' he agreed. 'Love you, too. And, yes, we will.'

The next day, she was reading Rosemary's notes, a cup of coffee in her hand, when the silence was shattered by a bang.

No – not just a bang, she thought as she dabbed at the coffee she'd spilt. An explosion. It had been loud enough to send birds flying from the woods.

A few minutes later, there was another one, followed by another clattering of birds. She tensed, waiting for it to happen again. But it didn't, and she slowly relaxed.

After twenty minutes, there was another, equally deafening bang from the same direction.

Bugger this, she thought. I'm not going to just sit here while things get blown up around me.

Pulling on some wellies, she set off down to the woods. At the treeline, she hesitated, wondering which way to go, but then yet another bang buffeted the air. It came from her left, deeper into the trees, so she headed that way.

When she reached the track to Gordon's farm, she saw there were two propane gas canisters next to it. Each was attached to a metal tube resembling a small cannon, pointing in the direction of Trade Cottage.

They were gas-powered bird scarers, she realised, though they must be extra-powerful ones: the bangs had been louder than any she'd heard before. Well, two could play at this game.

Going up to the canisters, she turned the valves clockwise until they were fully off.

For a few hours, there was peace. But that afternoon, the bangs started up again.

She googled 'gas gun regulations'. To her amazement, there didn't seem to be any. Or rather, there were 'Responsible Use Guidelines', but no actual rules about what farmers could do with them, or how often they could be set to go off. It seemed crazy that, in the countryside, you could deafen your neighbours or hand a child a shotgun without anyone giving a damn, but if you wanted to open an Airbnb or retile a bathroom, you had to jump through endless bureaucratic hoops.

She dialled the council's switchboard and got transferred from person to person, each time being put on hold. Eventually, she was put through to someone who wanted to know if the canisters were on a footpath.

She admitted they weren't.

'Well, your best bet is to speak to the farmer, to see why he's placed them where he has. Perhaps he'll agree to resite them.'

She knew it was going to be futile, but her blood was up from the frustration of being on the phone for so long, as well as from the bangs that had punctuated the on-hold music half a dozen times. Getting into the car, she drove down the muddy track that led to Park Farm, passing the gas guns on the way. Gordon must have put them there so he could check them as he drove past, she realised, and turn them back on if she'd turned them off.

She'd never been to the farmyard before. It was surprisingly large – the farmhouse was bigger even than Trade Cottage, surrounded by big, modern barns. For a moment she hesitated, not knowing which way to go. Then she saw Gordon, climbing down from a tractor.

'Hi, there,' she said as she walked over, deliberately making her voice as unconfrontational as possible.

'Oh, yes,' he said blankly.

'I've come about those gas guns. I was just wondering why they're where they are. According to the internet, it's not usual to have them going at this time of year. Quite apart from anything else, they must be scaring off the pheasants.'

'Must they?' he said. 'Interesting.'

She waited for him to continue – an uncomfortably long time.

'The pheasants are eating my winter barley,' he said at last. 'What time of year does the internet think I should be sowing that? Clue's in the name, I'd say, but maybe Facebook knows better.'

'Look,' she said desperately, 'you came to our party. You said yourself, it was great we were getting on so well with Paul and Rosemary, when you'd thought they'd find it impossible to leave. You know how much of an effort we've made.'

Gordon shrugged. 'I don't know the ins and outs, and I don't really care. But Rosemary wants the house back, and you're being as stubborn as an old ewe that doesn't want to go up the loading ramp. It's nothing personal, but we'll have you out in the end, so you might as well go sooner rather than later.'

She could feel herself flushing with anger. She wanted to hit him, and to hell with the consequences, but she managed to restrain herself.

'You won't,' she heard herself say. 'You really won't. We're not leaving, so *you* might as well stop these stupid games.'

She turned on her heel and went back to her car, getting in quickly so he wouldn't see she was trying not to cry. As she drove out of the farmyard, he was still there, standing by his tractor, watching her go.

# TWENTY-SEVEN

He did at least turn the gas guns off when night fell – probably as much to preserve his own sleep, Kate thought wearily, as theirs. But before then, the children had to endure having their homework time disturbed, made worse by the way the interval between the first and second bangs was maddeningly unpredictable. Will claimed to be unbothered by them, but Tilly hated it, waiting anxiously for the next explosion, unable to concentrate on her spellings.

The next morning, at six thirty, the guns started again. It was like the precursor to a battle, Kate thought wearily – she'd read somewhere that, in the First World War, both sides liked to start the morning of a big offensive with a barrage. She resigned herself to simply having to get used to them.

Around eight, there was a new development. Three men appeared among the trees at the bottom of the garden. They were wearing hi-vis vests and hard hats with ear defenders, and they were nailing something to the tree trunks.

She set off down the garden, but they'd already vanished back into the wood. Moments later, chainsaws started up – like loud, angry hornets. The noise deepened as the blades met timber, an anguished snarl.

As she got closer, she got a better look at what they'd been doing before. Arranged in a line, so they faced directly up the garden, were three large signs, each bearing the words: *PRIVATE – KEEP OUT*.

# TWENTY-EIGHT

'In planning terms,' Nikolas Katsaros said, 'this ought to be pretty straightforward. Yes, the conversions are in the curtilage of a listed building, but we'll argue our proposals for them are sensitive and proportionate. And yes, you've neglected to get listed building consent for some minor renovations to the house.'

The architect gazed around their kitchen. 'You've done a really good job, though. It's just the kind of approach I'd have taken myself.'

Despite the seriousness of the situation, Kate couldn't help feeling pleased.

'You're saying we'll win, then,' Matt said hopefully.

Nikolas shrugged. 'I'm saying you *should* win. But it's never that simple. So many people don't bother applying for listed building consent for internal works that, when the council does catch someone, they like to make an example of them. As for the issue around short-term lets . . . It's nonsense, but the planning committee members are elected councillors who generally want to be re-elected, so they like to be seen to be listening to their communities. Sometimes, it's quite literally a popularity contest.'

'And, unfortunately, we're the least popular people in this village,' Kate said. As if to underline her words, the chainsaws started up again in the woods. Matt had snuck down at first light to see what they were up to: they seemed to be cutting some kind of path or track through the trees, he'd reported, though for what purpose was anybody's guess.

'It may not be quite as bad as you think,' Nikolas said. 'Councillors usually affiliate themselves to a political party, so decisions often split along political lines. And you can research the committee members and write to them individually, to lobby them.'

She and Matt looked at each other. It was obvious Matt wasn't going to have time for that.

'I can write to them,' she said. 'Anything's better than just sitting here while Rosemary and Paul's minions run rings round us.'

She started her email campaign that afternoon. It soon became clear just how big a task it was. The district councillors' details were readily available online, but so was information about every decision they'd ever been involved in. It took her two hours to research the first name on her list – Susan Green, the planning committee chair – and another hour to compose an email to her.

She was just getting a coffee when she glanced out at the garden. They'd decided to keep Robert the gardener on for the autumn, to help them deal with the grass and the amount of fruit still falling in the orchard. He was standing beside one of the flower beds, talking with someone she couldn't quite see. Then he moved, and Kate realised it was Rosemary. She must have come through the gate in the hedge. She was gesturing at the border, and Robert was nodding. It looked very much like she was telling him what to do.

Kate put down her coffee and went outside. 'Hello,' she called firmly. 'What's going on?'

'Oh, Kate.' Rosemary turned. 'I couldn't help noticing you haven't pruned these.' She gestured at the long hedge of lavender plants that fringed the border. It had been in bloom when Kate came to measure for curtains, a mist of intense dark blue that had given the garden a lovely Provençal feel. The blossoms were all dead and grey now.

'No,' Kate said incredulously. 'I haven't.' It seemed completely bizarre that they were having this conversation, given everything else that was happening. 'So what?'

'Well, it needs doing, or the plants will turn into awful woody bushes. I could see from up there –' she gestured up at The Old Tennis Court – 'and I said to Paul, "She'll probably get round to it soon," but more and more time went by and in the end, I thought it would be easier if I just popped over and got it sorted. If Robert does one side and I do the other . . .' She gestured again, and Kate saw there were two pairs of secateurs in her hand. 'It would be such a shame to miss a year.'

For a moment, Kate was speechless. Then she said, 'Rosemary, you're in our garden.'

The other woman looked confused. 'Yes?'

'You can't just walk in and start pruning.'

'But you were clearly too busy, or you'd have done it yourself,' Rosemary said reasonably. 'And you did say you wanted to stay friends.' She gazed at the lavender. 'I planted these fifteen years ago. They've lasted rather well, haven't they? But it hasn't happened by accident.'

Robert was staring fixedly at the lavender. News of their falling-out had probably already reached him, Kate realised. And, although most of the local tradesmen tried to remain studiously neutral when it came to village matters, no doubt whatever she said now would be all round the area by nightfall.

She forced herself to match Rosemary's civil tone. 'That's very kind of you. But Robert's actually quite busy. Why don't you and I tackle the lavender? I can do one side while you do the other.'

Rosemary beamed. 'Perfect.'

'Incidentally,' Kate said as she took the proffered pair of secateurs, 'you don't happen to know what they're doing down there, do you?' She gestured at the woods, where the chainsaws had started shrieking again. 'I'd go and ask, but Gordon's put up all those *Private* signs.'

'Oh . . .' Rosemary looked vague. 'Yes, he did mention someone had been tampering with his bangers. And he likes to give the wood a tidy-up once in a while. It's a bit like the lavender – if you don't, it runs away with you.'

'It looked to me as if those woods hadn't been touched in twenty years,' Kate said sceptically. 'Will's devasted that he can't get to his dens.'

Just for a moment, she thought she'd got through to her. Rosemary's expression softened, and a flash of what might have been guilt crossed her face.

Then she said firmly, 'They're not really Will's dens, though, are they? It was Jamie who started them. I'm sure Will'll get over it.'

# TWENTY-NINE

That evening, the chainsaws fell silent. Nor did they start up again the next morning. Had Rosemary had a word? Kate wondered. Or – more likely – had the workmen simply finished whatever it was they were doing?

The next day was a Saturday. First thing after breakfast, Matt went and nailed shut the gate between The Old Tennis Court and Trade Cottage.

'That should keep her out,' he said with some satisfaction, when he came back inside.

Kate couldn't help feeling sad. For a short time, that gate had seemed such a symbol of her and Rosemary's friendship – the easy, informal popping back and forth between the two houses. There was still a part of her that didn't want to escalate things, even as another part of her acknowledged that it was too late: Paul and Rosemary and their allies were all in, and would do whatever it took to get her and Matt out.

She looked around her, at the interior of Trade Cottage. God, I love you so much, she thought wistfully. You are absolutely worth fighting for.

Another chainsaw started up in the woods. It sounded different from the previous ones – higher pitched, more whiney. Moments later, another, also high in pitch, joined it. And then another, and another . . .

'What the—?' Matt said, outraged. He pointed. 'Are those what I think they are?'

She followed his gaze. They weren't chainsaws at all, she realised. Down in the wood, behind the *KEEP OUT* signs, a figure on a tiny moped was skidding and sliding at high speed through the trees. It looked like a teenager, wearing a crash helmet and tight-fitting leathers. Behind it, two more bikes were battling it out for second place.

# THIRTY

Gordon was completely within his rights, the internet informed her. As the farmer, he could rent the wood out to a motocross club for twenty-eight days a year without even applying for a permit – effectively, every other Saturday.

Later that morning, Mary Snow, Fresco's owner, turned up with a trailer to take the pony away. There was a field that urgently needed grazing, apparently, or the weeds would take over. Tilly was inconsolable, weeping into the horse rug that was all she'd been left with.

And Will got a message from Andy, the boy in his class he'd gone beating with. The shoot was going to be on the far side of Pelham Park for the rest of the season, and Will was no longer invited.

Will didn't cry, but he went and turned on his Nintendo Switch in a furious silence.

'I did this,' Kate said, with a stab of horror. She turned to Matt. 'The pony, the shoot – it's all my fault.'

'What do you mean?' he said, puzzled. 'Of course it isn't.'

'I told Guy Pelham I'm not leaving because the children are my number-one priority and they love it here. So now they've decided to make the children miserable.'

Matt swore quietly. 'I can't believe Rosemary and Paul could be so *evil*. They said they adored our kids.'

'Not as much as they adore Jamie's. And I don't suppose Paul's giving any actual orders in all this, anyway. This is just the hangers-on, doing everything they can to winkle us out.'

Matt was silent a moment. 'They're right, though, aren't they? We can't go on like this. *Keep Out* signs at the bottom of our garden, not being able to go to our own local pub without being stared at . . . Everything we liked about this place is slowly being taken away. I could talk to Paul – we could name a steeper price, find somewhere even better, start again—'

'No!' she cried. 'I'm not leaving Trade Cottage!'

He stared at her, silenced by her vehemence.

She added, 'I just refuse to be forced out like this.'

'You should know . . .' Matt took a breath. 'I've been meaning to tell you – we're having some problems at work. Financial stuff. There's a possibility I might have to repay some of the loan. If we sold up for a really good price, it would mean, in the next place, we'd be a lot more secure.'

She didn't know what to say. Everything was falling apart.

'Sorry,' he added.

She shook her head. 'Don't be. It's not your fault.'

'I feel a failure,' he admitted. 'The truth is, I let us get overstretched.'

'Of course you're not a failure,' she said, going to hug him. 'You've worked so hard. We both have. And we're not going to let these bullies win.'

Something occurred to her. 'If we get that planning permission, it'll increase Trade Cottage's value, yes?'

He nodded. 'Should do.'

'Well, then. Let's fight as hard as we can for that. If we get it, hopefully the objectors will just give up and we can get on with our lives. But if for some reason they don't, we can choose to sell up if we want to, knowing we've made a good profit on the place. Either way, let's not make any decisions until after the committee meeting – yes?'

'And if we lose?' he said quietly.

She knew there was only one logical answer to that, but her mind didn't want to go there. 'We're not going to lose. We're just feeling low because everything's piling in on us at once. Look, let's get out of here for today. You try to cheer Will up, and I'll go and work on Tilly. And then we'll go out as a family for lunch and a movie, somewhere we don't have to listen to this racket.'

# THIRTY-ONE

Sunday was blissfully quiet. No motorbikes, no chainsaws. Even the gas guns seemed to have been given the day off. If it wasn't for the bait boxes the pest controller had left scattered around the terrace and garden, she could almost have persuaded herself that these last few weeks hadn't happened.

On Monday, she dropped the kids off as usual at the bus stop. When she came back, she saw the postman had been – there was an envelope on the mat, with her name and address printed on it in capital letters.

Inside was a single sheet of paper, folded.

*DEAR WHORE,*

*I WILL CALL YOU A WHORE BECAUSE THAT IS WHAT YOU ARE. YOU HAVE BEEN WATCHED LEERING AT YOUR GARDNER, HE IS ONLY DOING HIS JOB. IF YOU WAS A MAN, YOU WOULD BE CALLED A SICK PERVERT. THEY SAY YOU ARE GOING TO HOLD YOUR FILTHY SWINGER ORGIES AT YOUR HOUSE, WELL IF YOU STAY, YOU WILL BE ASKING FOR IT.*

*YOU HAVE BEEN WARNED.*

*GOODBYE SLUT.*

She felt, not so much disgust, as resignation. This too was Paul's doing. Oh, not directly – writing poison-pen letters was undoubtedly far beneath him; his preferred method was to expertly manipulate the planning system, which he clearly knew inside out. But he'd made Matt and her a target for the local trolls and bullies, and now they had her in their sights.

This was probably what passed for entertainment here, she thought wearily as she balled the letter up and pushed it deep into the rubbish. She ought to keep it, she knew, and show Matt. But he might want her to take it to the police, and she didn't want to think about it for a moment longer than she had to.

Even so, she couldn't shake off the awful, sick-making realisation that, for some people, this was clearly becoming personal. Support for Rosemary and Paul was changing, little by little, into hatred of her and Matt.

And yet, and yet . . . A little later, when she walked down to see if, by any miracle, the *Keep Out* signs had been removed, now the chain-sawing was finished – they hadn't – she came across a glistening, iridescent snakeskin, right on the edge of the wood. It was almost three feet long, as fat as a sausage. There was even a bulbous eye, or at least what had once been the film over one, regarding her watchfully from where the skin lay on the grass. It was as pale and ghostly as gossamer, freshly shed that very morning.

She crouched down and carefully picked it up with a twig, so she could take it back to show the children later. Will, she knew, would be thrilled, and even Tilly was losing her city-girl fear of such things.

Looking up at the house as it squatted protectively over her, she instinctively felt it was a gift, a reminder of all that was special about the place. '*Thank you*,' she mouthed, and in her heart she felt Trade Cottage answer that everything was going to be all right.

# THIRTY-TWO

The respite didn't last long. On Wednesday, Matt got a call from the solicitor who'd handled the purchase of Trade Cottage. He was up in the attic room, working from home, but he came down with his phone on speaker so she could hear.

'This is unbelievable,' he told her. 'Anwar, say that again.'

'I've had an email from your vendors' solicitor,' Anwar said. 'They're claiming you've impeded an easement benefiting their property.'

'What does that mean in English?' she asked.

'An easement is a right of way. When they sold themselves the tennis court, they put a covenant on Trade Cottage giving the owners of their new property access to its garden and orchard, specifically to gather fruit from the latter. The sale was done back-to-back with the sale of Trade Cottage – literally, the same week – which was why it didn't show up in my searches.'

'But what does this actually mean?' she asked again.

'In theory, they can force you to keep the right of way open.'

'What?' she said, outraged. 'And just come into our garden whenever they like?'

'We must be able to fight that,' Matt said immediately. 'The fact it was done so sneakily, without telling you – that must be some kind of misrepresentation, surely.'

'Well, possibly,' the solicitor said. 'But, in the meantime, they could get a court to grant them an injunction. And you need to think very carefully before getting into a legal dispute with a neighbour – you're obliged to declare it when you come to sell, and that could knock a substantial chunk off the value of your house.'

'In other words, this is a trap,' Matt said heavily. 'They *want* us to sue them.'

'It looks that way,' Anwar agreed. 'It might be wiser to unseal that door again, at least for the time being. In the meantime, document their use of it, along with any other nuisance activity. In neighbour disputes, the party with the most evidence usually wins, regardless of the actual rights or wrongs.'

At lunchtime, Matt went and took out the nails he'd hammered into the gate. Then he came back and got a saw from his toolbox.

'What are you doing?' she asked.

'I'm going to cut down most of those fruit trees,' he said grimly. 'It'll serve them right, and who needs a whole tree of cooking apples, anyway?'

But it was a bigger job than he'd anticipated – after a couple of hours, he'd only managed to fell a single tree.

'I need a chainsaw,' he said, coming back inside and throwing down the saw. 'This thing's blunt.'

He went online and ordered an electric chainsaw. He wasn't

going to run amok with it, he promised her, just take out the trees that were surplus to requirements.

Together, they went down to the orchard and chose which ones to get rid of, tying tags around the ones they didn't want. As they fastened the last one, Kate glanced up and saw the telescope in The Old Tennis Court's window dip towards them.

The next morning, there was a knock on the door. When she opened it, a young man with a shock of curly black hair nodded politely at her. 'Hi. I'm Tom Nichols, the council's tree officer. We've had a report you might be doing some arboreal work?'

'We're cutting down some old fruit trees,' she said. Already, there was a sinking feeling in the pit of her stomach.

'Mind if I take a look?'

She showed him the trees they'd marked. Once again, she was very conscious of the telescope over their heads.

'As you can see, there are way too many for one family,' she told him. 'And we've had a problem with rats.'

'OK,' he said slowly. 'But this is a conservation area. You have to give at least six weeks' notice before you carry out work on a tree, in case there are objections.'

'What – even pruning?' she said, startled.

He nodded. 'And the tree surgeon would be expected to submit details of what pruning they were going to do and when. Fruit trees like these are best cut back in spring, for example, when they're dormant.'

She gestured furiously at the woods. 'The farmer's been felling trees down there all last week. You're not telling me he got permission.'

'There are different rules for farmers.' Tom Nichols looked up at the hedge separating Trade Cottage's garden from The Old Tennis Court. 'For leylandii too, come to that. If your neighbours complain, we'd have to issue an enforcement notice requiring you to trim the rest of that hedge.'

'This is crazy!' she said, appalled. 'What happened to "an Englishman's home is his castle"?'

'I don't think there's a castle in England that isn't a grade-I listed building these days, and probably a scheduled monument as well,' Tom Nichols said mildly. He eyed the fruit trees. 'You can download the tree-works form online. It's pretty straightforward. Although, in the case of these particular trees, there's been an application for a Tree Preservation Order, so we'll have to consider that, as well.'

# THIRTY-THREE

The next day, she opened the front door to find a dead rat on her doorstep. It was lying on its side, its sharp teeth bared in a snarl. She couldn't help jumping back, the same cry of shock and disgust springing to her lips as when she'd first seen them, that time in the fruit cage.

She looked around. There was no one there. And, of course, the pest controller had put down poison. So it could just be a coincidence – the rat might have died here, in this very spot.

Or someone might have found it and placed it here. Someone who knew how much she loathed rats.

Either way, it needed to be dealt with. She went inside and tore off some kitchen roll. Gingerly, she picked the rat up by the tail and swung it into a skip.

She'd just got back from getting the children off to the bus stop when her phone rang. She glanced at the screen and saw the caller's name: *Paul Finch*.

Surprised and a little apprehensive, she put it to her ear. 'Yes?'

'It's Paul, from The Old Tennis Court,' he announced cheerily.

'I was looking through the telescope just now, and I couldn't help noticing – you've got moles.'

'Moles?' she repeated.

'On Trade Cottage's lower lawn. You'll need to sort them out, or they'll work their way up and ruin the whole damn thing.' He chuckled. 'I spent years getting that lawn into the shape it's in now. It's a lot more effort than it looks – you're fighting moss, drought, mushroom rings, weeds . . . But the blasted moles come back every autumn, when the males leave the nests. You want to put a crushed garlic clove down every molehill, and stick one of those foil pinwheels in the top – they don't like the vibration. The village shop sells them. It's perfectly humane. The little blighters just go and annoy someone else.'

There was a time when she'd appreciated his advice about Trade Cottage. Now, it just seemed patronising. 'What if we don't mind moles?'

'Don't mind them?' He sounded baffled. 'But they'll spoil the look of the lawn.'

'We're digging the lawn up soon, anyway. For a drainage field.'

There was a short silence. 'Yes, I saw an application had gone in for that. Along with all the other things.' His voice, though still jovial, had a harder edge to it. 'You don't need one, you know. Those drainage chaps always try to talk people into them, particularly if they think you don't know much about it. That soil at the bottom of the garden is loamy – it's a natural soakaway.'

'That's not the advice we've been given,' she retorted. 'Particularly as there'll be extra drains to connect from the outbuildings, once they're converted.'

This time the silence was even longer. Then he said patiently, 'Well, if you don't get permission for that – and from what I'm hearing from various members of the committee, you don't stand a chance – perhaps you should think about a cheaper drainage set-up, one that doesn't trash the lawn I spent years nurturing. I'd be very happy to recommend someone. In the meantime, take a look at those molehills, won't you? Pinwheels and garlic.'

He rang off. She stood there for a moment, furious, phone in hand, wondering what the real purpose of his call had been. To let her know he had friends on the planning committee? To remind her that he was constantly watching? Or was he genuinely offended by the sight of a few molehills? Again, it was so patronising to be told that she and Matt were being taken advantage of by Mick, the drainage contractor. She'd trust Mick's advice over Paul's any day.

Even so, the next time she went past the village shop, she went in and bought some pinwheels, then stuck one in each molehill, along with a crushed garlic clove. Both Matt and Robert would be upset if the moles came any higher up the lawn. And the little foil windmills actually looked quite jaunty, whirring away at the bottom of the garden.

As she went back up to the house, she remembered something. When she'd thrown the dead pheasants over the beam in the barn that time, she'd noticed some curious metal contraptions hanging on nails hammered into the timber. She went to take a look. Yes, she'd remembered right – there were five of them, each about eight inches long, with spring-loaded handles and sharp interlocking blades.

They were mole traps – she was sure of it. They looked like

they'd been well used, too – some had dried earth on them. Or was that brown stuff really blood?

She looked at the blades, clearly designed to break a mole's back, and shuddered. It said so much about Paul and Rosemary's time at Trade Cottage, she thought: the lawn, so effortlessly perfect on the surface, was kept that way by ruthlessly controlling anything beneath it that wasn't to Paul's liking. What was the betting he told guests that his pretty pinwheels were gently shooing the little beasts away, even as his buried traps were lurking below to slice them in two?

# THIRTY-FOUR

They struggled on towards the planning committee meeting. Unable to do any more painting until the retrospective applications were approved, Kate busied herself with getting builders' quotes and making sure that, this time, all the paperwork was in order. If they won, they'd start work straight away. Steve would come back to finish the bathrooms; the drainage contractor would get machinery in to dig the drainage field; roofers would erect scaffolding and start work on the rotten beams; and a second, larger firm of builders would get cracking on the barns.

Five days before the hearing, she got a call from the broker who'd arranged their mortgage. 'I've just been emailed by the lender,' he told her. 'They've got a concern you might be operating short-term lets at the property.'

'We're not, but we are planning to, one day,' she said, puzzled. 'Why?'

'There's a clause in the mortgage that says you can't do that without their permission. And that comes at a price, in the form of a higher interest rate.'

More expensive bureaucracy she hadn't known about. 'All right, send me the forms,' she said resignedly. A thought occurred to her. 'How did they even know?'

'Hang on.' There was a pause while he consulted the email. 'It says here they were sent a link to the listing.'

'Well, that's nonsense. Those outbuildings haven't even been converted yet, let alone listed online.'

'Odd. I'll tell them they've got it wrong.' He rang off.

She sat there for a moment, thinking. Then she opened the browser on her phone and, already nervous of what she might find, typed in 'Trade Cottage Pelham letting'.

It came up straight away, at the top of the search results, on some booking app she'd never heard of, let alone signed up for. The photographs had been copied from the Rightmove advert. Even more strangely, this non-existent letting already had a dozen reviews.

Then she realised. All were one star.

She read the topmost one: *Whatever you do, stay away from this place. The host is arrogant and rude . . .*

She scrolled down to the next: *The sheets hadn't been changed. I found a hair in my bed . . .*

She knew she should stop, that reading more would only make her feel even worse, but she couldn't help herself.

*Shower was dirty . . . Hot water didn't work . . . Toilet hadn't been cleaned . . . Mouse droppings in the closet . . .*

She felt sick. Back when she was Airbnb-hosting, her five-star reviews had been her pride and joy. The fact these were fake almost made it worse – things like this could hang around on the internet forever.

She tried to delete the listing, but it required a username and password. She used the *Report* button instead, and got an automatic response informing her that the site aimed to process complaints within ten working days.

She wondered who on earth had done this. It was surely well beyond the capabilities of Rosemary or Paul. But it wasn't illiterate, like the poison-pen letter. And that word 'closet' was an Americanism.

She recalled Rosemary saying that Jamie's children had American accents now. Paul couldn't possibly have got his grandchildren involved in this campaign, could he?

Something else occurred to her. She got up her Instagram account. She'd been posting the occasional picture of life at Trade Cottage – some jars of home-made gooseberry jam, a bowl of blood peaches, the downstairs loo after she'd colour-drenched it in silky cocoa-brown paint.

Beneath the pictures of the loo were fourteen comments. *HORRIBLE COLOR*, someone had written. *HORRIBLE PEOPLE*, another had added. *Gross and tacky*, a third had said, while *Looks like someone's smeared shit on the walls* had received seven likes.

She was still working out how to change her account settings when there was a brisk double knock at the front door. It was probably one of the builders she was getting a quote from, she thought – one had said he might pop round. She went to let him in.

On the doorstep was a tall, good-looking man of around fifty, wearing a quilted green jacket. She recognised him from somewhere. Perhaps he'd been at the party. But, of course, that didn't mean he couldn't be the builder as well.

'Stuart?' she said tentatively.

The tall man shook his head. 'I'm Jamie. Jamie Finch.' He looked up at Trade Cottage, then smiled at her. 'I'm the man whose house you're living in.'

# THIRTY-FIVE

'It's not your house,' she said automatically. 'Not anymore. It's ours.'

'Perhaps I should have said "childhood home",' he conceded. He gazed around appreciatively. 'It's good to see it again, actually. The last time I was here was almost a year ago. And – this will sound crazy, but I miss it. Wherever in the world I go for work, some dusty corrupt hellhole or other, this is where I think about. My happy place, to use that awful phrase they have back in the US. You probably think my family's obsession with it is baffling – and it is, in a way. But you're the lucky beneficiary.'

'The *beneficiary*?' she echoed incredulously. 'The recipient of a campaign of hate, you mean.'

'What?' He looked genuinely puzzled. 'What campaign?'

'You really don't know?' she said sceptically.

He shook his head. He looked extraordinarily like his father when he did that – the same comma of hair flopping over his blue eyes – though, where Paul's hair was white, Jamie's was brown and thick. Automatically, he pushed it off his forehead with his hand – again, very like his father.

'People round here can get a bit carried away sometimes. That's not my style, I promise. I'd rather tempt you with a whopping great carrot.' He reached into his pocket for an envelope. 'Which is what I think you'll find this is. Can I come in and talk it through?'

A little reluctantly, she led him into the kitchen.

'This is nice,' he said, gazing around. 'Whatever happens, I hope the permission for the work you've done in the house gets granted. The place needed some TLC.'

She refrained from pointing out that it was his own parents who'd shopped her to the council over that. He was trying to charm her, she knew. He was clearly used to getting what he wanted that way – he had the same twinkle in his eye as Paul, the same affable bonhomie. But, having discovered that the father's charm coexisted with a ruthless streak, she wasn't ready to trust the son just yet.

'See that?' he said fondly, tapping the wall. Around waist height, there was a gouge in the plaster that she'd wondered about when she was painting. 'When it was too wet to go out, me and Tess used to cycle round and round the dining table, trying to catch each other up. That's where our brake levers caught against the wall.' He pointed even lower, to the ancient skirting board. 'And those holes aren't woodworm. If you dig into them, you'll find airgun pellets. I used to put a Coke can down there for target practice. That's where I missed.'

'You said you wanted to discuss your offer,' she said firmly.

'Oh – of course.' He slid the envelope across the island. 'Basically, when I got here and talked it over with the aged parents, I realised the amount Dad had proposed wasn't quite enough. You've made improvements – that's obvious. And if you succeed in getting permission to develop the outbuildings, you'll add a hundred grand to Trade Cottage's value before you even put a spade in the ground. Dad's convinced you won't get it, of course, but there's always the possibility he's wrong. So –' he nodded at the envelope – 'we've increased our offer by a hundred and twenty thou. But it expires the moment that planning meeting starts. Think of it as a bonus for resolving this quickly.'

She tried to push the envelope back at him. 'We don't want it.'

'"We"?' he repeated. 'Or just you?' His blue eyes regarded her thoughtfully. 'I hear your husband's company's struggling, now it's been saddled with all the debt its new owners used to buy it.'

'Who told you that?' she said, furious.

Jamie shrugged. 'He pretty much told Dad himself, the first time they met. I emailed a couple of guys I know in London and they confirmed it – that deal he did was a stinker, unfortunately.'

When she didn't say anything, he added, 'Look, this is a win–win situation. I happen to have a lot of money, and you have something I'm prepared to spend big on. This house has sentimental value to me, but it can't possibly hold the same memories for you. So I've made you an offer you can't refuse.'

'Don't tell me what I can and can't do,' she snapped.

He looked at her calmly. 'Sorry – obviously, I didn't mean it like that. It's just that I can't see what you're holding out for.'

'We're not "holding out" for anything,' she retorted. 'We simply want to be left alone to enjoy our new home.'

He said patiently, 'It's a very good offer.'

'I'm not disputing that. But this isn't about money.'

He nodded. 'OK. So what *is* it about?'

She didn't answer. How could she put her attachment to Trade Cottage into words, or explain the depth of her love for it? But the more people like Jamie tried to take it away from her, the more resolved she was not to be trampled over.

He sighed. 'At least discuss it with Matt, will you? Maybe he can talk some sense into you. I'll see myself out.'

She bristled. 'No, I'll see *you* out.'

As they went through the entrance hall, he glanced at the console table and stopped. 'Isn't that ours?'

'It was,' she said defiantly. 'Your parents gave it to us. Along with a whole lot of other things.'

He looked baffled. 'Why?'

'Perhaps they thought we'd be better custodians of them than you would.' She saw him flinch, and realised she'd offended him. Well, tough. How dare he walk into her home and think he could just schmooze her out of it? 'When we first looked round, your mother told your father that Trade Cottage had found its rightful heirs.'

Jamie flinched again. Then he turned and left without another word.

# THIRTY-SIX

That evening, she told Matt about Jamie Finch's visit, leaving what he'd said about Matt's company until the end.

'There's some truth in it,' Matt admitted. He looked tired. 'Seems I'm not as good at negotiations as I thought.'

'If we have to . . .' she began, then stopped.

'Yes?'

'If you need the money, and there's no other way, then let's accept his offer.' She spoke calmly, but inwardly she was screaming, like that mythical plant Rosemary had written about in one of her emails.

For a long moment, Matt considered. Then he shook his head. 'No. We stick to the plan. If we win, we can always go back to him with a counter. Besides, I don't like time-expiring offers. They always feel like someone's trying to jump you into making the wrong decision.'

# THIRTY-SEVEN

The planning committee meeting was held at the district council's offices, in a large chamber that was like a cross between a lecture theatre and a courtroom. At the front was a raised platform for the chair, Susan Green, with the planning officer and a minute-taker directly in front of her. Facing them were tiers of desks, with district councillors in the front row and members of the public behind. It was about half full. Paul, as a wheelchair user, had been given a place at the front. A dozen or so supporters sat behind him in a little claque. Jason from the pub was among them, but not, Kate noticed, Gordon or Guy Pelham. Rosemary was there, her expression unreadable, as was Jamie, looking confident and relaxed.

Their own little group had taken seats on the other side of the aisle – just Kate, Matt and Nikolas, their architect. Already, nerves were shredding Kate's stomach at the prospect of having to speak.

Susan Green opened the meeting with a preamble about emergency exits and toilets. Then came apologies for absence and approval of the last meeting's minutes. After that, she asked for declarations of interest. Only then did the meeting start to deal with planning applications. Yet, somehow, the very slowness of it – the elaborate courtesy with which the chair thanked every speaker for their contribution, the way every decision had to be proposed, seconded, voted on and minuted – made it all the more tense.

The first application was for a change of use, from a private dwelling to a home for looked-after children. Local residents were strongly objecting. But it wasn't as clear-cut a case of Nimbyism as it first appeared: their argument was that they wouldn't let their own children near that particular street, which was notorious for conflicts between two county-lines drugs gangs, so didn't believe the looked-after children would be safe there either. The company applying for the change of use pointed to their good track record and the Ofsted ratings of the other homes they ran. They had the support of the county council, who desperately needed more children's homes, while the residents had the support of their ward councillor, who agreed it was the wrong place. It was all surprisingly gripping, not least because Kate had no idea which way it was going to go.

Eventually, Susan Green called for a vote, starting with 'All those against', raising her own hand as she did so. But when the votes were counted, the applicants had won by five votes to three.

An application for a disused shop to be turned into a hotel was dealt with more swiftly – the applicants had taken on board all the committee's previous objections and the planning officer now recommended approval. Then, at last, it was the turn of Trade Cottage.

Susan Green asked the planning officer to summarise the application. He did so briefly, adding that he recommended approval. So that was the first hurdle cleared, Kate thought with relief. She gave Matt's hand a little squeeze.

'However, the parish council has strong objections,' the planning officer added. 'Their letter is in your bundle at page fifty-two, along with a large number of comments supporting them.'

'Thank you. Mr Paul Finch will now speak for the objectors,' the chair said. Looking at Paul, she added, 'You have three minutes.'

Paul was handed a microphone. He scooted his wheelchair forward before he spoke, turning in slow circles so he could look the councillors in the eye, one by one.

'We have a pub in Pelham.' He spoke slowly, articulating clearly despite the slurring his voice always had these days, his left hand tucked against his chest to keep the microphone steady. 'The Pelham Arms. Four years ago, after the third tenant in six years went bust, the brewery put it up for sale. The village clubbed together and raised seven hundred thousand pounds to buy it.'

He paused. 'We own it, but that doesn't make it profitable. Everyone knows how tough it is in hospitality at the moment. Last year, the pub made a loss. It'll probably make a loss again this year. The income it makes from letting out rooms is vital to its survival. That's why we don't want more short-term lets in the village – the best way to live like a local is to *stay* in the local.'

His supporters applauded at that, although the chair immediately silenced them.

'Of course, that's not the only reason we oppose this application,' Paul continued. 'The government has given councils the power to block short-term lets precisely because of what they do to communities. Local people thrown out of their houses because short lets are more lucrative for landlords. Villages empty out of season. House prices through the roof. We saw what happened in the Cotswolds when they went down *that* road. It's nothing personal. But Pelham wants to send a very clear message that we intend to stay as we are.'

'Thank you,' the chair said. She consulted her agenda. 'We now have Kate Crowther for the applicants.' She repeated the rubric about the time, and a microphone was passed to Kate.

She stood up. The silence as everyone waited for her to start felt like vertigo, like looking over the side of a building and preparing to jump. But it was too late to back out now.

'On our first night in Pelham,' she began, and wondered if everyone else could hear the nervous tremor in her voice, 'we went to the pub. It was great. The landlord gave us a warm welcome and we had a couple of drinks while we waited for our takeaway pizzas. Since then, we've eaten there many times. We've had fish and chips from there. We've had friends down to stay and gone as a group for Sunday lunch.'

She paused. 'My point is, more people coming to the village – tourists, if you want to call them that – can only benefit the Pelham Arms. You'll see from the plans that these outbuilding conversions don't even have kitchens, only a microwave and a kettle. Our guests might not stay at the pub, but they'll eat there, drink there, buy bread at the village shop, pick fruit and veg at the pick-your-own. And as for rowdy behaviour, it's us who'll be nearest to them, so of course we're not going to allow that.'

She stopped and glanced across the aisle. Jamie was watching her fixedly, a slight smile on his face.

He thinks they've won, she realised. He thinks it's in the bag.

She said slowly, 'And when Mr Finch says it isn't personal, that isn't true. He's our next-door neighbour and the only reason he's objecting is because he's trying to force us out.'

'Ms Crowther,' the chair said immediately. 'You should stop right there. That's quite possibly slander. If Mr Finch had a personal interest, he would have declared it at the start of the meeting.'

'I can prove it,' she said. She reached into her folder for two pieces of paper. 'These are offers, in writing, to buy our house – one from Paul Finch and one from his son, Jamie. The one from Jamie Finch says –' she lifted it and read aloud – '*This offer expires the moment the planning committee sits. We want you out by the end of November, so we can be in Trade Cottage by Christmas. We have a lot of traditions around the holiday season, which we intend to enjoy as a family after your departure.*' She took a breath. 'He knows we can't afford to stay there if we don't get this planning permission. He's using you – this committee – as part of his own private vendetta.'

# THIRTY-EIGHT

After the decision, she, Matt and Nikolas quietly got to their feet and tiptoed out while the planning officer was introducing the next application. Only when the heavy door had swung shut behind them did she allow herself to let out a whoop.

'We did it! We bloody did it!'

Matt was laughing and hugging her. '*You* did it! Where the hell did *that* come from? My warrior wife!'

'I've no idea,' she confessed. 'It just sort of happened.'

'But you had those offers with you,' he pointed out.

'Yes,' she admitted. 'That is, they were in my folder with all the other paperwork. But it hadn't really crossed my mind I might use them like that.'

Nikolas held out his hand. 'Congratulations. You totally blind-sided them.'

'Thank you,' she said, shaking it. 'We couldn't have done it without you.'

'And you'll be pleased to know,' he added, 'that I've already had an email from the conservation officer. On the back of the planning permission, and the understanding that I'll be supervising things from now on, she's prepared to approve everything you've done so far. But she made clear it isn't a free pass – she'll be scrutinising every detail in future, to make sure you're playing by the rules.'

Kate held up her hands. 'I absolutely promise.'

'We should find a pub,' Matt said. 'Followed by a really nice restaurant. On us, of course,' he added to Nikolas.

The architect shook his head. 'Thanks, but go ahead without me. I've got another of these with a different council tomorrow.'

They found a nice little gastropub and had an early dinner, still basking in the relief of victory. After they'd eaten, Kate made calls to the mothers of the schoolfriends Tilly and Will were with, who reported they were happy and there was no rush to pick them up.

Even so, it felt like time to head home. As they walked through Trade Cottage's front door, Kate paused and put her palm on the wall. *I did this for you.*

In the kitchen, Matt had already put the kettle on. 'Tea?'

She shook her head. 'I'll have some juice.' Going to the fridge, she pulled it open. Then she froze.

In the fridge door, nestled between the milk and the grapefruit juice, was a bottle of Pol Roger.

'Did you put this here?' she asked slowly. Matt couldn't hear her over the noise of the kettle, and she had to repeat the question.

Alerted by her tone, he came over. 'No,' he said quietly.

She felt the bottle. It was cold. But that didn't mean anything. It might have been cold when it was put there.

'You locked the house, right?' she asked. 'And took the key with us?'

'Of course.' A lot of people round here didn't bother, or left the key under a stone, but Matt, like her, still had the ingrained London habit of always securing their property.

'I'll check the windows,' he added.

'I'll come with you.' She didn't want to be left downstairs alone.

They went round the whole house, checking the windows and doors. All were closed and secure.

Eventually, Matt said, 'Maybe someone put it there before, and we didn't notice—'

'I put the milk back in the fridge when we left for the meeting. I'd have noticed a bottle of champagne.' She shuddered. 'No. Someone's been in here. Trying to freak us out. It's the house rule, right? "Always have some champers in the fridge."' She thought, then added, 'And, by "someone" . . . Paul couldn't have managed it. And it isn't Rosemary's style. It must be Jamie. His way of saying, "Enjoy your moment, because it isn't over."'

'But how the hell did he get in?' Matt said, frowning.

'Maybe they kept a key when they moved out. Maybe he had his own copy.'

'Shit.' Matt took a breath. 'I'll get the locks changed tomorrow.'

'You can't,' she pointed out. 'That one on the front door is ancient. The back door, too. There's no way we'll be allowed to replace them.'

'We'll add bolts, then. And a deadlock.'

'Even those will need permission, now the conservation officer's got us in her sights. A brand-new deadlock on the front door is the first thing she'd spot.'

'Well, I'm calling the police.' Matt pulled out his phone and dialled 999. When it was answered, he put the phone on speaker and explained there'd been an intruder.

'Is the person still there?' the call handler asked.

'We don't believe so. But we're pretty sure we know who it was. The son of a neighbour.'

'Has there been a dispute?'

'You could say that.' Matt's voice was grim.

'Are there any signs of forced entry?'

'No. But he left a bottle of champagne in the fridge.' Briefly, Matt explained the context – the house rule, the committee meeting. Even to Kate's ears, it sounded surreal. Crazy, perhaps.

'So, to summarise,' the call handler interrupted, 'there's no evidence of forced entry, no theft, no threats of violence, but someone's left you a gift.'

Matt admitted that was the case.

'You can call 101 in the morning if you want to discuss home security,' the voice said. 'In future, please only use this number for emergencies.' The line went dead.

Kate went to the fridge and took out the bottle.

Matt looked surprised. 'You're not going to drink it?'

She shook her head. 'I don't want it in the house.'

She took it to the sink and opened it. As she did so, she remembered Rosemary's instructions for wringing a duck's neck: *Twist and pull – firmly, like you're pulling a cork out of a champagne bottle.* She felt faintly sick as the bronze-coloured liquid fizzed and hissed down the plughole. Then she dropped the empty bottle into the recycling bin.

'We still won,' Matt said, watching her face.

'We humiliated him,' she said. 'That written offer of his was stupid and entitled, and that was what undid them.' She thought back to the look of cold fury with which Jamie had listened to his words being read out, the glance of startled dismay Paul had directed at his son before slumping down in his wheelchair.

'It's not just the house he's going to want now,' she added. 'It's revenge.'

# THIRTY-NINE

Having taken a day off for the hearing, Matt had little choice but to go into the office the next morning. Kate saw the children on to their buses, then went back to Trade Cottage with a new sense of trepidation. The first thing she did was to check every room and window, to make sure no one had got in while she was out.

The very last room she looked in was the downstairs loo. She opened the door and recoiled. Splayed across the floor was a dead rat, a huge one, lying on its side, as if it was running.

Having one on the doorstep had been bad enough, but having one in the house felt even more of an invasion. On the other hand, at least it was dead. It must have come up through the drains – although she'd been careful about keeping all the other toilet lids closed, the ancient thunderbox-style seat in here didn't have one.

Or, she thought, the person who'd left them the Pol Roger might also have left them this. But, if so, it must have been this morning – she and Matt definitely checked in here last night.

With a shiver of disgust, she grabbed some loo paper so she didn't have to touch the long, scaly tail as she picked it up.

*

After she'd disposed of the rat, she went back inside. It was very quiet – no gas guns, no motocross bikes, no chainsaws, just the silence of Trade Cottage. Somehow, that only made it spookier, as if the house itself was holding its breath. She'd feel safer when the builders and other contractors came back, but even Steve wouldn't be restarting until later that day.

It was almost lunchtime when she heard footsteps crunching on the gravel. Going to the oriel window, she leaned forward slightly to see who it was.

Jamie Finch.

She watched as he pulled an envelope from his jacket and pushed it into their letter box. Just before he let it go, he pulled it out again, as if changing his mind, and reached for the knocker instead.

A sharp knock echoed down the corridor, followed by three more. For a moment, she thought about hiding. Then she reconsidered. *Fuck it.* We *won, not you.*

Going to the front door, she pulled it half open. 'What do you want?'

He regarded her calmly. 'I suppose I should congratulate you.'

'I want your key,' she said angrily. 'You have no right to just walk in here and leave things.'

'What?' he said, frowning. 'Of course I don't still have a key.' He looked around the front garden. 'I think my parents did keep a spare somewhere, though. You'll have to ask them about it.'

'We're changing the locks.'

'Well, make sure you get permission this time,' he said, amused.

He indicated the door she was still holding. 'That's eighteenth century.'

When she didn't respond, he added impatiently, 'Look, fair dos. You won and we lost. But that doesn't change the fact that I want to buy this house. So, this is my best and final offer. Everything my parents originally proposed, plus an extra two hundred thousand.'

'We don't want it,' she heard herself say, even as she blinked at the sheer amount of money she was turning down.

'You'll see it comes with a couple of conditions,' he continued, as if she hadn't spoken. 'For one thing, it goes down five thousand pounds every day. In four weeks' time, in other words, it'll be worth a hundred and forty thousand less than if you accept today.'

'Then we want it even less,' she said scornfully. 'Take it away.'

'And by the time I come back from America with my family in December, it'll be down by almost a quarter of a million.' He paused. 'These are big sums, Kate. I suggest you don't leave it too long.'

'Why on earth,' she said incredulously, 'would we be interested in an offer that gets smaller?'

He smiled. 'Seems counterintuitive, doesn't it? But I think you will be.'

When she still didn't take the envelope, he tossed it casually on to the mat. 'Oh, and would you mind getting the rest of that leylandii cut? Dad says it's blocking his light.'

This so-called final offer was just a parting shot, of that she was certain. A feeble attempt to make it look as if he was the one in control, rather than the sore loser.

Even so, she spent an hour searching for that key. It soon became clear it wasn't anywhere obvious, like under a flowerpot. She recalled Damon telling her that Rosemary and Paul didn't even lock up when they went out. That suggested the spare wasn't in frequent use either. It could be almost anywhere in Trade Cottage's garden.

Or in Jamie's pocket, for that matter.

She was washing earth off her hands when her phone rang. It was Nikolas.

'The decision's been officially published on the council's website now,' he told her. 'You should go through it carefully, so you're aware of all the conditions, but basically you've got the green light.'

'That's great,' she said. 'Again, thank you so much.'

'You're welcome.' He hesitated. 'Look, this may be nothing, but . . .'

'Yes?' she prompted.

'I was at a different committee meeting this morning, and afterwards I got chatting to a planning consultant I know. He does a lot of work on green-energy applications – landowners who want to invest in wind power, solar, that kind of thing. It's pretty much an open door at the moment, given how ambitious the government's net-zero targets are. He's just taken on a client who wants to set up a solar farm. I don't have the details, obviously, but the name and site location made me think of you.'

He paused. 'The company's called Pelham Park Clean Energy Limited, and the location is Pelham Park Farm.'

# FORTY

'It isn't Nikolas's speciality, but he knows a fair bit about it,' she told Matt despondently when he got home. 'The government prioritises less-productive land for solar farms – which basically means anything currently used for grazing. So it'll be the fields with sheep on, not the ones with crops.'

'The ones we look out at, in other words,' Matt said heavily.

'Exactly. But it gets worse. I went on the Companies House website and looked up Pelham Park Clean Energy. Guess who the directors are?'

Matt stared at her. 'Oh, no . . .'

She nodded. 'Guy told me he was at school with Jamie, and Rosemary mentioned they used to play in the woods together. The company was incorporated three weeks ago, and Guy and Jamie are the only directors.'

'But it must take years to get a project like that off the ground,' Matt objected. 'And from what you've told me of Jamie, he's not one for playing a waiting game – that grab-it-quick offer of his proves that. What's he up to?'

She sighed. 'First of all, he's helping Guy make money. According to Nikolas, solar farms are incredibly lucrative – landowners can count on getting over a thousand pounds per acre, as opposed to less than a hundred from grazing. But I reckon his short-term objective is just to reduce the value of Trade Cottage. Even if he hasn't declared exactly where the solar farm will go, just the threat of having those fields covered in panels means no one will touch this place with a barge pole.' She tried to speak calmly, but there was a lump in her throat. Those beautiful views, those lovely rolling fields dotted with white sheep she'd fallen in love with, back in April – at the thought of them being invaded by row after row of mirror-glass black panes, staring blankly in Trade Cottage's direction, she almost started crying again, just as she'd done after Nikolas's call – weeping with impotence and fury, as well as rage at an enemy who refused to be beaten. That smile Jamie had given her at the planning meeting – that hadn't been arrogant certainty the decision would go the Finches' way, she'd belatedly realised: it was knowing that, even if it didn't, it didn't matter.

'So his offer will be the only one in town,' Matt said thoughtfully. 'And it's getting smaller by the day. Smart. Horrible, but smart. And if he does get us out, he'll simply tuck the panels behind the woods, where he won't see them.' He took a deep breath. 'Well, it's not going to work. The village will never accept a solar farm on their doorstep.'

'You'd think not. But us and The Old Tennis Court are the only ones who'd be directly affected. And Nikolas says most of the district councils round here have formally declared a climate emergency. They can hardly turn round and say they don't want clean energy if it's being produced in their own back yard.'

'We could start a petition.'

She shrugged. 'Somehow, I don't think the Pelham Preservation Committee is going to be coming out against this.'

'Arrgh.' Matt rubbed his eyes wearily. 'This is a nightmare.'

'There is one thing . . .' she began hesitantly.

He looked up. 'What?'

'It may be nothing, but . . . while I was online, I googled him – Jamie Finch. "Know your enemy" and all that.'

'And?'

'According to his LinkedIn page, he's chief investment officer for emerging nations at the International Monetary Fund. Which is a pretty big job, right? But when you go to the IMF's website, there's no mention of him – not a single one.'

'Which makes you think what?' Matt asked.

She pulled a face. 'That maybe they fired him, and it was over something bad enough for them to cancel him completely? International development's having a real MeToo moment right now – there's been a lot of talk about toxic work cultures, bullying and so on. Maybe that's what's really behind relocating his family to the UK.'

Matt considered. 'OK. But it doesn't really help us, does it? Even if he *was* fired, I'm sure he'll spin coming home as being because he wants to see more of his dying father.'

'I know,' she said miserably. 'But it all just seems so hopeless.'

'You'll feel better once the builders are back at work.'

'Will I?' she wondered. 'Or are we just tarting up Trade Cottage for Jamie and his family to live in?'

'They're not going to beat us,' Matt said gently. 'Look at the way you saw him off at that committee meeting.'

Reassured by his confidence, she nodded. 'You're right – maybe things will look better in the morning. I'll phone Liv – she's very into conservation and the environment, and she's friends with Sally, Gordon's wife. I'll see what she knows about this solar farm.'

# FORTY-ONE

Matt was right: she did feel better in the morning, helped by the fact that the house's silence was broken by the army of tradesmen who arrived shortly before eight. Three small mechanical diggers trundled down the garden to begin excavating the drainage field; another started on the groundworks for the outbuilding conversions; Steve and his two sidekicks resumed work on the bathroom, while the roofers started to erect scaffolding at the front of the house, the chinking of their metal poles somehow redolent of the sound of an army hammering its weapons. Sitting in the captain's chair, watching men with huge spanners shimmy up and down the ladders outside the oriel window, she couldn't help thinking of sailors manning a ship's rigging, cutlasses at the ready. Trade Cottage, she felt, was girding itself for battle.

Buoyed, she phoned Liv, on the pretext of asking about the next book club. Liv sounded pleased to have been called – relieved, even, as if recognising that things had got slightly out of hand before.

'We're doing *Where the Crawdads Sing*,' she told Kate. 'Sally chose it.'

'Great choice – it's been on my TBR list for ages.' Kate hesitated, then said casually, 'Has Sally said anything about Guy Pelham putting in an application for a solar farm, by the way?'

'She did mention something, yes. It's great, isn't it? Apparently, they can build them off the ground now, so Gordon will still be able to graze his sheep. I don't know why more people aren't doing them.'

'I guess it's an aesthetic thing?' Kate ventured. 'I mean, they're not exactly nice to look at.'

'Oh, I love them,' Liv said breathlessly. 'Just the thought of all that beautiful clean energy. And if it helps to make a place like Pelham Park financially sustainable too . . . It's win–win, really.'

Kate agreed that it probably was, and rang off, frustrated. She knew Liv was completely sincere. It was going to be hard to oppose the solar farm without coming across as selfish Nimbys.

While she was thinking about that, her phone rang. It was Mary Snow, the woman who'd lent Fresco to Tilly, before taking him back again.

'I'm having to use my stable for a neighbour's horse that's damaged its leg,' she told Kate. 'And, now it's getting colder, Fresco should really come in at night. I don't suppose you still have room for him?'

'Of course,' Kate said, surprised. 'Tilly would love to have him back. She adores him.'

'Well, in that case, she might as well ride him, too. I'll arrange some lessons with Izzy.'

Kate had absolutely no idea who Izzy was – Rosemary taught Tilly when Fresco was with them before – but, once again, she had the feeling that she and Matt were being talked about, and perhaps, she thought, in a slightly more nuanced way than before the planning meeting.

Later that morning, she went down to the bottom of the garden. As expected, Paul's pinwheels had proved completely ineffectual at addressing the mole problem, but the pest controller had suggested sonic mole repellents, which seemed to be working. To her surprise, the *Keep Out* signs had vanished from the edge of the wood. So Will was being allowed to access his dens, as well.

This could only be Rosemary's doing, she realised. Was it because, now that the planning battle was lost, she wanted to let bygones be bygones? Or because Jamie was going back to America, at least for the time being? Or had Kate's own plea about the children, that time by the lavender bushes, had an effect after all? Whatever was behind it, it felt like an olive branch.

She looked up at The Old Tennis Court, wondering if she'd catch sight of her, but its big plate-glass windows were filled only with reflected clouds.

Any hopes that the truce might be extended to Kate and Matt too, though, were scuppered the next day when a letter arrived from the council, enclosing a 'Remedial Action Notice'. An officer had visited the property next door, it said, and agreed that the leylandii hedge was blocking the light. The notice required the entire hedge to be reduced to two metres.

'Quite why Rosemary and Paul want it done now, when all they'll see is diggers trashing Trade Cottage's garden, beats me,' Matt grumbled. 'But it looks like we don't have a choice.' So a team of tree surgeons was added to all the other contractors. It only took two days of men with chainsaws hanging like mountaineers off the leylandii, and the great green cliff was gone, exposing the end wall of the bungalow completely.

At least The Old Tennis Court didn't have any windows on that side, Kate thought, only a large pane of frosted glass that must be a bathroom. But she felt exposed, all the same.

That evening, she was startled to see Rosemary walking up the lawn, carrying a tray covered in a tea towel. It looked as if she was bringing them a freshly baked cake, or a lasagne perhaps, that the towel was helping to keep warm. A peace offering, Kate immediately thought. Rosemary was about to make another of her apologies – to say what an idiot she was for letting Paul get carried away with that petition, or that she was going to put a stop to this solar-farm nonsense.

Hurrying to the back door, Kate set off to meet her, striding down the lawn, ready to take the tray so she could put it down and envelop Rosemary's tiny frame in a hug . . .

Then she got close enough to see the older woman's shell-shocked expression, and that her beautiful wrinkled face was streaked with tears. 'What is it?' Kate asked desperately. 'What's wrong?'

Mutely, the other woman held out the tray. Kate lifted the tea towel. She saw a heart-shaped face, a stubby curved beak, a mass of fluffy white feathers, and gasped.

It was the owl, dead.

'He lived in the barn,' Rosemary said hoarsely. 'I suppose the work disturbed him. But it's the rat poison that'll have done for him. The mice would have eaten it too, and then, when they were dying, they'd have been easier to catch, and if he ate a few of them, the poison would have got him as well.'

'Oh, Rosemary,' Kate said miserably, 'I'm so sorry.'

She meant it. That Rosemary had wrung a duck's neck with barely a flicker of emotion, and that the woods were full of pheasants raised solely to be shot, was beside the point. She understood completely that owls were as different from those birds as a lion was from a hyena. It felt as if Trade Cottage had been desecrated, somehow – as if a household god had been slain.

'I'm so, so sorry,' she repeated. 'But the rats were so gross . . . I couldn't not do anything.'

'You could have used live traps.'

Kate hadn't even known there were such things – she'd left it completely to the pest controller. She stayed silent, horrified at her own lack of forethought.

'They say it's a curse to kill an owl,' Rosemary added. 'They say it brings death. Let's hope that's not true.'

Turning, she walked back down towards the gate to The Old Tennis Court, leaving Kate still holding the tea tray with the owl on it, like a tiny bier.

# FORTY-TWO

For the next two weeks things were calmer. That is, they were full-on, frenetic, noisy and exhausting – Kate hadn't realised just how much work supervising so many builders would be. Although Nikolas was nominally in charge of the conversions, he was only visiting weekly, and it seemed like every other minute someone had a question for her about how a hole should be dug or whether a beam could be salvaged. She was careful to refer anything she wasn't sure about to Annie, the conservation officer, who was turning out to be quite helpful, now Matt and Kate were playing by the rules. Kate had got hold of heritage paints, too, and was busy finishing off the rooms she'd had to abandon before. But, on the village front, there were no more developments, and no more poison-pen letters either. She and Matt even started getting takeaway pizzas from the Pelham Arms again, although she noticed that Jason always managed to contrive things so it was one of the other staff who served them.

By unspoken agreement, she and Matt didn't speak about Jamie Finch's offer. There was no point – they'd resolved not to take it, and that was that. But occasionally, lying awake in the small hours, she'd find herself trying to work out how many days had passed since he'd made it, and what it was now worth – like a hideous doomsday clock, counting down in the background. Then she'd firmly push the thought away. It would be unthinkable to leave Trade Cottage now. They'd just have to find some way of scotching this solar farm.

It was mid-afternoon on Thursday when she heard a bang – loud enough to puncture the constant low rattling of the diggers and to echo off the woods below, scattering birds into the air. Involuntarily, she flinched. She hadn't heard the gas guns for a while, though she was always slightly on edge, knowing they could start again at any moment. But this had sounded different, somehow. Nearer, and higher pitched than the bird scarers' booming explosions.

Putting down her paintbrush, she went into the garden to see if it was something to do with the contractors. But the digger drivers were all wearing helmets with ear defenders, and none of them seemed to have noticed anything over the din.

She glanced up at the side of The Old Tennis Court. That big pane of frosted glass facing Trade Cottage, last time she'd looked at it, had been a pristine, milky white, almost velvety in texture. Now, it was piebald, spattered with dark patches on the inside, some almost blackberry-juice coloured . . .

It took a moment for it to sink in, for her to realise what she was seeing. Dashing to the gate in the hedge, she ran up to The Old Tennis Court's side door.

'Rosemary?' she called into the house, panting. 'Rosemary – are you all right?'

Rosemary came out of the shadows towards her. Her face was

covered in blood, her clothes smeared and streaked with it, as if she'd tried to wipe her hands clean on herself. In one bloodied hand was a phone.

'It's Paul,' she said hoarsely. 'He's dead. He's shot himself in the wet room.'

# FORTY-THREE

The minutes that followed were a blur. She should go and check, she dimly thought, in case there was any possibility Rosemary was mistaken and Paul could still be saved. But, even through the wet room's open door, she could immediately see it was hopeless. On the floor, to one side, was a small double-barrelled shotgun – she recognised it with a jolt of horror as the one Will had carried around so proudly after his shooting lessons, barrels open and tucked over his arm as Paul had taught him:

*Never, never let your gun*
*Pointed be at anyone.*
*That it might unloaded be*
*Matters not the least to me.*

Paul's wheelchair was there too, empty. He was lying on the floor in his pyjamas – Kate glimpsed one bare foot, the toes surprisingly long, pointed in her direction. His face was intact, but the back of his head had been completely blown apart. There was blood and worse up the wall, and more blood on the floor, puddled and streaked, as if someone – Rosemary, presumably – had attempted to reach his body. Beside the door, a blood-soaked towel showed where she'd tried to clean herself.

'My hands were all covered with it,' Rosemary said, behind her. 'I couldn't get my blasted phone to work. I had to . . .' She indicated her filthy clothes.

Kate nodded numbly. 'You did the right thing.' She had no idea if that was true, but she wanted the other woman to hear some words of reassurance.

'I've only called the police. Not the children yet. They're sending an ambulance anyway.' Rosemary sounded as if she was on autopilot. 'Perhaps they'll know what happens next.'

'I'm sure they will,' Kate said gently. She heard sirens. 'Is the electric gate open?'

'Oh!' Rosemary gasped. 'No – they mustn't ring the bell—' She hurried to the controls for the gate, just beside the front door.

'It sends Jamie an alert,' she added. 'If he sees police and an ambulance, he'll realise.'

As soon as the gate had trundled open, the ambulance came in, followed by a police car. Two young women in dark-green uniforms jumped out of the ambulance, calm but purposeful, grabbing bags of equipment and canisters of oxygen. Already the air was crackling with radio traffic.

At the front door, the two paramedics hesitated.

'Please, come in,' Rosemary said. 'I mean, there's nothing you can do, but come in anyway. He's through there.' She pointed. Kate half-expected her to offer them a scone and raspberry jam. But of course, Rosemary was in shock, they both were, and this surreal this-can't-be-happening feeling must be what shock felt like.

Two police officers followed – one female, one male. They took in Rosemary's bloodied clothes.

'Was it you who called 999?' the female officer asked gently.

Rosemary nodded. 'I'm his wife.' Perhaps it was the word 'wife' that did it, the awful finality of a lifetime together coming to an end, because she blinked and gasped, her composure finally cracking. She turned away, her shoulders shaking.

The officer turned to Kate. 'And you are . . . ?'

'A neighbour. I heard the shot.'

The male officer cocked his head. 'Is that your property next door? With the machinery I can hear?'

'Yes. I only just heard the bang over the noise – that was why it took me—'

'If you could tell them to stop work, but to stay at the property until someone's spoken to them,' he said gently, and Kate realised she'd been about to gabble incontinently at him.

The paramedics came back from the wet room. 'We'll need to get a doctor out,' one of them said quietly to the police officers, and for a single, mad, dizzying moment, Kate thought, *He's still alive*, then realised the woman was actually saying the opposite, that they'd need a doctor to come and certify Paul's death. Dimly, she grasped that a whole vast machinery was about to swing into action. Suicides, she'd read somewhere, were treated no differently from any other violent death. There would be police photographs, forensic evidence collected; the body would be taken to a hospital for a post-mortem. Paul's computer and phone would be analysed for evidence of his state of mind. And finally, many months or even years from now, there would be an inquest.

A Land Rover pulled into the drive at speed, squeezing in between the ambulance and police car. Sally, Gordon's wife, jumped out of the passenger side and came towards the house, followed closely by Gordon. The male police officer moved to head them off.

'It's all right,' Rosemary said, noticing. 'They're friends. Oh, Sally – Gordon,' she called desperately. 'Paul's gone and killed himself.'

Sally came and enveloped Rosemary in a hug, bloody clothes and all, while Gordon surprised Kate by letting out a terrible, bellowing wail.

'If you could all move into the sitting room,' the policeman said. 'We need to cordon this area off.'

Rosemary allowed herself to be led towards the sofa. As Sally urged her to sit down, the farmer's wife shot a look back towards Kate that was, Kate was surprised to see, almost accusatory.

# FORTY-FOUR

She'd wanted to wait for Matt to get home before breaking the news to the children, but The Old Tennis Court was still a hive of activity when she went to pick them up from their buses – as well as the police car and ambulance, there was now the unmistakeable glossy bulk of a hearse. So she told them in the car, as gently as she could, without mentioning that it was suicide.

'How did it happen? Did he have a heart attack?' Will asked.

'I don't think they know yet,' she lied. She suspected the children would find out in the end, but she instinctively wanted to protect them from the truth as long as possible. Tilly was already in tears. Perhaps more worryingly, Will wasn't – he was just at that age where he wasn't sure if crying was unmanly. She suspected it might happen later, when he was alone. He'd adored Paul. It wasn't just the shooting lessons or the eagerness to hear about dens and forts and walks with Biddy. Paul's larger-than-life bonhomie had acted as a foil for Will's pre-teen shyness.

For her part, she kept getting flashbacks to the carnage behind Paul's head, the awful dripping of bloody matter down the wet-room wall. It was a huge relief when Matt arrived and she could cry over him. He, too, was devastated. He'd never taken Paul out for that bury-the-hatchet drink – he'd been too busy with work – and felt guilty as a result.

'I wish now I'd taken his advice about the French, too,' he added. 'Not that I could have changed the deal by then, but I could have been firmer with them at the beginning.'

Already, he said, flowers and cards were being left outside The Old Tennis Court's front gate. Presumably Rosemary was taking them in, since there were none the next morning when Kate took Will and Tilly to the bus. But when she collected the children that afternoon, there were masses – bouquets, cards, even some teddy bears and bottles of Pol Roger: a spontaneous outpouring of local compassion.

She wondered how quickly Jamie and Tessa would get there. Soon, she assumed – if Jamie was currently jobless, presumably there'd been nothing stopping him from jumping on a plane as soon as he heard, while Tessa, she recalled Rosemary saying, was in Wales, so even nearer. For that reason, she didn't go back to The Old Tennis Court to see how Rosemary was. Instead, she bought flowers and a card. *Thinking of you at this awful time. I won't pester you, but please, PLEASE, if you would like a cup of tea or a glass of wine or just to talk, I'm around.* She used the gate in the hedge, leaving the flowers and card beside Rosemary's door.

As she walked back to Trade Cottage, the ignominious thought crossed her mind that, once the dust had settled, things might actually be easier now. With Rosemary grieving – lonely, even – she might be more approachable than when Paul, energetic chair of the Pelham Preservation Committee, had been alive. Kate tried to think back. What had Rosemary's involvement in all that discord been? She'd been at the planning committee meeting, true, but she hadn't spoken. There'd been that 'fucking barbarians' comment, and the subsequent apology, but, now Kate thought about it, all the excitement about Jamie relocating to the UK, and the request to buy back Trade Cottage, had been led by Paul – Rosemary's reaction had actually been quite muted. So perhaps this death would be . . . not a good thing, of course not that, but it might reset the relationship between Trade Cottage and The Old Tennis Court somewhat.

An even more ignominious thought occurred to her: Jamie wouldn't be able to dress up coming back to the UK as a selfless act for the benefit of his terminally ill father now. Was it too much to hope he might even decide to stay where he was, and look for a job in the US instead? God, she hoped so. But first, of course, there would be the funeral, probably delayed a little by the need for a post-mortem. He'd certainly want to stay in Pelham until after that. At the thought of him being in her vicinity once again, she felt a shudder of dislike. She must have another look for that key.

She'd given a statement to the female police officer on the day of Paul's suicide, and was visited a few days later by a man in plain clothes who introduced himself as Oliver Wray, the coroner's officer. He was equivalent in rank to a detective sergeant, he told her, and was responsible for gathering information for the inquest.

'There is one thing I want to check,' he added. 'You told the officer you heard a shot over the noise of machinery in your garden?'

'That's right. I was painting, and the window was open because of the fumes.'

'And it was definitely a single report you heard? One bang, rather than two?'

'Yes, of course,' she said, puzzled. 'Why?'

'The shotgun in question has two barrels and two triggers – it's what's called a side-by-side,' he explained. 'Both barrels were fired. The reason I'm checking is that one of the men working on your roof also remembers hearing the gun. But he says that, to the best of his recollection, there were two bangs, in quick succession.'

'But that's . . .' She stopped, rendered speechless by the implication. Then she breathed a sigh of relief. 'He heard the echo.'

'The echo?' Oliver Wray repeated.

'Yes. Acoustically, the woods at the bottom of the garden act like a cliff – any really loud noise bounces back a moment later. We've noticed it with gas guns, the shoot, even party noise from The Old Tennis Court.'

'And you definitely heard the echo when the gun was fired?' Oliver Wray asked.

'I'm certain of it. I remember the birds coming out of the trees.'

'It would have been a doubly loud bang, of course, even though it was just a .410,' he said thoughtfully, making a note. 'So that explanation does make sense.'

For reasons that weren't entirely clear to her, the police asked that the builders hold off work for two more weeks. With time on her hands, she started walking again. On one of these excursions, she saw a notice in the window of the village shop: *The funeral of Paul Finch will be held at noon on Tuesday 16th and afterwards at the Pelham Arms. Due to anticipated high numbers, it will also be streamed online.*

Perhaps because funerals were in her thoughts, on her way back she went into the church to see if there was a book of condolence. As she came in, she heard someone crying. She looked around. At the back, sitting in one of the pews, was Rosemary. She'd clearly been weeping for some time – her face was wet, and she was rocking, her shoulders heaving.

'Oh, Rosemary!' Kate exclaimed. Hurrying over, she slid into the pew alongside her. 'I'm so, so sorry. This must be awful for you.'

She put her arm around Rosemary's shoulder. The older woman turned and buried her face in Kate's jumper, bawling without restraint. Like a child, Kate thought – it was like having Tilly or Will in her arms, making the kind of unfettered, full-throttle, unselfconscious wailing that adults almost never did: mucussy, anguished, full of horror. Kate pressed her hand against Rosemary's tiny back and rocked her, making motherly sounds in an instinctive effort to soothe her.

Eventually, the other woman struggled upright and stared bleakly at the altar.

'I only came to choose hymns.' She gestured at an open hymn book on the ledge in front of her. 'He'd have hated some awful dirge in a key no one could manage. Jolly sing-songs were more his thing.'

'It must be so overwhelming,' Kate ventured. 'But it's good you can let your emotions out.'

Rosemary shot her an angry glance. 'Oh, I wasn't crying for *him*.'

'Really?' Kate said, surprised. 'What, then?'

'I was crying for Tray,' Rosemary said bleakly. 'If he'd only done this a year ago, I wouldn't have had to move out.'

# FORTY-FIVE

'Apparently, being angry with someone who's killed themselves is quite a common reaction,' she told Matt. 'I read a blog post about it. People are upset that the dead person didn't realise, or didn't apparently care, how much they were loved.'

'I get that,' Matt said doubtfully. 'But, from what you've told me, Rosemary's anger was different. It was specifically about leaving here.'

They were in the kitchen at Trade Cottage, while the children were upstairs, getting on with homework. At least, Kate hoped they were. Will in particular was still taking Paul's death very hard. Someone at school had told him that Paul shot himself, and, although he didn't seem to have made the connection with the gun he'd learnt to shoot clay pigeons with, Kate had noticed he wasn't playing video games just now. Normally, she'd have been pleased by that, but this listless, quiet child wasn't the Will she knew.

'True,' she admitted, bringing her attention back to Matt. 'But Tray isn't just a house, it's a whole way of life. I think she's been grieving for that ever since they moved out – Paul's death has just given it a focus. It's not necessarily even rational. After all, even if he *had* killed himself a year ago, she'd still have needed to move out in the end. This house is way too big for an eighty-three-year-old woman on her own.'

'Perhaps she'd have moved into a granny annexe, and Jamie and family would have been in here,' Matt said.

Kate shuddered. 'Horrible thought. I can't believe she'd have been happy with that kind of set-up.'

Another thought struck her. 'She said something, actually – just after Paul died. At the time, I was too shocked by everything to take much notice, but . . . She said, if the ambulance crew rang the doorbell, Jamie would get an alert and be able to see them. She was in a real panic to get the gates open so they wouldn't have to use the Ring.'

'That's understandable, though, surely?' Matt said. 'She wanted to tell him about his father's death herself.'

'Yes, but setting up doorbell alerts so he can see who's visiting? I could understand if she was some frail old lady who might let scammers in, but Rosemary's hardly at a stage where she needs her son in America overseeing who visits her house.'

'They were probably just future-proofing it for when she *is* old and frail,' Matt said gently. 'We already know he takes an interest. The first time we came, Rosemary said it was him who'd been pestering them to get a wet room.'

'I guess.' She sighed. 'I'm not looking forward to seeing him at the funeral, let alone Guy and Gordon and the rest. But I suppose it's inevitable.'

Matt shot her a look. 'You're going?'

She nodded. 'I feel I should, to support Rosemary. It's clearly going to be rammed, so hopefully I can just sit at the back and keep my head down. And obviously I won't go to the wake afterwards.'

There was a sound from the direction of the front door – not a knock, more like the soft thump of a package hitting the mat. 'Did you hear that?' she asked.

Matt frowned. 'What?'

'Never mind – I'll go.' Getting up, she followed the passageway round to the front door and opened it.

There was no one there. And – she glanced down – no package. Just something red and liquid, dripping—

She gasped as she saw that more red liquid was dripping from the open door on to the flagstones. She had to go outside and step back to look at it properly, to see the great scar of red paint that had been flung across Trade Cottage's ancient oak door. No, not paint, she realised a moment later: it was too thin. Their door had been covered with blood.

Matt heard her cry and came running. Taking the situation in with a glance, he said, 'It'll stain. We need to get it off before it dries.' He darted into the loo and came out a few moments later with the hand towel, which he'd run under the tap. He wiped the door swiftly, then went back to rinse the towel so he could do it again. Kate, meanwhile, stayed rooted helplessly to the spot, trying and failing to get the image of the wet-room wall out of her head.

'It's fake,' Matt added, as he dabbed and swabbed. 'Fake blood. It was in all the shops for Halloween.'

She didn't ask him how he could be so sure. She could think of half a dozen locals who could get hold of real animal blood.

'Even if it is,' she said slowly, 'the message isn't.'

He glanced at her. 'What do you mean?'

'Blood on our doorstep,' she said. 'I think someone's trying to say we bear responsibility for Paul's death.'

# FORTY-SIX

*TO THE SLAG AT TRADE COTTAGE AND HER COCKOLD HUSBAND.*

*SCREWING AROUND IS ONE THING BUT YOU HAVE GONE TO FAR THIS TIME. AN INNOCENT MAN & RESPECTED PERSON IS DEAD, ALL BECAUSE OF YOUR PLANS TO OPEN A BROTHEL IN OUR AREA.*

*WHAT GOES AROUND COMES AROUND. GOODBYE SLAG. YOU HAVE ONLY YOURSELF TO BLAME.*

# FORTY-SEVEN

She didn't go to the funeral, after that. Jamie she could just about cope with. But anonymous letters and attacks on their property were something else. She remembered the accusatory look Sally had given her when she and Gordon swept into The Old Tennis Court after Paul's death. At the time, it hadn't even occurred to Kate that anyone could think her and Matt's small – and, given the solar farm, short-lived – victory in getting permission for a couple of outbuilding conversions could have been a factor in Paul killing himself. But clearly a toxic narrative was forming, fuelled by pints of Bowman's and Longdog, that suited the village's ravenous appetite for gossip and feuds.

She left Rosemary a card and another bunch of flowers. *Probably best if I don't attend today, but I'll be thinking of you and watching online. All my love, K xx*

A quick search for 'Paul Finch funeral' brought up the live stream inside the church. The rubric informed her that it was being filmed so Paul's many friends from Botswana and the US could be part of it. Already, sixty people were logged in, and it was only 11.30.

It was strangely fascinating, being able to scrutinise the villagers as they arrived while remaining unseen herself. There was Gordon, in a slightly unlikely grey double-breasted suit, muttering something to Guy Pelham as they passed in front of the camera. Sally, wearing a black version of the kind of hat you might expect to see at a wedding, was with Liv and Elizabeth. Jason from the pub looked as if he was struggling not to cry. Kate recognised the couple who ran the village shop, the woman who delivered the papers, a bunch of people she'd met at the housewarming party. A group of elderly men – Paul's ex-colleagues, perhaps – arrived together and took up two rows. People were dragging stacks of chairs out from the vestry and putting them at the back of the church, at the end of pews – anywhere they could pack them in. But soon even that wasn't enough, and those who arrived with less than ten minutes to spare had to stand.

Eventually, the family appeared. Jamie, dressed in a dark suit, was accompanied by a woman with immaculate short blonde hair, wearing an expensive-looking dark trouser suit. That must be Courtney, his wife. Their children – Hamish and Flora, Kate remembered – were also smartly turned out, in a black suit and black dress respectively. Hamish looked to be about thirteen, Flora around eleven. Behind them was a slight, grey-haired woman, wearing a baggy brown dress. That must be Tessa, Jamie's younger sister, although she actually looked older than him – now Kate thought about it, Jamie had probably had a little bit of work done round his eyes. Tessa had Biddy with her, on a lead. Beside her, Rosemary was smiling politely at people, thanking them for coming.

Donna, the vicar, came out of the vestry in her ceremonial

robes. The organ fell silent, and she spoke a few words of welcome. Then the door of the church opened and the pallbearers came in, marching slowly in step, with the coffin on their shoulders. It was only when it had been lowered on to trestles in front of the altar that Kate felt the awful reality of the situation – that Paul, who she'd last seen lying in a pool of his own blood on the wet-room floor, had since then been cut up, put back together, boxed up, and was now right there, in front of them. She kept thinking of that naked foot with the surprisingly long toes, sticking out of his pyjama leg, and those dripping wet-room walls.

After the first hymn – 'He Who Would Valiant Be': Rosemary had succeeded in her mission to choose some thumping tunes – Tessa gave a reading from the Bible, her voice dry and firm. Then Donna announced that Flora was going to play a piano piece she'd composed herself, entitled 'For Grandpappy Paulie'. It was staggeringly good, not least because Flora sang a wordless melody over it, her voice floating pure and true through the church's Gothic arches.

Donna thanked her and introduced Hamish. For a moment, Kate felt sorry for him, having to follow that stellar performance by his sister, but she needn't have worried. Hamish boldly announced that there was only one way to do justice to Grandpappy Paulie's famous sense of fun. 'Other families have dad jokes,' he said. 'The Finch crew have grandpappy jokes. Here's a couple of his faves. What do you call a magician's dog? A Labracadabrador. What did the pony say when it caught a cold? Forgive me, I'm a little hoarse.' It was a tough crowd – Kate could tell people were unsure, to begin with, whether it was all right to laugh out loud at a funeral – but Hamish had a stand-up's precision of timing and by the third one-liner it was impossible to hold back. He quite literally had them rolling in the aisles when, again with an orator's timing, he flipped the mood. 'What do you call a man who takes his own life?' he asked, and for a moment the shocked silence was so palpable, Kate could feel it through the camera. 'A giant,' he answered himself. 'A legend. A tragedy. But, most of all, one of the greatest men I have had the privilege of knowing.'

My God, Kate thought. These children are titans. She felt a stab of envy that Jamie and Courtney had somehow raised such self-assured, talented creatures.

There was a second hymn – another belter: 'Lord of All Hopefulness' – then it was Jamie's turn. He walked confidently to the lectern and, even more confidently, made them all wait while he unfolded his notes. Then he glanced up at the packed aisles.

'The terrible thing is, he would have loved this bit.'

He paused for that to sink in. 'Imagine – almost two hundred of his closest family, friends, colleagues and neighbours, all gathered in one place, and he's stuck in there and can't greet you properly.

'And by "properly", I mean, of course, with a welcoming smile and a glass of Pol Roger.' Jamie looked around. 'I can see a few glum faces here today, but if there was ever a man who could have had this place rocking, it was Dad. "Guests!" he'd have said. "Party!"'

People chuckled at that. Anecdotes followed – in-jokes and punchlines that meant nothing to Kate, but which had the congregation in stitches. Occasionally, though, Jamie's voice cracked and he had to pause, turning away for a moment to hide his grief, then resuming as if nothing had happened.

She was about to get up and put the kettle on when she heard him say, 'Of course, there were difficulties at the end of his life. He felt – wrongly – that he'd let Mum down by having to move. And it never occurred to either of them, when they sold their beloved Trade Cottage, that their new neighbours would turn out to be developers.'

Kate froze. A couple of heads in the congregation, she saw, were nodding.

'Developers,' Jamie continued, 'who would rip out period features without bothering to obtain the proper consent, apparently believing the old adage that it is easier to seek forgiveness than permission.'

He paused. 'Not that they ever did. Seek forgiveness, that is.'

Kate stared at the screen, rage starting to boil. How could he possibly be doing this? Using a eulogy to his dead father to attack her and Matt – it was simply grotesque.

'Even so, Mum and Dad tried hard to welcome them into the village. Many of you will remember the housewarming party they so generously arranged.' Jamie paused again. 'Although you may also remember how the village was chucked out at ten p.m. sharp, and had to decamp next door to The Old Tennis Court.'

A few people laughed out loud at that. She couldn't believe what she was hearing. He was weaponising a party he hadn't even been at!

'A campaign of harassment,' Jamie was saying. 'Noise disturbances at all hours of day and night . . . The antidepressants he had to take, to try to deal with it all . . . The final straw, when the hedge between the two properties was razed almost to the ground, and he was forced to watch the pointless destruction of the garden he'd spent a lifetime creating—'

'That wasn't us, you prick!' Kate shouted. 'That was *you*!'

'There had already been the revelation that they were intending to open multiple short-term lets on the site. In a last, desperate attempt to preserve the character of the house – and the village – he loved so much, he even made a generous offer to buy it back – an offer that was instantly thrown back in his face, and subsequently misrepresented.' Jamie's voice had changed now – it was clipped and curt, his anger unmistakeable. As he looked round, making eye contact with his listeners for emphasis, he happened to glance straight at the camera. Even though he couldn't see her, Kate recoiled at the boiling fury in his eyes, so different from the wry twinkle they'd had when he was trying to charm her.

'We had some anguished phone calls in those last, dark weeks,' he said quietly. 'I had already decided to give up my job at the IMF and return to the UK with my family, to do what I could to help. On top of everything else, there were the worries he'd confided about my mother's health. But, sadly, the burden and the sense of failure were just too much to bear; and, tragically, we were just too late—'

'AAARGH!' she shouted at the screen, enraged. 'YOU ARE KIDDING ME!'

Jamie was listing Paul's many achievements: the charities he'd chaired; the one he'd founded himself to supply schoolbooks to Botswana; the industry bodies he'd served on; the CBE he was too modest to mention to people; the parish council; the pub; the Pelham Preservation Committee . . . There hadn't been a single mention of his illness, she realised. If it didn't suit Jamie's narrative, it was ignored.

'Yet his greatest talent, and the one he was proudest of, was his skill as a host. If he were here, he'd be going round the pews with a bottle of Pol by now, topping you all up and telling me to hurry up and get to the toast.'

Jamie paused. 'So, by special kind permission of Donna and the PCC, that's what we're going to do.'

Hamish and Flora pushed two trolleys laden with champagne flutes out of the vestry. The glasses were already half-full; Courtney and Tessa followed with bottles, topping up any that needed it. People were laughing and chattering as they passed the glasses down the pews; corks popped as more bottles were opened. Jamie had to raise his voice to shout, 'There's a hymn that's not on the printed order of service. But I think most of you know the words.'

He started to sing. It was the drinking song, she realised, that Paul had sung on the night of the party. By the second line, everyone was joining in, just as they had around the firepit, all the way to the rousing final words:

'*Cos we've always got some champers,*

*Always got some champers,*

*We've always got some champers in the fridge!*'

'To a great man: Paul Finch!' Jamie said, and there was a moment before the toast was echoed to the rafters, and another before the congregation, cheering and stamping their feet on the wooden floor, gave Paul's son a massive round of applause.

# FORTY-EIGHT

Matt watched it later, on the train. If anything, he was even angrier than she'd been. To be openly besmirched like that, in front of their neighbours – lie after lie – even as Paul's body lay in front of them, spoke to something atavistic in him, the tribe turning on its own. Or perhaps it was simply his fundamental sense of decency.

'He's gone too far this time,' he kept repeating. 'He's going to pay for this.'

But exactly how Jamie Finch was going to pay for it was still eluding them. His very lies had made him untouchable, the grieving son of the wronged king. Anything they did or said now was going to be seen as pure spite.

'What did he mean, about Rosemary having health issues too?' Matt asked.

'I've no idea,' Kate said, baffled. 'She did mention that she's been feeling her age, but so far as I know there's nothing specific, just some rheumatism and creaky bones. I'm not sure she'd have told me if there *was* something, though. She didn't even tell me they'd lost a child.' At the thought that Jamie, the prodigal son, might have more access to Rosemary's private thoughts than she did, she felt a visceral pang of jealousy. 'I wouldn't be surprised if he was making it up. It suits his version of events to portray her as a helpless old lady.'

There were already masses more flowers and cards outside The Old Tennis Court's front gate, Matt told her. 'And the Pelham Arms is heaving – cars parked down both sides of the road, right to the end of the village.'

'Oh, God.' If the funeral had been bad, she could only imagine how viciously tongues were wagging at the wake, fuelled no doubt by copious amounts of free Pol Roger. She felt a great weariness descend on her. 'I'm going to bed. Perhaps things will look better in the morning.'

She found it hard to sleep. Images kept coming back to her: the villagers' faces, the lip-smacking gusto with which they'd bellowed out that song; Jamie at the lectern, dapper in his expensive suit, angrily spinning his web of lies . . . But eventually she must have drifted off, because she was asleep when she felt a hand shaking her shoulder and heard Tilly whispering anxiously, 'Mummy, Mummy, wake up.'

Instantly, she was fully alert. 'What's wrong?'

'There are people outside. At the front. I'm frightened.'

'Get into bed with Daddy. I'll go and take a look.'

Tilly started to protest fearfully that she didn't want her to go, so Kate added, 'Just through the window. Is Will awake?'

'I don't think so.'

That frightened her – the scaffolding at the front of the house effectively gave access to both children's bedrooms. She waited until Tilly had climbed into bed, then woke Matt up. 'People outside,' she whispered as he rolled over. 'Don't worry – I'll be careful.'

She went downstairs, leaving the lights off. She could immediately see why Tilly had been woken up. There were two Land Rovers outside, headlights on and engines running. Voices were shouting instructions. Somehow, the fact they were making absolutely no effort to conceal their presence made it even more frightening. For one awful moment, she thought they might even have come to torch the place – Trade Cottage's old walls, all that wooden panelling, would go up in minutes.

But they were doing something else, she realised. There were more shouts, then the unmistakeable *beep-beep* of a large vehicle reversing – a lorry or tanker, perhaps. A clanking sound, the revving of a diesel engine, some strange squelching noises.

The noises stopped, and the lorry drove away. Moments later, car doors banged and the Land Rovers sped after it.

She waited until she was absolutely sure they'd gone. Then, tentatively, she opened the door.

It was dark, and she couldn't immediately see what they'd done. But she didn't need to. The acrid stench of human sewage hit her nostrils, and with a cry of disgust she slammed the door shut.

It turned out, when dawn finally broke, that a stinking pool of human slurry had been pumped over their gravel. At least, this time, the police took it seriously. Matt called the non-emergency number and was told someone would come out that morning. Sure enough, shortly after nine a.m., a police car turned up and two uniformed officers got out. Kate recognised one as Phillipa

Dickinson, the female officer who'd come to The Old Tennis Court after Paul's suicide and who'd later taken Kate's statement.

It soon became clear, though, that the reason for the speedy response had little to do with the harassment of Kate and her family. It was because improperly disposing of human waste – or 'sewage sludge', as Kate discovered it was called in legalese – was an offence under the same environmental laws that were necessitating a new drainage field at Trade Cottage.

Still, Sergeant Dickinson and her colleague listened sympathetically as Kate explained what had been happening. She showed them the most recent poison-pen letter, and the two officers exchanged a glance.

'Did you take photographs of the liquid that was thrown at your door?' Sergeant Dickinson asked.

Kate shook her head. 'We wanted to get it off before it stained.'

'Well, make sure you record that and all the other incidents in a logbook. And, in future, photograph everything, including what's happened now, and keep any letters.'

Anwar had said much the same thing, Kate recalled, back in the days when the worst that was being done to them was some rogue lavender pruning. She resolved that, from now on, every attempt at intimidation was going to be documented in full.

'Given that there's nothing to identify anyone, it doesn't reach the threshold for involving a detective,' the sergeant added. 'But if it escalates, or an ID becomes clearer, it'll be useful to have all the evidence.'

'What do we do next? About the slurry, I mean?'

'Your drainage contractor can deal with that. He'll need to test the pond, too, to see if it's been contaminated. If it has, it'll have to be drained and refilled. From the look of it, that effluent's biosolids – that's human waste that's been minimally treated, so farmers can use it as manure.'

'There's a farmer involved in the harassment,' Kate said. 'He's been setting off gas guns. And he's holding motocross competitions in the wood beside our garden, which he never used to.'

Sergeant Dickinson made a note. 'I'll have a word. Obviously, if there's no proof he was responsible, he's unlikely to admit it, but sometimes just knowing the police are asking questions is enough to make people think twice.'

# FORTY-NINE

*HEY SLAG*

*KARMA = SHITTY PEOPLE GETTING THE SHIT THEY DESERVE.*

*NOW FUCK OFF WHILE YOU STILL CAN.*

# FIFTY

So the letter writer and the sewage dumpers were working in concert, she thought resignedly as she read the latest missive. She wasn't surprised. But, once again, she had the unsettling sense of matters escalating, pressure mounting, the locals becoming ever more determined to force her and Matt out.

And Jamie would make another move soon, she was certain. The solar farm, though devastating, was a long-term manoeuvre – she'd read on the internet they could take years to get through planning. No: having so effectively turned the village against Matt and Kate, he'd want to press home his advantage.

It was almost a relief, then, when she saw a white Tesla pull up outside the house one morning and Jamie climb out. In his hand was an envelope. She saw him screw up his face at the smell – even though Mick had pumped the effluent away and drenched the area with hoses, it still stank. A moment later, there were three loud raps on the front door.

She left him standing there almost a minute. Perhaps childishly, she wanted him to breathe as much of that excrement-scented air as possible.

'Christ, what have you done out here?' he said disgustedly

when she finally opened the door. 'It smells like the drains are blocked.'

'What do you want?' She ought to tell him she was sorry for his loss, she knew, but, after that eulogy, she was damned if she would.

He handed her the envelope. 'This, for starters.'

She opened it. The document inside was headed *MISSING CHATTELS*. Underneath was a list. *Portrait of Captain Pelham by George Hayter . . . Meiji-period oriental vase . . . Jacobean console table . . .* He'd put down everything Rosemary and Paul had left, plus all the junk she and Matt had cleared from the cellar. *Ibanez electric guitar . . . Box of schoolbooks . . . Shop display mannequin . . .*

'Don't be ridiculous,' she scoffed. 'The stuff in the cellar was just rubbish that Rosemary asked us to get rid of. The other things were gifts.'

'Gifts that should never have been made. That portrait's worth over thirty grand. That alone should have alerted you to what was going on with my mother.'

'What do you mean?' she said, puzzled. 'There's nothing "going on" with her.'

He regarded her coldly. 'Mum's been given a formal diagnosis of stage-three dementia, most likely Alzheimer's. She didn't have the mental capacity to give away anything, let alone precious family heirlooms.'

Kate gaped at him, speechless.

'You didn't think she really liked you, did you?' he said scathingly. 'She was just confused and trying to be polite. Which you repaid by getting your rapacious little claws into her just as fast as you could.' He nodded at the list. 'You can have all that delivered to Pelham House. Guy's kindly putting me up until you vacate.'

'We're not vacating,' she said automatically, her mind still reeling as she tried to get her head around what he'd just said about Rosemary's diagnosis.

'Of course you are. You can't possibly stay here after all this. The only question is, when and at what price.' He considered. 'I haven't checked recently, but I think the offer still comes to just about what you paid for it. And it'll be much better to sell now, while things are still reasonably civil.'

'This is hardly civil,' she snapped.

'Believe me, this is positively friendly compared with how it ought to be.' His face hardened even further – she could see muscles pulsing in his forehead. 'You've not only taken advantage of a frail old lady with dementia, you've effectively murdered my father. I'm not likely to forgive you either of those.'

He was serious, she realised with a shock. Somehow, he had actually convinced himself that the narrative he'd constructed to denigrate her and Matt was true. It was preposterous – absurd, even – but also so barefaced, so self-deluding, that it was impossible to find the right words to dismantle it.

When she didn't say anything, he indicated the list. 'A copy of that's been sent to your solicitor, along with some other matters that require his attention. I suggest you take it up with him.'

It took two hours to pin Matt down between meetings, and another hour after that to organise a Zoom with their solicitor.

'The chattels that were left in the house aren't an issue,' Anwar told them. 'If anything, it was the sellers' responsibility to deal with them. The Hayter portrait is a different matter, because Mrs Finch apparently gave that to you without consulting her husband. On the face of it, it does seem unusual behaviour. But it's a stretch to say that it's evidence she doesn't have capacity. People are entitled to make bad decisions.'

'I don't believe for one moment she has dementia,' Matt said.

'Well, they've managed to find a private doctor who says she does. And they're claiming you should have known from the start that her decision-making was disordered – as proof of which, they point to the fact you weren't even the highest bidder for Trade Cottage. Kate, apparently you yourself told a neighbour you thought she might have Alzheimer's.'

'I don't think I did,' Kate said, puzzled.

Anwar consulted the documents. 'Olivia Hoggart, who runs the village book club?'

'Oh,' Kate said, outraged. 'Liv. I didn't tell her – I *asked* her. Rosemary had been behaving oddly about a fireplace. But it all got cleared up – and, anyway, Liv said she was sure she didn't.'

'And there was an incident at a party, where she didn't recognise you? Several people saw that, their lawyer claims.'

'Well – yes,' Kate admitted. 'But it was the first time she'd seen me wearing make-up.'

'And, apparently, on more than one occasion, she completely forgot they'd moved out of Trade Cottage and was found pruning plants in your garden. The gardener's confirmed that part of it.'

'That's totally twisting it! She comes and prunes things because she doesn't think I'm a very good gardener. And because they sneakily gave themselves that access.'

'Yes,' Anwar said. 'I was coming to the access.'

Something about the way he said it alerted her that there was worse to come. 'What about it?'

'Well, that right of way is for their benefit, not yours. Apparently, you've been going on to their property uninvited.'

'That's rubbish,' Kate said. Then she remembered. 'I've left a card and some flowers a couple of times. And, of course, there was the time I heard the gunshot.'

'There's a formal warning to desist – *harassing a vulnerable elderly woman living on her own*, is how they describe it. But, to be honest, all this is just chaff to pad out their main demand.'

'Which is?' Matt asked.

'They're applying for a judicial review of the contract to purchase Trade Cottage. They want the judge to order a rescission.'

'A rescission?' Kate echoed. 'What's that?'

'It's when a contract is wound up and it's as if it never happened. So they would pay back the purchase price, minus a reasonable deduction as rent for the time you've been living there, and then they would own it again. There are very, very few grounds for rescinding a property contract like that. But, unfortunately, lack of mental capacity is one of them.'

'What – so we'd just *give it back*? But that's madness!' she exclaimed. 'What about Paul? His name was on that contract too.'

'Yes, but they both had to have capacity for it to be valid. And, apparently, there's evidence he'd realised his wife was getting dementia and was covering up for her.'

Suddenly, that line of Jamie's at the funeral made sense: *On top of everything else, there were the worries he'd confided about my mother's health. But, sadly, the burden and the sense of failure were just too much to bear . . .* 'The bastard's been planning this for weeks,' she said bitterly. 'He even built it into his eulogy.'

'There are various other bits of so-called evidence, too,' Anwar added. 'They've got a handwriting expert to look at some notes she wrote, dating back over the last year; apparently, there's a marked deterioration, consistent with neurological decline—'

'And also consistent,' Kate interrupted, 'with her having arthritis in her fingers from fifty-odd years of gardening, which is what she told me she'd got.'

'I don't doubt it,' Anwar said. 'But I think gathering all this material is more about convincing you that they're deadly serious about pursuing it, than convincing a judge. They'll be hoping you'll balk at the cost of fighting them and try to reach a settlement instead.'

'Accept his offer for the house, you mean? Never,' she said firmly.

'When you say, "the cost of fighting them",' Matt said quietly, 'how much are we talking about?'

Anwar shrugged his shoulders. 'It's hard to say. But you're going to need a whole team of lawyers now – as well as the property and contract issues, there's the capacity aspect, which will need a court-of-protection specialist, and probably a KC too, and a junior if they really throw the works at it. Potentially, it could all reach half a million, and, if they win, you might have to pay their costs as well.'

Kate's jaw dropped.

Matt said, 'And is that also true in reverse – if we win, we could claim our costs from them?'

'You could certainly try.'

'So it's a gamble, then,' Matt said heavily. 'A million-pound game of chicken.'

Anwar nodded. '"Lawfare", it's sometimes called – using the courts, and the threat of litigation, to bully people. I'd like to say it doesn't work, but unfortunately there's a depressingly large number of cases where it does.'

# FIFTY-ONE

She hated doing Zooms like that, with her at home and Matt in the office. It was a reminder how much of his life went on in that other world, separate from her. Although they managed a quick chat after Anwar had left the call, she could see there were already other people around him, setting up for his next meeting.

She felt as if she'd been hit by a bus – even physically dragging herself from room to room was an effort. So Jamie's response to their refusal to sell Trade Cottage was to engage lawyers to simply take it from them. It was horrendous – arrogant, entitled and, yes, to use Anwar's word, bullying. But what could they do? Anwar had left them in no doubt that, in a case like this, the party most determined to double down and raise the stakes was the one most likely to win. She cursed Jamie Finch aloud, speaking his name to the house's walls as if willing Trade Cottage itself to take the problem and solve it for them – ideally, in a way that involved Jamie vanishing from the face of the earth forever.

She'd pulled herself together by the time Matt got home, but, even then, it wasn't possible to discuss it properly. Tilly wanted him to hear her ukelele practice, and he was making time to chat to Will every day, too, usually over a game of draughts or Uno. Their son still wasn't really talking about Paul's death, but they wanted him to feel supported, and to know he could discuss his feelings with them if he wanted to.

It was gone nine when they finally had some time to themselves. 'How are you feeling?' he asked gently.

She shrugged. 'Battered. And, I suppose, a bit guilty, now I've had a chance to think about it more. Rosemary and I talked about dementia a couple of times – she was clearly worried about it. Perhaps I should have pushed harder – found out if there were little signs she wasn't telling me about . . .'

'I still don't accept she has Alzheimer's,' Matt said, shaking his head. 'I was reading about it on the train – stages one and two are indistinguishable from normal ageing, and stage three is a bunch of tiny things that may or may not mean anything. And even if she does have the early signs of it, she knew exactly what she was doing back in April, when they accepted our offer. They both did.'

'She called Jason at the pub "Jake". And she hid the notes about Captain Pelham behind the bath, then forgot she'd put them there. And do you remember when she called Paul a stupid old cripple? He didn't seem surprised – maybe he'd seen mood swings like that before. Maybe Jamie had too, for that matter.' She was still smarting from the sneering way Jamie had told her that Rosemary didn't really like her. Was it possible he was right? He'd known his mother all his life, after all, whereas Kate had only known her a few months. Could their friendship really be nothing more than a figment of a confused, fading mind?

'Maybe,' Matt said. 'But all of that could also just be old age. I looked at the screening tool GPs use for dementia, and it's really big things, like whether you can draw a clock face, and if you know what month it is. If it comes to a court hearing, we'll have her checked out by a doctor from our own side.'

She caught the implication. 'So you're definitely thinking we'll fight it? Can we afford to?'

Matt sighed. 'Probably not, as things stand. We might be able to get a bigger mortgage, now we've got that planning permission. There'd be a cost for that, though – we'd have to pay an early repayment charge on our existing loan. Then there are all these builders – it's about twenty grand a month to keep them going, now. It's unfortunate he's hitting us with this just when we're at our most stretched.'

'Which of course is deliberate.' She glanced at him. 'Any news at work?'

'Nothing good,' he admitted. 'It looks like I might have to lawyer up for that as well.'

'Is there a chance we could go under?' She spoke calmly – she knew, if she sounded anxious, he'd immediately clam up and say everything was going to be fine.

'A chance, yes.' He exhaled. 'Sometimes, it's like staring into an abyss.'

'I could go back to work part-time. I know it won't bring in much, but . . .'

Matt shook his head. 'You're project-managing the builders. Not to mention running the children around, supervising homework and fixing up the house. No, you keep doing what you're doing. We'll just have to play Jamie at his own game, and hope something turns up in the meantime.'

'Whatever happens,' she said, reaching for his hand, 'at least we've got each other, and the children. He can't take our family away from us. We're going to be fine.'

They were meant as words of reassurance, for him, but she was surprised to discover that she really meant them; that what she felt, when she contemplated taking on Jamie now, was not so much fear, as the adrenalin of battle.

# FIFTY-TWO

The next morning, she was making the children's breakfast when she heard several loud thumps on the front door, like the sound a rubber mallet would make. For a moment, she froze. But ignoring it wasn't an option – the children would be leaving through that door soon, and if it was something unpleasant, she'd need to get it out of the way.

She pulled the door open. 'Oh, Jesus,' she said aloud.

It was another dead pheasant. But, unlike the brace that had been slung over her knocker that time, this one was actually nailed to the door – two nails, great big steel things with oversized square heads, had been hammered through its spreadeagled wings into the oak. It made the dead bird look eerily like a crucified angel, its head drooping on to one shoulder, those splayed wings ridiculously beautiful, running the gamut of colours from conker-brown to grey, with a pattern inside them like a myriad of overlapping eyes.

She was about to go and find some pliers, to pull the nails out, when she remembered Sergeant Dickinson's advice: *Document everything*. Pulling out her phone, she snapped a picture first, and only then went in search of tools.

The tradesmen arrived soon after, filling the house and garden with their reassuring presence. The drainage contractor, Mick, had brought a tanker.

'The test results from the pond came back,' he told her. 'It's not good, unfortunately – it needs draining.'

More expense. She nodded. 'OK. Best get on with it.'

On an impulse, she took the nails from her pocket and showed him. 'Incidentally, do you know what these are? I haven't seen ones like this before.'

He peered at them. 'Nor me.' He looked around. 'Dougie – know what these are?'

The man he'd called came over. 'Horseshoe nails,' he said confidently. 'Farriers use them. Sometimes they fall out of the shoe, but then they're dirty. Those ones you've got there are brand new.'

'Thanks,' she said, making a mental note to add that information to the incident log. Even in the countryside, she suspected, horseshoe nails weren't something that everybody had to hand.

The tanker driver was still laying hoses to the pond when a car drove up and two men got out. She recognised one as Oliver Wray, the coroner's officer. He came over to speak to her.

'I'd like to carry out an acoustic test,' he said. 'I'm still trying to get to the bottom of whether the man on the scaffolding heard two bangs or not.'

'I guess that's fine,' she said, a little flustered. 'I'll go and tell everyone to be quiet—'

He stopped her. 'Actually, I'd like anyone who was operating machinery the day it happened to operate it again. That way, the ambient noise will be similar.'

The other man was taking a gun bag out of the car's boot. 'Before we start, can you confirm this was the gun you saw next to Mr Finch's body?' Oliver Wray asked her formally.

The man slid the gun halfway out of the bag to show her, and she nodded, feeling slightly sick at the sight of Paul's .410. 'Yes.'

'I'll take it over to The Old Tennis Court,' the second man said. He glanced at her. 'We'll run the test at least twice, so don't be alarmed if you hear more than one shot.'

As the man drove off, Oliver Wray made a phone call, and one of the roofers came down the scaffolding to speak to him. That must be the person who thought he'd heard two bangs, she guessed.

She was asked to go to the room she'd been painting on the day of Paul's death and open the window. She did as she was instructed, feeling strangely nervous. A little later, a loud bang came from the direction of The Old Tennis Court, followed immediately by the echo from the woods.

She stayed where she was. A minute or so after the first gunshot, there was a second bang and another loud, rolling echo.

A little later, Oliver Wray knocked on the front door. 'Could I have a few more minutes of your time?'

'Of course.' She led him to the kitchen.

'So you've heard the echo for yourself, now,' she said as they sat down. 'It's quite pronounced, isn't it?'

'Very.' He hesitated. 'Actually, so pronounced that it raises another question.'

'What's that?'

'That second test . . . How many shots would you say were fired?'

She shrugged. 'Well – there was just the one bang, I think.'

He shook his head. 'There were two shots that time, a second apart. The echo of the first one coincided with the second barrel being fired. It must have masked the sound, slightly.'

'But that's impossible—' she began.

He started to explain, and she added, 'No – I'm sure your test is accurate. It's what you're implying that's impossible. There's no way Rosemary killed her own husband.'

There was a short silence before Oliver Wray said, 'She was trying to care for him on her own, I understand.'

'She could easily have afforded help, if she'd wanted it. We only bought this place off them earlier this year, and, believe me, it wasn't cheap.'

After a moment, he nodded. 'I'm sorry to have to raise it. But it's important these questions are asked.'

'For what it's worth,' Kate added, 'I found her in the church, about a week after he died, crying. She said, quite apart from anything else, why wait until he'd moved out of here to do it?' She felt disloyal telling Oliver Wray about that private conversation with Rosemary, but it did show how absurd it was to think she might have been involved.

'Interesting,' Oliver said, making a note. 'But there are other possible scenarios to consider, too. An assisted suicide, for example.'

Kate had a sudden memory of Rosemary snapping the neck of that injured duck. *I'm afraid the only option is to put the poor thing out of its misery.* And then, just before she chucked its body in the skip:

*Poor old chap. It happens to them all, in the end.* But putting a duck out of its pain was very different from killing a human being.

Even so, she decided not to tell Oliver about that particular incident.

'How quickly would you say you got there, after you heard the shot?' he asked.

'Very quickly. That is, it probably took me about thirty seconds to go outside, then about ten seconds to realise what had happened, then I ran down to that hedge, there – there's a door into The Old Tennis Court's garden. I was probably inside their house within a minute.'

'Did anyone see you?'

She shrugged. 'I assume so. The garden was full of contractors, and there were men on the roof as well. None of them seemed to have heard the bang, but they probably noticed me running. You could ask them.'

'I already have.' He paused. 'So far, nobody I've spoken to did see you.'

She didn't understand what he was saying. 'But I was there.'

'Yes,' he agreed. 'The point is, I can't actually prove whether you were there just after Mr Finch's death. Or just before.'

She frowned. '*What?* You cannot think—'

'I don't think anything,' he interrupted. 'I just have to examine all the possibilities.'

He let that sink in, then added, 'Mrs Finch says she remembers being in the kitchen when she heard the shot. She then went into the wet room and found him. As she did that, she noticed the side door was open – the one nearest the garden. And I gather you were in the habit of coming in that way.'

Kate stared at him mutely, aghast at where he was going with this.

'And then Mrs Finch had, she says, a minute or so of panic when she couldn't operate her phone to call the emergency services, because her hands were wet with blood. She had to go back to the kitchen to clean herself up.'

'Yes,' Kate said. 'That's when I arrived. She said she'd just called them.'

'She doesn't actually recall seeing you come up the garden, though. The sink in the kitchen overlooks the back lawn, so that's odd, isn't it?'

'She'd just found her husband dead!'

'Yes,' Oliver Wray agreed. 'But I think she'd have noticed you, the first person on the scene. Instead, she says the first time she saw you was at the open door.'

'I can only assume,' Kate said desperately, 'that she was concentrating on trying to make that call.' She remembered something else. 'She takes her glasses off to use her phone – she has to bring the screen close to her face to see it properly. So anything in the garden would probably be out of focus.'

He made a note. 'You've been having some disagreements with your neighbours, I gather.'

'We've been subjected to a campaign of harassment,' she retorted, 'ever since the Finches asked if their son could buy our house back.'

The coroner's officer nodded. 'He grew up here, as I understand it.'

'That doesn't give him the right to walk in and take it from us!'

'Indeed not . . . So things got unpleasant, would you say?'

'Very. I've kept a log, actually. The reason that tanker's having to drain the pond, for example, is because we had human slurry dumped on our drive. And, just this morning, I found this.'

She showed him the photo she'd taken of the pheasant nailed to the front door. He raised his eyebrows. 'Could you send me this?'

'Of course.'

'I've also been sent this video of the planning committee meeting.' He got his own phone out and showed her. It was a clip of Kate making her speech: *'When Mr Finch says it isn't personal, that isn't true . . .'* She looked so fearless, she thought – that moment of clarity and purpose when she'd realised what reading out those offers would prove. *'He's using this committee as part of his private vendetta . . .'*

'*Vendetta*,' Oliver repeated, pausing the clip. 'That's a strong word.'

She shrugged. 'I was angry.'

He made another note. She wondered what on earth Jamie thought he stood to gain by sending him that video. Then she realised.

'You've spoken to Jamie Finch, haven't you?' she said slowly.

Oliver Wray looked up. 'I've interviewed the deceased's son, yes.'

'And he, no doubt, told you that I killed his father. Either figuratively or literally. Because of our so-called vendetta.' If it weren't so serious, she could almost laugh out loud at the sheer audacity of it. If it was suicide, it must be Kate and Matt's fault for not giving in to the pressure to sell; but if by any chance it could be construed as an actual murder – well, that must be Kate as well, snapping under the strain.

The coroner's officer looked at her steadily. 'Did you?'

She took a deep breath. 'Paul was like a grandfather to my son. I like Rosemary. I've never even held a shotgun, let alone fired one. And Paul had a terminal illness, for goodness' sake – he told me himself, the doctors had given him no more than two years to live. And, yes, perhaps discovering that his plan to force us out and spend his last months surrounded by his family had come to nothing – perhaps that was part of it, too. But this community trying to somehow pin it all on me – that's just madness.'

# FIFTY-THREE

After the coroner's officer had gone back outside, she stayed in the kitchen, trying to get her head round all this. How had things become so crazy? Dead pheasants were one thing, but suggestions of murder? And how could a house – any house – be worth all this?

Yet she knew in her bones she would fight for Trade Cottage, fight to her dying breath. The more Jamie and his cronies threw at her, the more resolute she would become.

She'd never really fought for anything before. In London, she'd slipped through life avoiding confrontation. She'd been the one who kept quiet when drunken youths kicked off on the Tube, or who apologised when someone trod on her heel on the escalators. But Trade Cottage had brought out another side to her. *Here, I make my stand.*

It occurred to her that, if Oliver Wray's reconstruction and interview had been hard for her, it must have been doubly traumatic for Rosemary. Kate had a sudden image of her, sitting all alone in that barren modern house, and her heart went out to her.

She jumped up. It wasn't Rosemary's fault that Jamie was being so horrible. And, on top of the shock of her husband's death, there was that diagnosis – Rosemary would be devasted about that. Kate couldn't not go to her, whatever lawyers or Jamie might say.

She went to the gate in the hedge. Once inside The Old Tennis Court's garden, she stopped, looking up at the house. In the window, she could see Paul's telescope and, next to it, his motorised wheelchair, empty now.

As she hesitated, she saw Rosemary walking towards the big plate-glass pane. Seeing Kate, she also stopped.

Tentatively, Kate waved up at her. For a long moment, Rosemary didn't respond. Then she raised her arm and waved back.

'I suppose he's only doing his job,' Rosemary said with a sigh. 'But it's not as if any of it's going to bring Paul back.'

Instinctively, Kate reached out and squeezed Rosemary's hand. 'It must be so hard.'

They were drinking tea in The Old Tennis Court's kitchen. Below them, in Trade Cottage's garden, mechanical diggers toiled away, making trenches for the drainage field.

'I had no idea he was going to do it,' Rosemary said bleakly. 'Absolutely none. It's funny, isn't it? You think you know someone – what they're like, what they're thinking – but, really, you never do. Even when you've been married to them almost sixty years.'

Kate tried to think of any crumbs of comfort. 'Perhaps he was thinking of you. You know – not wanting to become a burden.'

'Perhaps.' Rosemary was silent a moment. 'Though, actually, I don't think it was that. If anything, Paul rather took me looking after him for granted – he was quite old-fashioned in some ways. But Oliver can't find any evidence of depression or anxiety – nothing on the computer to suggest he'd been building up to it, for example. And, of course, it probably *is* harder to pull a shotgun trigger with MND, let alone two at once. But he'd had that little .410 since he was a boy. If anyone knew how to handle it, he did.'

'At the funeral,' Kate said carefully, 'Jamie said something about how Paul had been worried about your health. And now . . .' She hesitated. 'We've been told you've been diagnosed with dementia.'

'Ah. Yes, I have.' Rosemary pursed her lips. 'So I suppose *my* future is that I shall gradually turn into a shuffling, vacant husk. Like something out of those awful zombie movies Hamish and Flora like to watch. Will I be aware of it, do you suppose? Or does one forget what one used to be?'

She considered for a moment. 'It's probably kinder if you do just forget, isn't it? But, somehow, I don't think one does. I think you're probably always aware everything's slipping away from you. Such a shame. I have some lovely memories of the children growing up at Trade Cottage, for example. Playing in the woods, helping with lambing . . . It will be sad not to be able to remember all that.'

'And, Rosemary . . . About this solar-farm business . . .' Kate began.

'Oh, that.' Rosemary's eyes went to the fields. 'Well, *I* don't want to look at solar panels either – of course I don't. But family has to come first.'

'Does it?' Kate ventured. 'What about . . . friendship?'

'Friendship?' For a moment, Kate thought Jamie had been right, and Rosemary was going to deny that was what the two of them had, and she braced herself for the inevitable hurt that would cause her. But the other woman only said bleakly, 'I've had friends in the village before. Some of them for decades. But then the grandchildren come along and they get busy. You see less and less of them, and eventually they move away to be near where their children live, and by then you hardly notice they've gone. And so it goes on – everyone else, preoccupied with family, and you treading water. No one ever talks about that, do they? The . . . *grief* of not having your grandchildren around you. Having all this energy, and nothing to put it into except making jam no one will eat and working the till in a charity shop where the only customers are other old people. Don't you see? Jamie and his family are all I've got now. If he doesn't move into Trade Cottage, I don't know what I'll do with myself. Let alone how I'll cope with what's coming my way.'

'But he *isn't* all you've got,' Kate insisted. 'You've got me – *us* – Tilly and Will, who adore you—'

Rosemary shook her head. 'Even so. You wouldn't want to be responsible for a dribbling, incontinent zombie.'

'It would be a privilege,' Kate said gently. 'And anyway, all that could be years away. Did the doctor—'

'What the fuck is going on here?' Jamie's voice said incredulously.

She looked up. He was about ten feet away, his face a mask of fury, striding towards them as if he meant to lay hands on her and physically pull her away from his mother.

She jumped up. He had his father's height, and if he did get violent there'd be nothing she could do, but she didn't want him towering over her when he did it.

'You were told to stay away from here,' he snarled.

'It's not up to you,' she retorted. 'It isn't your house.'

'Nor yours.' He looked at Rosemary. 'What's she been saying to you?'

Rosemary said meekly, 'Kate just popped in to see if I was all right. The coroner's officer has been suggesting all sorts of nonsense—'

Jamie's face darkened. 'He shouldn't be talking to you without me here, either. I'll have a word with our lawyer.' He gestured to Kate. 'Now hop it, before I call the police.'

# FIFTY-FOUR

She walked back to Trade Cottage the long way round, so as not to give Jamie the chance to berate her for going through the forbidden gate. As she walked up the dilapidated drive – some of the potholes seemed to be growing, she noticed, and even joining together in places – she considered what she'd just witnessed. Apart from Paul's funeral, when the Finches had been on show, it was the first time she'd seen Jamie and his mother together. It had been brief, but she couldn't help thinking how directive he'd been with her – disrespectful, even. Of course, he'd been angry. And he'd previously been a big beast at the IMF, used to telling people what to do. But if Will had spoken to Kate the way Jamie had just spoken to Rosemary, she'd have pulled him up on it immediately.

Once again, she had the feeling that this wasn't just a battle for Trade Cottage. It was a battle for its former owner, too.

A few minutes after she got home, there was a knock on the front door. It was Oliver Wray, the coroner's officer, again.

'I've now spoken to all the contractors who were here when Mr Finch died,' he said, 'and I've still not found anyone who saw you reacting to the sound of the shot. I'd like to take the clothes you were wearing that day, please.'

He caught her puzzled look and explained, 'To test for gunshot residue.'

'Oh . . . But I've washed them.' For a moment, she wondered if that looked suspicious. But she hadn't been able to shake the idea that some of Paul's blood might have got on them.

'If it was an ordinary wash, that doesn't necessarily negate the tests. I'll wait here, if that's all right.' Politely but firmly, he stepped inside the house.

She went to get the clothes. At least this should prove she had nothing to do with it, she thought. Or were tests like this more ambiguous than that? It was impossible to prove a negative, after all. She wondered if Rosemary had also been asked to provide what she was wearing.

When she came back downstairs, Oliver already had a clear bag open for her to put the clothes in. 'We'll need a DNA swab, as well,' he added.

They went into the kitchen. It was as he was scrubbing the swab against the soft tissue inside her cheek, with her jaws open wide and feeling at her most vulnerable, that she heard a frantic banging on the front door and shouts from the men outside. The drainage tanker, she realised, had been turned off – the noise of its pumps had stopped. Through the window, she could see men in hard hats abandoning their diggers and running up the lawn.

'There must have been an accident,' she said, as Oliver put the swab into a container. 'I'd better go and see what's happened.'

'Of course.' He placed the container in a bag and wrote her name on it. 'In any case, I'm done.'

She went to the front door. The drainage contractor, Mick, was there, his face ashen. 'What is it?' she asked.

But he was looking past her, into the house. 'Is he still here – the coroner's officer?'

'Yes. Why?'

'We've called the police, but he'll want to know about this.' He hesitated. 'We've found a body in the pond.'

# FIFTY-FIVE

Oliver Wray's immediate concern was to make everyone move back, so nothing was disturbed before the police got there. Even so, Kate, glancing involuntarily at the pond as she was shepherded past with the others, got a horrific glimpse of some white bones – a ribcage and what looked like a jaw, still wrapped in a leather jacket with a fur hood, lying half-submerged in the mud. Nearby, gold glinted from the buckles of what might have been a handbag.

'Everyone back behind the tanker,' Oliver ordered as one or two workmen still pressed forward to see. 'Right back. Now!'

Kate saw the drainage contractor, Mick, turn to Steve, the builder. 'It's her, isn't it?' he said quietly. 'Martina. It must be.'

The builder nodded. 'I remember the police circulating a picture of that jacket. Fake leather and fur, they said. Must be why it hasn't rotted. And if she was in that pond, it must be—'

'Probably best not to speculate,' Mick said quickly.

Kate saw Steve bite back his words. He'd been about to say *it must be murder*, she realised with a shock of horror. And who was Martina? She turned to Steve, to ask him, but he and Mick had already moved away, back behind the tanker.

Moments later, the police arrived – two squad cars, followed by a van. They made everyone move further back still, then began taping the area off. Kate recognised Sergeant Dickinson. She was getting the builders to move their vehicles. Only the drainage tanker stayed where it was, its hoses still in the pond. Nearby, two scenes of crime officers were already pulling on the white paper overalls familiar from a thousand TV shows.

Sergeant Dickinson came over to speak to Kate. 'We may need you to evacuate the property, so you should go and pack a bag, in case. If we don't require that, we'll put screens around the retrieval scene, so your children don't have to see it. But you should be aware that going past those tapes under any circumstances is a criminal offence.'

'I understand,' Kate said. She hesitated. 'One of the tradesmen seemed to think he knew who it was. He mentioned the name Martina.'

'It's obviously much too early to speculate,' Sergeant Dickinson said firmly.

'Of course. But . . . who was Martina?'

There was a pause before the sergeant answered. 'It was way before I joined. Back in the nineties, as I understand it, there was a young woman who went missing from this area. Her name was Martina Boban. But it's far too soon to say that's who it might be.'

'She had a distinctive fake leather jacket, apparently,' Kate persisted, but she was trying the officer's patience now.

'You need to go back inside. We'll let you know if we need anything else.'

Aware she was more likely to be told to leave Trade Cottage

altogether if she made a nuisance of herself, Kate nodded meekly and did as she was instructed.

She packed a suitcase, then called Matt. They considered taking the children to a hotel even if they weren't told to evacuate, but decided against it. Will and Tilly would hear about the discovery of a body at Trade Cottage eventually, in any case. Better to explain before they got home, then make sure they stayed inside the house until the remains had been taken away.

She told Matt about the acoustic test earlier, and Oliver Wray taking a DNA swab and her clothes, apparently as a result of Jamie's insinuations.

'It'll just be process,' Matt said reassuringly. 'They have to eliminate possibilities, that's all.'

'Let's hope that's all it is.' A sudden thought hit her, and she gasped. 'What if it's connected?'

'What is?'

'This body and Paul's suicide. We've been assuming he killed himself because of his MND, yes? While Jamie's been implying it's because we got permission to make all these changes to his beloved Trade Cottage. But what if Jamie's actually right? What if Paul shot himself now because he was worried about what we might find when the building work started?'

There was a pause while Matt digested that. 'That seems pretty far-fetched,' he said at last.

'Is it, though? It would explain why he was always so against Trade Cottage being bought by developers. *And* why he was so keen for Jamie to buy it back. He even had a go at me about digging up the garden. His standing in this community has always been so high. Losing that, over something as awful as this – the shame would be devastating.'

'But he couldn't have known for certain the pond was going to be drained,' Matt objected. 'It's complete chance that body was ever found.'

'True,' Kate admitted. 'But what if he didn't know its precise location? What if he only knew it was somewhere in Trade Cottage's grounds?' She hesitated, knowing that what she was about to say was so momentous, it might even sound a little crazy. 'What if he suspected Jamie of killing this Martina woman all along?'

# FIFTY-SIX

Matt had a meeting, but promised to get home early. Meanwhile, Kate googled the name 'Martina Boban'. To begin with, she sat at her usual spot to do it, at the captain's desk. But the oriel window looked over the pond, screened off now with large barriers, and the constant activity as scenes of crime officers went back and forth was too distracting. She took her laptop to the kitchen instead.

There was almost nothing online. In a way, that wasn't surprising. As someone who'd been a teenager herself in the 1990s, Kate often struggled to explain to Will and Tilly just how different it had been. Mobile phones were the preserve of people who needed them for work, and in any case, didn't connect to the internet. To do that, you had to make an expensive phone call down a landline, from a computer the size of a suitcase. There was no WhatsApp, no Facebook, no digital cameras – no portable digital music player, even, apart from maybe a Sony Discman, if your parents were rich enough. And no digital news sources. Whereas today a missing person's details would be plastered over newsfeeds and social media within hours, back then there simply weren't any websites carrying that kind of information. There'd been the BBC's Ceefax service, but, when she tried to search that, she discovered it had been mothballed years ago.

She did find the National Crime Agency's missing persons register, which had a brief entry for Martina Boban and a photograph. The photo, which was grainy and looked as if it had been cropped from a larger image, showed a dark-haired young woman in a shiny black jacket that had a hood with a fur trim. She was wearing big hoop earrings and a lot of make-up, although her eyes, below her heavily shaped eyebrows, were somehow younger-looking than the rest of her face. The entry read: *Martina Boban, F. Age last seen: 21 yrs. Nationality: Croatia (Former Yugoslavia). Last known location: Pelham, Hampshire. Date: September 1993. Constabulary: Hampshire and Isle of Wight.*

An idea occurred to her. She brought up the website of the local paper, the *Hampshire Chronicle*, to see if it had a searchable archive. She was in luck – it did. She typed in 'Martina Boban'.

There were three articles. The first was headed *HAMPSHIRE WELCOMES REFUGEES FROM BALKAN TROUBLES*. It was dated 1991 and was mainly about three families who'd fled fierce fighting in Yugoslavia, where both Slovenia and Croatia had declared independence from Serbia. The reference to Martina was a brief one:

> **Several young women from the former Soviet country are believed to have come to Hampshire by applying for nanny and au-pair visas at the UK border. One, Martina Boban, from Vukovar, recently contacted the *Chronicle* for help with finding employment.**

The next, from September 1993, was headed *POLICE INVESTIGATE MISSING AU PAIR:*

**Croatian au pair Martina Boban, 21, has not been seen for two weeks after a night in her local pub with friends. Anyone with information should contact Hampshire and Isle of Wight Constabulary.**

The third article was from November 1993 and was headed *MISSING AU PAIR 'FEARED RETURN TO CROATIA', POLICE SAY.*

**Martina Boban, 21, who has not been seen since 7 September, was nearing the end of her two-year au-pair visa, police say. She had told a friend she was worried about being refused refugee status in the UK, which would have meant returning to her country of origin, Croatia. Over the last year, the UK has become less receptive to refugees from the region, with local MPs and others saying there are insufficient resources to cope with the current influx of asylum seekers, many of whom find work illegally if their claims are refused.**

Kate sat back, thinking. Reading between the lines, there'd been less of an outcry, and therefore perhaps less of an investigation into Martina's disappearance, because she was from war-torn Eastern Europe, her family quite possibly displaced by conflict themselves. Kate remembered those wars only very dimly. Decades on, of course, Croatia had become a smart holiday destination and a fully fledged member of the EU, but back then, like the other former Soviet Union countries, it had seemed very far away and unknown. She did recall, though, that those were the conflicts which introduced the term 'ethnic cleansing' to the world, and that there had been war crimes alleged on all sides – Serbian, Bosnian, Kosovan, Croatian. And – again, reading between the lines – perhaps, when the police drew a blank, it had been easy to conclude that Martina had simply decided to vanish, rather than return home to an uncertain future.

There was a knock at Trade Cottage's front door. On the doorstep was Sergeant Dickinson, accompanied by two white-suited SOCOs. They were both wearing masks and hairnets, and carrying what looked like large battery-powered torches.

'This is Martha and Kim,' Sergeant Dickinson said. 'Would it be all right if they looked round? I've told them you've recently redecorated, but they'd like to do a quick sweep for residues all the same.'

'Of course,' Kate said. She registered the startling implication that, if there had been foul play, the person in the pond might have been killed in Trade Cottage. It was obvious, when you thought about it, but somehow she hadn't connected the gruesome discovery outside with the possibility of violent murder in these very rooms. 'But if it was so long ago . . . ?'

'Even so, it might be useful,' either Martha or Kim said through her mask. 'Is it all right if we draw the curtains?'

The reason for that request became clear when they closed the wooden shutters in the entrance hall. Their torches produced powerful beams of ultraviolet light, which they passed slowly over the oak panelling. Any patches that lit up were examined more closely and, in a couple of cases, scraped with a scalpel for further testing.

Kate waited in the kitchen with Sergeant Dickinson while they did the rest of the house – the police officer resisting most of Kate's attempts to find out more about the investigation, although she did let slip that a forensic archaeologist was now on site, and that they hoped to remove the remains later that day.

After about forty minutes, Martha and Kim returned. 'You really have redecorated,' one of them said to Kate with a sigh.

'Top to bottom,' she agreed. Then she thought of something. 'Did you do the cellar?'

The SOCOs exchanged glances. 'What cellar?' one asked.

'We call it the secret cellar,' Kate explained, 'because it's so hard to find. The entrance is under the stairs, but you'd never know unless you were looking for it. It's the only place I haven't painted – I just cleared out some of the junk.'

'Could you show us?' one of the SOCOs asked.

She took them to the understairs cupboard and showed them how the floor lifted up to reveal steps down into the darkness, and how the light switch in the cupboard turned on bulbs to illuminate the descent.

'I can stay here and turn them off once you're down there, if you like,' she suggested.

The SOCOs made their way down, then shouted back to her when they were ready. She turned off the light. After a moment, the cellar glowed with ultraviolet as their torch beams roved back and forth.

There was a shout: 'Could you turn the light on again?'

She did as she was asked. She heard some muttered conversation, a grunt as something was moved. Then another shout: 'And off?'

This time, the ultraviolet was only on for about thirty seconds before she was asked to turn the lights back on. The SOCOs emerged tight-lipped, but Kate could tell something was up when they asked her not to go into the cellar before they got back.

They returned a few minutes later with two more white-suited figures, men this time, and between them heaved something up the cellar steps. It was, she saw, the battered old sofa.

Kate recalled what Rosemary had said, when they'd asked her about the cellar's contents: *Jamie used to have parties down there, before he and his friends were old enough for the pub.* If they'd found residues on the sofa, she realised, there was a very good chance they were connected to him.

# FIFTY-SEVEN

She took the children to a café to break the gruesome news about the pond. Both were upset before she even started. Will was being teased at school, he told her miserably – other boys were making a gun shape with their fingers, putting it into their mouths and pretending to pull the trigger – while Tilly reported that girls in her class were saying she had nasty parents. Kate spent a bit of time unpicking those developments first – people didn't necessarily mean to be cruel, they were just insensitive and trying to get a reaction, and so on – but inwardly she was seething. If it got any worse, she'd definitely be marching into both schools to demand the heads did something. They made such a big deal of having counsellors and pastoral care on tap for tragedies these days; how could they let their pupils be so brutal to two children who'd been traumatised by suicide?

The news about the body in the pond, therefore, fell on already poisoned ground. Will said immediately, 'It's like Trade Cottage is cursed,' and Tilly started crying.

'It would have been a very long time ago,' Kate said, trying to reassure them. 'Before you were even born.'

'That makes it *worse*,' Will said. 'Think how long it's been lying there, with no one even knowing.' He shuddered. 'I fell in that pond once. I could have *stood* on it.'

'I want to go back to London,' Tilly said wistfully. 'Nothing bad ever happened there.'

Strictly speaking, that wasn't true, but right now Kate didn't feel like disagreeing.

By the time they got home, most of the police vehicles had gone. That was something, at least. There was just one left – occupied, Kate saw as they passed it, by Sergeant Dickinson. On guard duty, presumably, to make sure no one interfered with the scene. Kate waved as she passed, and made a mental note to go out later, to see if there was anything she needed. It might be the pond the sergeant was officially guarding, but Kate couldn't help feeling safer for having a police presence at Trade Cottage.

As the three of them went towards the front door, she glanced back and saw Liv Hoggart from the book club, carrying a bunch of flowers. Assuming she was coming to the house, Kate waited for her. Then she realised Liv was heading for the police barrier tape round the pond. Crouching down, she placed the flowers on the ground next to it.

As she stood up, she saw Kate. 'I hope you don't mind,' she said, indicating the flowers.

'Of course not,' Kate said. 'That's a lovely thing to do. She might be a stranger, but we can still treat her with respect.'

To her surprise, Liv started to cry.

'What is it?' Kate asked.

Liv gulped. 'I don't think she was. A stranger, I mean. People are saying it's Martina.' She saw Kate's puzzled look and explained, 'Our au pair.'

Kate took her inside. She knew Liv had been in the area a long time, but she hadn't realised that she grew up in Roley, just a few miles away.

'Lots of people had au pairs, in those days,' Liv said, as Kate made a pot of tea. 'Even if you didn't work, like my mum, having four kids was exhausting and an extra pair of hands really helped. They didn't get paid much – around fifty pounds a week, I think – but they got bed and board and the chance to travel. Mostly they came through agencies, but Martina had been in the local paper, so Mum contacted her through that.'

'And when she went missing, it was completely out of the blue?' Kate asked, bringing the tea over to the island. 'There was nothing that led up to it?'

Liv wiped away a tear with her finger. 'I didn't think there was, at the time. I mean, I was only eleven. I really liked her. She was quite glamorous – she wore a lot of make-up, and she had all these miniskirts and tight tops. Guy Pelham used to come by in his sports car sometimes, to take her to the pub.'

'She knew Guy?'

Liv nodded. 'There was this whole group of young people, seventeen-, eighteen-, nineteen-year-olds knocking about, a bit bored and getting up to mischief. I mean, it's not like there's that much to do in the country, so people made their own entertainment.'

'What kind of entertainment?' Kate asked, thinking of the party venue in the cellar.

Liv shrugged. 'So, for example, Guy's car was low enough that he could come up alongside a pheasant and then Jamie could quickly whack the passenger door open to kill it. Or they'd drive round shooting at the road signs with air rifles. Classic young farmers' stuff.'

'Sounds lovely,' Kate said. 'But they were neither of them farmers, surely?'

'Oh – no, I meant the Young Farmers' Club. It was them who organised most of the social stuff round here. It had a pretty rowdy reputation.'

'And Martina was part of that scene?'

Liv pulled a face. 'Kind of. She certainly went out a lot. My parents weren't very happy about it, but the arrangement was she had to stay in two nights a week to babysit, and the other evenings were her own. Once, Mum made a comment about her burning the candle at both ends, and she just shrugged and said, 'I've only got two years to find myself a husband.'

'She actually said that?' Kate asked, surprised.

Liv nodded. 'It was half a joke. But that was the thing with Martina – you couldn't always tell when she was joking. And she also talked about applying for refugee status, or about this friend of hers who'd moved to London and was waitressing without papers – no one ever checked, apparently. But, when she vanished, we were sure it wasn't that – she'd left most of her stuff behind, for one thing. And she'd told Mum she'd only be gone a couple of days. That was something she did sometimes – went away for a night or two. They assumed it was with a boyfriend, but she was quite cagey about it – she never gave them a name.'

Liv was silent a moment. 'I used to ask her about boys. I mean, I was just at the age where I'd have loved to hear her go on about her Prince Charming or whatever. But she'd just laugh and say, "Oh, I don't have time for *boyfriends*." Like that would have been soppy.'

'Could she have been seeing Jamie Finch?' Kate asked.

Liv looked startled. 'It's possible, I suppose. But if so, it was very under-the-radar. All the girls were after Jamie – you should have seen the way they flocked round him at the tennis courts or in the pub. He never had a girlfriend for more than a week or two. He and Guy and their friends from private school were like this herd of young gods, all headed for Oxford or Cirencester or wherever. They didn't want to tie themselves down before they got there.'

A thought occurred to Kate. 'What if she was pregnant?'

Liv's eyes widened. 'Martina?'

Kate nodded. 'This is pure speculation, obviously, but what if she was? And then told the father she was going to keep it . . . I'm pretty sure the authorities wouldn't be able to send her back to a war zone then. And she'd be entitled to child support from the father, too.'

Liv looked shocked. 'You can't know that's what happened.'

'No,' Kate admitted. 'But it could explain a lot, couldn't it? Why she died – maybe even why she was here, in Trade Cottage's pond—'

'You're saying *Jamie* might have killed her?' Liv said, appalled. 'I know you and he haven't been getting on since he came back, but that's a wicked thing to suggest. Particularly with no evidence whatsoever.'

Oh dear, Kate thought. Liv was right, of course – she might dislike Jamie, but she had absolutely no grounds for pinning a decades-old death on him. And, caught up in following her own, undoubtedly biased, train of thought, she'd voiced out loud suspicions that were probably better kept to herself, given the febrile atmosphere in Pelham just then.

She said quickly, 'I shouldn't have said that – you're right, it's just idle speculation and I'm probably letting everything that's been going on colour my judgement.'

But she couldn't help adding, 'The police have taken away an old sofa from the cellar, for forensic examination. Whatever happened, I'm sure they'll get to the bottom of it.'

Liv nodded, mollified. 'Will you be coming to the next book club? It's at Sally's house.'

'Oh . . .' Kate was tempted to snap that of course she wasn't going to book club, not when Sally seemed to be one of those who thought she was responsible for Paul's death, but she decided, this time, to keep her own counsel.

'I'd love to,' she lied, 'but I'm just a bit busy with everything that's going on.'

# FIFTY-EIGHT

She updated Matt after he got home. But he also had some news for her.

'I've been asking round about Jamie. It turns out a couple of people I know in finance know him too, from way back.'

'And?' she prompted.

Matt shrugged. 'The consensus is, he's a great guy. Likeable, sporty, a bit wild in his youth, but a solid family man now who you'd definitely go out for a beer with, if you found yourself in Washington. But you were right – he got thrown out of the IMF for inappropriate behaviour. Or, more accurately, comments. My informant put it down to strait-laced Americans not getting British banter, but apparently he described an intern as "gratifyingly slutty", and she found out and complained. It wasn't the first time, either – after that complaint, a whole bunch of women started coming forward about what my contact called "colourful language".'

'Somehow that doesn't surprise me.'

'There were complaints about him taking an overly hard line with juniors, too,' Matt added. 'Expecting them to get his lunch, bawling them out in front of the whole team, that kind of thing. Stuff that, a few years back, might have been acceptable alpha-male behaviour. But it seems he failed to realise that the world's moved on.'

That might explain the latent anger she sensed in him, Kate thought. If Jamie believed he'd lost his high-flying, high-status job unjustly, and had decided to retreat to his childhood home to lick his wounds – the place where, in Liv's words, he and his friends had once been like 'a herd of young gods' – it must have been galling, to say the least, to discover that Trade Cottage, too, had moved on, and he couldn't just stroll back into his former life. And to have her refusing to be charmed or bullied into giving him what he wanted, when it had also been a woman, a lowly intern, who'd triggered his disgrace at the IMF – perhaps that, too, helped to explain why the ownership of Trade Cottage had become such a totemic fight, one he was determined to win at all costs.

'That all fits,' she said, nodding. 'I'm sure there's a link between him and those human remains, too. I just don't know what it is yet.'

'But you'll leave it to the police to deal with, yes?' Matt said gently. 'I know it sounds awful to say it, but, in some ways, this is really good for us. If he *is* investigated over Martina's death, it would completely alter the context around those Alzheimer's claims, for example. It feels as if the system might actually be on our side for once.'

'Of course,' she agreed. 'The best thing all round is if the police nail him themselves.'

But that didn't mean not doing all she could to give them a

helping hand. After she'd got the children to bed, she took a mug of tea and some biscuits out to Sergeant Dickinson, still maintaining her lonely vigil in the police car.

'Thanks,' the policewoman said, winding down her window and accepting them gratefully.

'Will you be here all night?' Kate asked.

Sergeant Dickinson nodded. 'They're going to sieve through the mud tomorrow. After that, we should be out of your hair.'

'Look,' Kate said tentatively, 'this may be none of my business, but that woman who was here earlier, with the flowers – her name's Liv Hoggart. If it turns out it *was* Martina Boban they found, you might want to talk to her.'

She explained what Liv had said about Martina's connection with Jamie and Guy Pelham.

'Also,' she added, 'and again, none of my business, but . . . Would the forensic people have any way of knowing if she was pregnant when she died? Because, from what Liv was saying, that might have been a possibility, too.'

Sergeant Dickinson cocked an eye at her, and for a moment Kate thought she was going to be told off again for being nosey. But the policewoman only said, 'I probably shouldn't tell you this, but there's going to be a presser first thing tomorrow anyway, to try to jog people's memories. It's more than a possibility she was pregnant – it's a near-certainty. They found some forensic evidence with the body.'

# FIFTY-NINE

'Apparently, there's a particular bone that only starts to form at around twelve weeks,' Kate told Matt when she was back inside. 'If Oliver Wray hadn't been here, making everyone get back, it would probably have been trampled into the mud.'

'We can't know for sure the baby was Jamie's, though,' Matt objected.

'No, but they'll be able to get DNA from it. That's partly why they're doing a press conference – they want every man who had contact with Martina to come forward to be swabbed, for a screening programme.'

'Wow.' Matt was silent a moment. 'But, whoever the father was, they won't come forward, will they? They've spent the last thirty-odd years thinking they've got away with it.'

'There'll be some people the police approach directly. "Persons of interest," as the sergeant put it. So if Jamie refuses, it'll look pretty suspicious. And that's even before they examine that sofa.'

Later, as they were getting ready for bed, Matt said, 'By the way, I've told Will he can download *Fortnite*. It's a shooting game, and it's rated 12, but it's what he wanted for Christmas anyway and I think having it a bit early might cheer him up. His friend Andy plays it and he's said Will can join his team. He heard through the gun club what a good shot Will is, apparently, so that seems to have smoothed things over between them.'

'That's a good idea,' she agreed. 'He certainly needs a boost.'

'I'll play with him the first few times, to make sure he's got it set up safely. From the sound of it, it's quite like a shooter called *Quake* I wasted far too much time on, back in the day.' Matt was silent a moment. 'Though if I'd never got into gaming, I'd never have started the company, so perhaps it wasn't completely wasted time.'

She shot him a glance. 'Is all that still horrible? Work, I mean?'

'Still tough,' he said with a sigh. 'Perhaps ironically, I'm learning a lot more than I ever wanted to about contract-dispute law. It looks like we'll have to go to mediation.'

She got into bed and hugged him. 'Poor you. The last thing you need right now is this distraction with Jamie Finch.'

'On the plus side, if we do end up in court over the sale of the house,' he said grimly, 'at least I now know a very good contract lawyer.'

The next morning, after breakfast, she dropped the children off at the bus stop as usual. They were still getting their kit out of the car when a white Tesla going in the opposite direction screeched to a halt, then did a U-turn, blocking her in.

Jamie Finch jumped out of the driver's seat. Striding towards her, he banged on her window with the side of his fist. He clearly expected her to open it. Instead, she checked the children were safely over at the bus stop, then locked all the doors.

'Open this,' he yelled through the glass.

'I can hear you fine, thank you,' she retorted. At the bus stop, a dozen or so children were watching, open-mouthed. A couple of the older ones had pulled out their phones to film it.

Jamie bent down so his face, just the other side of the glass, was very close to hers. 'Stop spreading your fucking lies,' he snarled. Flecks of his spit dotted the glass in front of her. 'I'm warning you – stop.'

He was incandescent with rage. Liv must have repeated Kate's speculation about him being the father of Martina's child, she realised, and that the sofa was being tested by the police. And, in a place like Pelham, unfortunately, telling one person was the same as telling everyone.

He hammered on the glass with the side of his fist again, more to make her flinch than anything. 'I fucking told you the gloves would come off. Well, now they have.'

He looked over the bonnet at Tilly and Will, who were watching the confrontation with a mixture of embarrassment and fear. Turning back to Kate, he said, 'You killed my father.' He was speaking more quietly now, so only she could hear. 'An eye for an eye?'

'Leave my family out of this!' she cried.

'Bit late for that.' He stood up to his full height. 'In the meantime, I'll tell the lawyer to add slander to the list. Believe me, he is really going to do a number on *you*.'

She was still shaking when she got home. As she got out of the car, she heard the sudden boom of a gas gun, which, in her current razzed-up state, made her jump. And, if she wasn't mistaken, that was the buzz of a motocross bike in the wood, too. Jamie's foot-soldiers, rallying to his defence.

With the police there, at least there was no likelihood of him following her back to Trade Cottage. But she'd be sure to log this latest incident, all the same. She made a mental note to ask Will if he knew any of the kids who'd been filming it.

Outside the house, she met Steve, the builder, getting some tools from his van.

'You were right,' she told him. 'It's almost certain it's Martina. There's going to be a press conference.'

He nodded, digesting that, then cast a glance at the pond, still screened off for the scenes of crime officers. 'Poor girl.'

'Did you know her?'

He shrugged. 'Only to say hello to. We all drank in the Pelham Arms – some of us were underage, but back then they weren't too worried about that. There was a group of older private-school kids who kept a bit separate from the rest of us. She used to hang out with them.'

'What sort of person was she?' Kate asked, curious.

'Nice enough.' He considered for a moment. 'I didn't think it at the time, but, in hindsight, maybe a bit naive. My mum would have called her tarty. You could tell the other girls in the group didn't like her, but the boys liked that about her, too. They'd wind the other girls up by talking about the things Martina would supposedly do for them – "Go on, Martina, flash us your tits again," that sort of stuff. I don't suppose half of it was true, but there was this atmosphere of them all egging each other on.'

'Did she hang out with anyone in particular?'

Steve thought. 'Well, they all wanted to buddy up to Guy Pelham. It's like that, round here – they try not to let it show, but the posh lot are all over anyone with a title. To be fair to Guy, he's not a snob – he'll talk to anyone – but the people who hang around him usually are. And they don't like other people getting too close.' He nodded and went on his way.

Inside the house, she went and checked her laptop. It looked as if the press conference had already happened – there was a short clip of it under 'Breaking News' on the *Hampshire Chronicle* website. The senior investigating officer, a woman about Kate's age, read out a short statement to the effect that human remains, believed to be those of a pregnant female, had been found at a location in Pelham. Tests were ongoing to determine whether the remains might be those of Martina Boban, missing from the area since 1993. A DNA screening programme was being established to try to identify the father, and any man who had contact with Martina was being asked to come forward for elimination purposes.

The SIO added, 'Because it is believed the pregnancy was at an early stage, the father may not have been aware of it. It's too soon to speculate about how she died, but at the moment we can't rule out natural causes.'

They were only saying that so people wouldn't be scared off from getting swabbed, Kate thought. Presumably they had no way to compel people. What was the betting Jamie would simply refuse – if necessary, hiding behind those expensive lawyers he was so fond of?

She drummed her fingers on the table in frustration. The fact the remains had been found at Trade Cottage pointed at him being involved in some way, but it certainly wasn't proof. That pond was right by the drive – anyone could have backed a car up to it and rolled a body, weighted with stones perhaps, into the water.

For want of anything more concrete to do, she went into the study and located the box of papers Rosemary had left under the bath. She vaguely recalled seeing some of Jamie's old school reports in it. Perhaps there would be something useful to be learnt from them.

She went through the box, putting everything relating to Jamie on one side. She wasn't even sure what she was looking for. A name, perhaps – some schoolfriend, still living in the area, who she could question for more information.

There was nothing, beyond the confirmation that Jamie had been academically bright as well as sporty, ultra-competitive, and successful in everything he did. But, as well as the reports, there were a dozen or so photographs celebrating rowing victories – Jamie and his fellow oarsmen, posing with their boats. They'd clearly been taken by the official school photographer: they were encased in cardboard frames that had the name of each crew member listed on them.

At least that gave her something to work with. She selected the photos from Jamie's last year at school, then googled the names. In most cases, there were simply too many hits to be useful, but when she added the name of the school – 'Townley's' – she found a few people who'd included their place of education in their LinkedIn profiles.

She started to draft an email to send them. But, after a few lines, she hesitated. What, really, was she asking? Whether their fellow rower was an arrogant, angry, bullying shit? Whether they'd ever seen him with Martina Boban? Whether he was capable of murder?

Mindful that Jamie had undoubtedly been telling the truth when he'd threatened to come after her for slander, she contented herself with sending a link to the press conference and saying that, if the recipient had any relevant information, please could they contact the police.

That done, she sighed and closed her laptop. If anything, her sense of impotence had only increased.

As she went into the kitchen, she glanced out of the window. Biddy, the black Lab, was trotting up the lawn, Rosemary following a few paces behind him. That was fortuitous – Kate might not be allowed through the gate herself, but there was nothing to stop her going and talking to Rosemary if she came through it. She went outside.

'Oh, Kate, there you are,' Rosemary called when she saw her. 'I'm so sorry – Biddy must have decided he'd get his tea at Trade Cottage's back door again. And you know how stubborn he is when he starts to think about food.'

'No problem,' Kate said. 'It's lovely to see you.' She glanced at Biddy. It didn't look to her as if the dog was thinking about food – he wasn't drooling, or thumping his tail, the way he usually did when he was hungry – and, in any case, it was far too early for his tea. It seemed more likely that Rosemary had wanted to come round to talk to her, and following a wandering Biddy was her cover story if Jamie found out.

'I take it you've heard the news?' she added.

Rosemary stopped. 'So it's true? A body in the pond? And they think it's Martina?'

Kate nodded. 'Why don't you come in, and I'll tell you what I know.'

She actually knew very little, of course, but she wanted to see what Rosemary remembered about Martina.

'I felt sorry for her,' Rosemary said simply, as Kate handed her a mug of tea. 'She was such a long way from home, and people she knew there were being killed – her own relatives, even. And being Pam Hoggart's au pair wasn't much fun, poor girl. Pam was completely chaotic – she couldn't make up her mind whether Martina was a refugee she was housing out of the goodness of her heart, or an incompetent employee who didn't know how to cook the children's meals properly. One minute she was saying, "You poor thing, it must be terrible," the next she was shouting at her. And she wasn't the only one who didn't know how to deal with her. This village can be a bit funny about outsiders.'

Don't I know it, Kate thought. 'And . . . Jamie?' she ventured. 'Liv thought perhaps there'd been something there. Or with Guy Pelham, perhaps?'

Rosemary was silent a moment. 'Well, possibly. I suppose I felt bad for her over all that, too.'

'Over all what?'

'Jamie and his friends . . . They were young men, and I don't suppose they were any crueller than other young men are, but they did rather make fun of her behind her back.'

Interesting, Kate thought – from what Liv had told her, it had sounded more like Guy and Jamie had almost pursued Martina. Or perhaps that was just how Martina had spun it to herself.

'They're saying she might have been pregnant,' she prompted gently. 'If so, is there any possibility Jamie could have been the father, do you think?'

Just for a moment, she thought she saw a flash of anger, deep in Rosemary's eyes.

'I've no idea,' she replied haughtily. 'I haven't asked him and I don't intend to. But if she *was* pregnant – well, I'd say more fool him, for not being more careful. He should have realised that was probably exactly what she wanted.'

'Rosemary!' Kate remonstrated. 'You can't know that.'

'Can't I?' Rosemary tutted. 'Oh, I know we're meant to say girls are always the victims and boys are in the wrong, but, whoever the father was, perhaps it was *him* who got taken advantage of.'

'Except that she *was* the victim,' Kate said gently. 'Somebody killed her.'

Rosemary shot her a glance. 'That's what they're saying, is it?'

'Not in so many words,' Kate admitted. 'But the circumstances look pretty suspicious.'

'Well, Jamie wouldn't have hurt her,' Rosemary said firmly. 'I can promise you that. He might not be perfect, but he believes in decency and fair play.'

Kate decided not to challenge that. 'When was the last time you saw Martina? Can you remember?'

There was another silence. Then Rosemary said angrily, 'Of course I can't. It was all so long ago – I can barely remember what she looked like. I'm sure you know I've been diagnosed with dementia. So I can't be expected to know anything about anything.'

# SIXTY

'You were right,' Kate told Matt later. 'That dementia diagnosis is definitely fake – or, at any rate, exaggerated. She hides behind it when she chooses to, but she seemed to recall events in the 1990s perfectly well before that.'

'Which makes you think what?' Matt asked, reaching into the fridge for a beer.

'Well – it did cross my mind that Rosemary herself might have killed her,' Kate admitted. 'I mean, she's definitely tough enough – look at the way she dispatched that duck. And the coroner's officer is asking all these questions about Paul's death. He says he's just being careful and considering the options, but something seems to have made him suspicious.'

'So your new friend might be a geriatric serial killer?' Matt said, amused. 'It seems a bit unlikely, though. And, anyway, *why* would she kill this au pair?'

Kate shrugged. 'To protect Jamie's glittering future, maybe? He was just about to go off to Oxford, after all – to become a champion rower like his father, and make all the connections that landed him a stellar career in international finance. That family – they're obsessed by success, aren't they? Or, at least, the appearance of it. Everything has to look as if it's perfect: the perfect childhood, in this, the perfect setting; the perfect hosts; successful, high-flying kids . . . Back then, a baby with Martina might have seemed like a terrible encumbrance for her golden boy to start his adult life with. And, although Rosemary claimed she felt sorry for Martina, she sounded pretty unsympathetic about her pregnancy.'

'OK. But you're doing exactly what you promised not to do,' Matt said gently. 'Trying to solve the mystery yourself. Leave it to the police, yes? We've got enough on our plates.'

# SIXTY-ONE

*THIS IS YOUR FINAL WARNING YOU FUCKING WHORE. YOU ARE TOO UGLY TO ENJOY RAPING BUT YOU WILL GET IT ALL THE SAME. AFTER THAT IT WILL BE BOTH BARRELS OF A SHOTGUN IN THE FACE – THEN AT LEAST YOU WON'T BE SO FUCKING UGLY*

# SIXTY-TWO

The police had left the previous evening, but Sergeant Dickinson had given Kate her phone number. Kate called her and read the contents of the latest note aloud, her voice shaking despite her efforts to control it.

'This must be something the police can follow up now, isn't it?' she added. 'I mean, it's clearly a death threat. Not to mention the other stuff.'

The sergeant sighed. 'Send me a photo of it and I'll pass it on to a detective. But, honestly? I know it's horrible to be on the receiving end of something like this, but the police are shown similar material all the time. Mostly online, admittedly, but gathering enough evidence to catch and charge the culprit over something like this is very, very hard.' She repeated her advice to keep everything, and told Kate to get back in touch if it escalated further.

The screens around the empty pond had been removed now, so Mick laid hoses to start refilling it. At least the ducks – who'd been marooned on their little island for the past few days – were grateful, paddling back and forth in the slowly rising water. But, looking at the sludge-brown liquid, stirred up even more than usual by the hoses, Kate couldn't shake off the thought of poor Martina, lying underneath the wych elm all those years, unseen and ignored. It somehow felt as if Trade Cottage itself had been violated, and was urging her to make some kind of restitution.

But what could she do? She had no way to compel Jamie to take a DNA test, and even if Martina's own DNA was found on that sofa, it wouldn't prove he was involved in her death.

Back in the study, her eye alighted on a second pile of papers she'd put aside as she'd separated out Jamie's school reports. There were no commemorative sports photos of Tessa, just a couple showing her dressed up for her school proms. She'd been pretty, but it seemed to Kate that her weight had yo-yoed more than was usual for a teenager. She recalled Rosemary saying something about an eating disorder. She wondered about that – at the very least, it hinted at a darker side to the sunny idyll of Trade Cottage.

She typed 'Tessa Finch' into her browser. Again, there were too many hits to be useful, so she narrowed it down with 'commune + Wales'.

She was in luck. The very first link was to the website of a self-styled 'intentional community' called Fawr Carreg, situated in the Preseli Hills, Pembrokeshire. She clicked on it. The home page showed twenty or so people gathered outside a large stone farmhouse – a mixture of adults and children, with a couple of dogs and half a dozen goats. Tessa was holding one of the goats in her arms.

Kate scrolled down to the blurb below: *We are diggers, dreamers, activists and educators. But first and foremost, we are the stewards of this ancient land – 90 acres of beautiful pasture, woodland, orchard and stream.*

*We strive to work in harmony with its needs and rhythms, and to be sustainable and self-sufficient in all we do.* A 'Donate Now' button suggested they weren't necessarily achieving the last of those aims.

Further pictures showed vegetable beds, polytunnels, more goats grazing in tiny fields, a coppiced hazel wood and a farmhouse kitchen with a huge communal table. It all looked stunningly beautiful – like a rugged version of Trade Cottage, perhaps.

She clicked on 'Visit'.

*We welcome visitors to Fawr Carreg, both to volunteer their labour and to learn from our community. We make a small charge to cover our expenses.*

She was going to Wales, Kate realised. She was going to go and speak to Tessa.

# SIXTY-THREE

Pembrokeshire was five hours away, so she had to wait until the next day, when Matt was working from home and could mind the children, who were breaking up for Christmas. She'd never been to the Preseli Hills, and was surprised to find herself, towards the end of her journey, on a high, wild, empty moor, scattered with massive rocks of blue granite. A brooding peak loomed over the village where, according to her satnav, Fawr Carreg was located. But, when she got a little closer, the farm turned out to be nestled in the foothills – still a harsh environment, but it would be glorious when the sky was blue. Today, though, it was as dark as Welsh slate, the December wind blowing cold and sharp. It looked like it mostly blew in this direction, in from the sea: the trees were shaped into elaborate quiffs, leaning forward on their trunks like so many inquisitive skulls.

She'd emailed ahead to say she was coming, but not why. She'd used her full name – she didn't want this conversation to be based on any kind of subterfuge. So she wasn't surprised when Tessa opened the farmhouse door and, in response to Kate introducing herself, nodded and said, 'Yes, I know who you are. Jamie could talk about no one else before Dad's funeral. After it, too, for that matter.'

'I'd say I'm flattered, but it wasn't all favourable, I imagine,' Kate said as she followed Tessa into the big farmhouse kitchen she'd seen on the website.

Tessa smiled, and for a moment she reminded Kate of Rosemary. 'Not all of it, no. The fact that it's a woman who's got the temerity to refuse to hand back his childhood home makes it even worse. So, you see, I was favourably predisposed towards you from the start.'

That was promising, Kate felt. 'You've heard the recent news, I take it?'

'About poor Martina?' Tessa nodded. 'I still have friends in the village. How horrible, to think she was there all that time. Do you want something to eat? I missed lunch, so I'm going to have some soup while we talk.'

'That would be lovely.' She watched as Tessa cut two slices of sourdough to toast on the Aga's boiling plate, warming a large saucepan of soup on the other one.

'It's all our own,' Tessa said matter-of-factly as she gave the soup a stir. 'Potatoes and leeks from the veg tunnels, bread made by Gareth. And this is my contribution.' She placed a slab of white cheese on the table. 'Home-made feta from the goats. Crumble some into the soup – it's great like that.'

It was all delicious. 'I once spent a very happy few days learning to make jam with your mother,' Kate said, cutting more bread. 'She was going to show me how to make wild garlic pesto, too, though I don't suppose that'll happen now.'

'Dad did love that pesto,' Tessa said, smiling. 'I used to pick the leaves every year with Mum. It's too rocky for wild garlic here, unfortunately. But I make a herb pesto sometimes.'

Kate hesitated. 'I was thinking about something, on the way here. Back in the summer, Jamie invited your parents to Washington, for Christmas. Rosemary told me they weren't sure they could manage it, what with Paul's wheelchair. But, looking back, I think she didn't really want to go.'

Tessa shrugged. 'She probably didn't. But I doubt she'd have admitted it, even to herself. She knows Jamie's a total shit, but she wants everything in and about Trade Cottage to be perfect. So she pushes it out of her mind. Her Rosemary-tinted spectacles, I used to call it.'

She caught Kate's look of surprise. 'Sorry. But if you didn't come all this way to hear me dissect our family dynamic, why have you come? And, yes, if you're thinking it's just sibling rivalry, you'd probably be right. Jamie's love-in with Dad was a hard act to follow. Particularly as I never had the height for rowing.'

'That was pretty much my reading of the situation, too,' Kate said. Tessa was more waspish than her mother, she thought. Not abrasive, exactly, but certainly forthright. It must have made for some interesting arguments with Jamie, growing up.

'I suppose I mostly came to find out about Martina,' she added. 'Whether Jamie ever hung out with her – went out with her, even – and if so, what they were like together.'

Tessa shook her head. 'They certainly never "went out" in any formal way. And I didn't see them together much – I was only fifteen or so when she was around. But you've got to understand what a toxic twosome my brother and Guy Pelham were. Always egging each other on to say or do gross things, particularly about girls. I think, after a while, they barely noticed they were doing it.'

'What sort of things?' Kate asked, curious.

'Oh . . .' Tessa thought, then said wearily, 'Well, they were completely obsessed with cum. I was there once when a girl called Fenella Croft said something about her mother getting a facial. God – Jamie and Guy thought that was *so* hilarious. But what they thought even funnier was making Fen realise what she'd said, then embarrassing her in front of everyone. After that, she was "Fenella Facial" for life. Guy used to tell me he'd give me a pearl necklace for my sixteenth birthday, and wouldn't that be nice? Luckily – or unluckily – you couldn't be around my brother for long and not know what *that* meant. So I just told him he wouldn't have enough for a bracelet, let alone a necklace.'

'Ugh . . . So what did they say about Martina?'

Tessa shrugged. 'To begin with, it was stuff like "double bagger".' She caught Kate's puzzled look. 'That's a girl you'd sleep with, but only with a bag over your head in case the bag over her head broke. Later on, it got even more unpleasant . . . I'll spare you the grisly details.'

'But either Guy or Jamie definitely did sleep with her?'

'Well, I never asked Jamie directly – he'd only have told me in graphic detail. But what Jamie wants, Jamie usually gets. Guy, too.' Tessa hesitated. 'In fact, I think they might even have done it together.'

'A *threesome*?'

Tessa nodded. 'One of the things they used to go on about was something they called a "spit roast". I mean, I don't know for sure that happened. But, afterwards, they started calling her Miss Piggy behind her back, or making *oink-oink* noises whenever her name was mentioned.'

'But, if something like that did happen . . . they'd have used condoms, surely?' Kate said, aghast. 'They'd have been mad not to.'

Tessa nodded. 'You'd think. But they were shagging the same girls, anyway. And Jamie always hated condoms. Said they were a waste of a good facial.'

# SIXTY-FOUR

She drove back to Hampshire feeling dispirited. Not because of Tessa, who she'd liked. She'd gone to Wales expecting to find some vague, unworldly hippy, only to meet a down-to-earth, slightly acerbic cheesemaker, who – it transpired, when she introduced Kate to her herd – knew every one of her goats by name. The irony was, Kate reflected, that Tessa had found herself somewhere genuinely idyllic in the end, quite unlike the poisoned paradise that Trade Cottage had turned out to be. Perhaps those nights spent lambing as a child with Gordon had been more formative than anyone realised.

No – her low mood was more because of what Tessa had told her. Of course, she'd been talking about a time over thirty years ago, long before MeToo, but Kate knew that the culture she'd described – teenage boys belittling the same girls they so desperately wanted to have sex with; girls going along with it purely to get the boys' approval – was still just as pervasive. It was one of the reasons she'd wanted to leave London – the very worst stories on Everyone's Invited seemed to be about London schools – but she realised in hindsight that had been naive of her. The problem was people, not places.

She was going to have to start talking to Will about things like porn, consent and respect soon, she reflected. He wasn't yet twelve, and she still thought of him as a child, but those conversations were probably best begun before the hormonal conflagration of puberty started raging through his brain. Tilly, too – she had to know she could always call out unacceptable behaviour.

There was another reason for feeling crestfallen. On the face of it, her trip to Pembrokeshire had been a waste of time – Tessa had told her nothing worth passing on to the police. The possibility that Martina might have had a threesome with Guy and Jamie was only that, a possibility. Even if true, it hardly provided a motive for murdering her—

A sudden thought flashed into her brain. There was one motive so massive, it would surely be worth killing for.

*Pelham Park.*

What if the baby wasn't Jamie's, after all? What if Guy Pelham was the father? It would have been difficult to know for sure before it was born, of course, particularly if the circumstances of its conception were as grim as Tessa had suggested. But even the possibility that the future heir to Pelham Park would be born to a Croatian au pair would provide a credible reason for killing her.

She examined the idea from different angles. What was the legal situation with aristocrats' illegitimate offspring, these days? She dimly recalled an Act of Parliament in the 1980s granting them the same rights as legitimate children. It would still have had to be a boy to inherit – when they abolished male primogeniture for the royal family, they'd specifically excluded the aristocracy, she knew. But the point was, there would have been a risk.

Tessa had called Jamie and Guy 'a toxic twosome'. In a situation like that, would Jamie help his friend by offering somewhere to hide the body? Might they even have killed Martina together, and together rolled her weighted body into the pond?

She was almost home now. On a sudden impulse, she decided to go and see Pelham House for herself. She'd often passed the grand stone gatehouse that guarded the park's entrance, but even though events were often held there – shows, country fairs and the like – she'd never gone through it.

She did so now. Ahead of her, the drive curved away through some woods, the house not immediately in view. It was several hundred yards before an artfully constructed gap in the trees framed a lake, with the house on a rise behind it, floodlit.

And what a house. It was Alconleigh, it was Pemberley, it was Brideshead, Manderley . . . She remembered the description of Pemberley in *Pride and Prejudice*: 'a large handsome stone building, standing well on rising ground.' It was so like Austen to use the word 'handsome' of a house. But, looking at Pelham House now, it seemed apt.

She thought of her own, possessive love for Trade Cottage. Yet, compared with Pelham House, Trade Cottage was almost insignificant – a mere "cottage", indeed. If she was prepared to fight tooth and nail for her own menial little hearth, she could only imagine how fiercely the owners of Pelham House would defend it from all comers.

She'd pulled up to look. There was a Land Rover parked nearby, but she'd already seen there was no one in it. She was just about to turn her own car round when Guy Pelham emerged from the trees, followed by two black Labradors.

'Park's closed,' he shouted, clearly annoyed. Then he saw who it was.

'What do *you* want?' he said, approaching.

She got out. 'I've been talking to Jamie's sister,' she said defiantly.

He frowned. 'Ten-ton Tessa? Why?'

'I suspected Jamie'd had sex with Martina, but I hadn't realised it was both of you. Or how badly you both treated her.'

He grunted. 'She got what she wanted out of it.'

Kate shook her head. 'Not what she really wanted. As you very well know. She might have been a couple of years older than you, but she was desperate and naive, and you took advantage.' She decided to take a long shot. 'Tessa told me about the threesome, too.'

Just for a moment, Guy Pelham couldn't help smirking. 'Yes, that was quite a night.'

'A night that could have had big consequences.' She turned her gaze towards Pelham House.

'What d'you mean?' he said, frowning. He seemed genuinely puzzled.

'I'm going to tell the police everything I know. If you haven't already had your DNA screened, you need to.'

'What? You are one mad bitch,' he said, shaking his head. 'As for the screening programme, haven't you heard? It's been called off. They've found a match.'

It was her turn to be puzzled. 'Already? Why? Did Jamie come forward?'

'Jamie? Christ, no. It turned out to be someone they already had on file.'

She was stunned. 'But – who?'

He shrugged. 'They haven't said. But she slept with dozens of people round here. There won't be any shortage of contenders.'

# SIXTY-FIVE

She got home even more demoralised. All her charging around the country had achieved precisely nothing. And, while it was great that the father of Martina's baby had been found, which would hopefully lead to some kind of justice being done for her, it seemed it wouldn't help Matt and Kate in their fight against Jamie for Trade Cottage after all.

'But I did discover that he's an even bigger sleazeball than we thought,' she told Matt. She relayed her conversation with Tessa, and her realisation that it was time to start talking to Will about relationships.

Matt nodded. 'I was thinking the same thing.'

The sound of their son's voice floated down the corridor. 'Round the back! Two of them behind the building! Take them out!'

'Though, right now,' Matt added, 'he does seem a lot more interested in killing people than sex.'

'*Fortnite*?'

Matt nodded. 'I've set it up in the small sitting room. I've been checking in on him – it all seems OK.'

'And Tilly?'

'Outside, getting Fresco his hay net.'

She nodded, reassured. 'You know, it's funny to think of them – Tessa and Jamie – living in these same four walls as us. Like ghosts, almost. Trade Cottage is a bit like one of those medieval manuscripts that got scraped down and reused, but which still bears the imprint of the previous writing if you look hard enough.'

'Or an old musical instrument,' Matt suggested. 'They say violins are changed by the people who've played them down the centuries. Maybe houses are the same.'

'And it's true the other way round, too, isn't it?' she said thoughtfully. 'Trade Cottage is still such a huge part of who its former occupants are today. Jamie believing he's entitled to whatever he wants in life, Tessa living off the land.' Something else occurred to her. 'You know, I wonder if some of Jamie's obsession with getting this place back isn't to do with Guy. Guy inherited his house, after all. Perhaps, by reclaiming Trade Cottage, Jamie can feel he's still almost his equal. When the truth is, he's just a failed banker with a grudge against women and too much money to throw at lawyers.'

Alerted by Matt's sigh, she added, 'Is there any news about that?'

Reluctantly, he nodded. 'Anwar was hoping the judicial review might get thrown out at the application stage. But, unfortunately, they've been given the green light. We'll need to start spending big on legal fees soon.'

She put her hand on his arm and squeezed. Then she added, 'Incidentally . . . When Jamie was ranting at me the other day, he said something about how I'd killed his father.'

'And?'

'Then he looked at the children and said, "an eye for an eye". I wonder if he meant . . . he should kill *you*.'

Matt said reassuringly, 'I'm sure he was just trying to scare you.'

She sighed. 'Well, he's succeeded. The way he looked at the kids . . . And those poison-pen letters are getting more and more deranged. Be careful, won't you?'

Matt nodded. 'Of course. But you too, yes? And make sure you put that threat of Jamie's in the log, along with everything else.'

# SIXTY-SIX

Most of Saturday passed without incident, unless you counted the motocross competition that was being noisily contested in the woods. The only silver lining was that Will, watching the little bikes from the kitchen, said thoughtfully, 'That looks quite cool.'

Kate glanced at him, surprised. 'Would you like to try it?'

He nodded. 'Maybe.' He wandered off, back to his game.

She spent some time putting up Christmas decorations with Tilly, while Matt went out and bought a tree, which they placed at the base of the stairs. At about five, the bikes finally packed it in. She heard Will shouting from the small sitting room, but assumed he was simply engrossed in a *Fortnite* battle. It was a moment or two before she caught the anguish in his tone and realised something was wrong.

She hurried to the sitting room. Matt was already there, holding a bawling Will. She glanced at the computer screen. It said in big letters: *ELIMINATED BY HAZHAM.*

'What's happened?' she asked. 'Did he lose?'

'Worse than that,' Matt said quietly. 'He was wiped out by his own teammates. They ganged up on him somehow – I didn't catch the details; it's quite hard to do, apparently. And it was this guy, Hazham, who did it.' He paused. 'He's another friend of Andy's – a bit older than Will, with an American accent, Will said. I think it might be Hamish Finch.'

Furious, she snatched up Will's headset and said into the microphone, 'How could you? That is completely despicable behaviour.' She heard laughter, barely suppressed, and flung the headset down again.

They were still consoling Will when Tilly came in. 'Mummy, something's wrong with Fresco,' she said anxiously. 'He's not eating and he looks uncomfy.'

Kate got a torch and went outside with her to see. She was no expert, but even she could tell, from the way the pony was pawing the ground and sweating, that it was in pain.

Abruptly, Fresco threw himself to the ground and rolled. When he got up, he was breathing hoarsely. The whites of his eyes looked red, as if they were bleeding.

'What's that?' Kate said, pointing. On the floor of the stable was some odd-looking blue grain. She'd seen something like it before, she was certain, but she couldn't remember where.

Tilly said nervously, 'I don't know. But he was eating it when I came to skip out. Didn't you give it to him?'

'No,' Kate said. Suddenly she remembered where she'd seen grain like that before. The pest controller had poured a couple of scoops into a bait box.

'Oh my God,' she said slowly. 'I think it's rat poison.'

Pulling out her phone, she called Fresco's owner, Mary Snow.

'Call the vet,' Mary said at once, when she'd explained. 'No, I'll do it – they know me and they'll come out straight away. In the meantime, try to get him to drink, and walk him in a circle. He'll want to roll, but it's best not to – he might twist his gut.'

'Got it.' And then, because Tilly, next to her, was desperately asking if Fresco was going to be all right, she said, 'How serious is it?'

Mary hesitated. 'It depends how much he's got hold of. A pony's a lot bigger than a rat, but they love grain, and that blue stuff's been coated with apple juice, so it's even more attractive. Horses can't vomit, either, so any kind of colic can be fatal. Is Tilly with you?'

'Yes.'

'Get her to walk him. Walking's to distract Fresco, as much as anything, but it'll distract her as well. And, if it is a bad outcome, at least she'll feel she did all she could.'

By the time the vet arrived, Fresco's head was drooping and Kate thought, when she shone the torch on him, that she saw blood glistening in one nostril. A tremor shuddered up the pony's neck.

'Yes, this looks like rat poison all right,' the vet said grimly as she prepared an intravenous drip. 'It's an anticoagulant, so we're going to get some saline and vitamin K into him, then you can walk him again.'

When the IV line went in, Fresco bled profusely from the puncture wound.

'That's to be expected,' the vet said. 'But if he fits, or comes off his feet, I'm afraid we're in a very different ball game.'

Fresco staggered, and for a moment Kate thought he was going to collapse. Then he shook his head and steadied himself.

'Tough little fellow,' the vet said, squeezing the bag to make the saline go in faster.

The vet stayed until midnight, by which time she thought Fresco was probably out of danger. But she still wanted him walked every half hour. Tilly was exhausted, but there was no way she was leaving the pony, so Kate took over with the promise that Tilly could lie down in the stable and keep an eye on things. She was asleep within minutes.

Matt came out with coffee.

'Jamie?' he asked quietly, handing it to her.

Kate nodded bitterly. 'Who else? Maybe when he knew we'd be distracted by what his son had just done to Will. He could have nipped through The Old Tennis Court's back gate, emptied a couple of pouches of grain on the stable floor, and been out of here within a minute.' She glanced up at The Old Tennis Court. All the lights were off, but that didn't mean much. 'You know, it's a good thing we don't have a shotgun. If we did, I think I'd have emptied it into him by now.'

# SIXTY-SEVEN

Christmas Day that year was a miserable affair. They tried to make the best of it, for the children, but Will's present of *Fortnite* was tainted now, and Tilly had asked for a new saddle for Fresco, which, after it was unwrapped, only reminded her of the attempted poisoning. Even the tree Matt had bought sat rather forlornly at the bottom of the main staircase, somehow too small and timid for its surroundings, its flashing lights more reminiscent of a warning beacon than the cheery twinkling of stars.

Kate recalled Jamie's letter, the one she'd read out to the planning committee: *We have a lot of traditions around the holiday season, which we intend to enjoy as a family after your departure* . . . She wondered whether they'd transplanted those customs to their temporary accommodation at Pelham Park, and, if so, whether their day was as muted as the Crowthers' was turning out to be. No doubt Jamie was reassuring them that, by this time next year, everything would be different and they'd be back in Trade Cottage again.

It was the day after Boxing Day when, taking a binload of peelings out to the composter, she heard the rumble of a male voice in The Old Tennis Court's garden. Hairs prickled on the back of her neck, even before she'd identified it as Jamie's.

But it *was* him, there was no question – that insistent, hectoring drawl, answered by Rosemary's higher tones. It sounded as if she was trying to disagree with him. Kate moved closer, stealthily pressing up against the leylandii.

'But if I did that, *I'd* have to see it,' Rosemary was saying.

'It's hardly a big price to pay,' Jamie replied dismissively.

'Dumping rubbish outside my window?' Rosemary sounded disgusted. 'Is that really necessary?'

'We want the rats to come back,' he said calmly. 'If you scatter it under the hedge, you'll hardly see it.'

'Aren't I doing enough already?' Rosemary asked wearily. 'You realise they might stop me driving? At the very most, they'll only give me a temporary licence now.'

'Why d'you need to drive? Everyone round here delivers. Besides, you'll soon have us next door. Courtney can run you around, if you need to go somewhere.'

'You know I don't like to impose. And I have things I like to do. Helping at the hospice shop, seeing my friends . . .'

'You'll have your hands full with the kids. That's what you wanted, isn't it?'

When Rosemary didn't reply, Jamie's voice became curt. 'They're having to leave behind the grandparents they're closest to, in America. This is *your* fault, for making Dad leave Trade Cottage. You need to help me put it right.'

'You know very well it was him who wanted to move—'

'I know he wanted us to get Trade Cottage back. If you don't work with me on this, you'll be betraying his legacy.'

'His legacy!' Rosemary exclaimed bitterly. 'We both know what his legacy was. And how long do you think it'll be before the whole village knows, too?'

Jamie said harshly, 'If anyone tries to spread rumours, I'll have the lawyers on to them. The police, too. They're not allowed to slander a dead man who can't defend himself.'

'It would hardly be—'

'End of,' he cut across her. 'Now, either you dump your rubbish out here, or I'll take away your bin. When there's a nice big pile, I'll take some photos.'

It sounded as if he was already walking back to the house, his voice fading as he tossed those last words over his shoulder. Rosemary stayed where she was for a few moments – Kate heard her sigh – then she followed Jamie back up to The Old Tennis Court.

Kate didn't move. Her brain was whirring as she processed what she'd just heard. What had Rosemary meant when she spoke so bitterly about Paul's legacy?

Then she realised.

The father of Martina's child wasn't Jamie, or Guy Pelham.

It was Paul.

That was why the police had access to the matching DNA – there would have been tissue samples from the post-mortem. That was why they were no longer hoping to interview the father. They knew he was dead.

And that was why Paul had killed himself. Not because of his terminal condition, and not because of Kate and Matt. But because he'd guessed the secrets of the past were about to resurface, and he'd be revealed for what he was.

She did a quick calculation. Paul would have been near enough fifty when Martina got pregnant – almost thirty years older than her, which was shocking enough in itself. Old enough to feel his good looks fading? A mid-life crisis, a young woman in distress . . . And for Martina's part, perhaps, desperation as well as misery, when the young men she'd set her cap at took advantage of her, then tossed her aside. Perhaps it had even seemed like sweet revenge, to sleep with the father instead.

She walked slowly back to the house, thinking it all through. That snippet of conversation had revealed other things, too. That Rosemary's dementia diagnosis was trumped-up was hardly a surprise. But the ugly tone Jamie had used with her confirmed what Kate had suspected before, when she'd seen them together at The Old Tennis Court.

He was contemptuous of her. The Finches, she realised, were one of those families that created a glittering façade for the outside world, but at the core were deeply rotten. And what was the betting Jamie had picked up that attitude towards his mother from the other male member of the household, his father?

She waited an hour, pacing up and down, to give Jamie time to leave. Then she went back to the hedge and eased open the wooden gate.

She looked up at The Old Tennis Court. All seemed quiet. Even so, she went and checked the front. There was no sign of Jamie's Tesla, only the Popemobile.

Keeping well away from the Ring doorbell, she knocked on the side door.

When Rosemary saw who it was, she looked shocked. 'Oh! Kate. I'm not sure you should—'

'I need to ask you something,' Kate interrupted. 'And a lot depends on the answer, so please tell me the truth. Do you actually want any of this?' She gestured over at Trade Cottage. 'Jamie, living next door? You, at his beck and call? Me and Matt and the children, out of your life completely?'

There was a long pause before Rosemary said quietly, 'No. I don't want him here. I don't want him in Tray. That was all Paul. But now I don't think I can stop him.'

'Yes, you can,' Kate said. 'I'm going to help you.'

# SIXTY-EIGHT

She got Rosemary an appointment at the GP's surgery. She thought it best she didn't go into the consulting room with her, but she sat with her in the waiting room until her name flashed up on the screen. *Rosemary Finch – Dr Hazel Ground, Room 3.*

When Rosemary came out, she was clutching a piece of paper and smiling. Kate waited until they were in the car park before asking. 'Well?'

'I'm forgetful, but there are absolutely no clinical signs of dementia,' Rosemary said proudly. She held up the piece of paper. 'She's going to put it in a letter, so it's all official, but this is the test she got me to do.'

'May I?' Kate took a photo of it on her phone. 'I'll get this to our lawyer.' She hesitated. 'That's if you're still sure you want me to. Jamie's going to go ballistic when he hears.'

'It's got to be done,' Rosemary said simply. 'I should have stood up to him years ago. But it's never too late, is it?'

# SIXTY-NINE

Back at Trade Cottage, Kate made them both a celebratory pot of tea.

'Oh, that's better,' Rosemary said, drinking deeply. 'Do you know, I don't even like champagne. But it was so much a part of Paul's thing. He did so want everything to be *fun*.'

She gave Kate a sideways glance. 'I suppose you think now we had an awful marriage. But actually, most of it was good. There was just this small part that was . . . Well, one had to turn a blind eye sometimes.'

Kate said nothing. She wasn't about to voice a judgement about Rosemary's marriage – what would be the point, now Paul was dead? But she couldn't imagine how betrayed she would feel if Matt slept with someone else, let alone fathered a child with them.

Just for a moment, she wondered if she'd feel so betrayed she'd want to kill that other woman. But, no – surely her anger would be directed more at her husband. And in any case, Rosemary appeared to be saying she'd been able to overlook Paul's infidelities.

'And you mustn't think . . .' Rosemary added. 'I mean, I'm sure Paul didn't kill her.'

'I agree,' Kate said, nodding. 'That is, I think he knew she was dead, or at least suspected it. But I don't think he knew exactly where her body had been hidden. It was the building work, after all, that prompted him to kill himself when he did – that, and the diggers in the garden. So I think he imagined that whoever did it had buried her, and that, once the contractors arrived, it was only a matter of time before she was found.' She paused. 'He might even have been protecting that person – hoping all the blame would rebound on him, instead.'

Rosemary shot her a hurt look. 'You're not still trying to say it was Jamie!'

Privately, Kate did think that was the most likely scenario, but again, it seemed unlikely she'd gain anything by saying so. Instead, she said, 'Anyway, I think we should tell people. About Paul being the father of Martina's child, I mean. And about your diagnosis being wrong.'

When Rosemary started to protest, she added, 'It's the only way Jamie's ever going to back off. Once it's out there, he's hardly likely to want Trade Cottage anymore. Most likely, he'll decide to start again somewhere new, where nobody knows the family history.'

Rosemary was silent for a moment. 'You're talking about trashing our reputation.'

'I'm talking about telling people the truth,' Kate said gently. 'It won't be hard to get the word out. If you tell Liv and Sally, for example, it'll be all round the village by nightfall.'

'Easy for you to say,' Rosemary said angrily. 'I've known my neighbours most of my life.'

'Then you know they'll rally round and support you,' Kate said. 'The decent ones, anyway. And I really do think it's the only way.'

After a moment, Rosemary sighed. 'All right. I'll call Sally this evening.'

# SEVENTY

Kate waited on tenterhooks for Jamie's reaction. How would he respond? She couldn't help fearing another assault on Trade Cottage, or – perhaps even worse – The Old Tennis Court.

But the days went by, and none came.

Perhaps it was true what they said about standing up to bullies, she thought. When you showed them you wouldn't be beaten, they just slunk away.

One evening, she and Matt were getting the children to bed when there was a loud knocking at the front door. They both stiffened.

Matt said quietly, 'I'll get it.'

She followed him downstairs. Abruptly, he pulled the door open.

But it wasn't Jamie. It was Jason from the pub.

'Sorry it's late. I just wanted to give you these.' He handed a startled Matt two pizza boxes.

Still fearing violence, perhaps, Matt handed them back to her, so he'd have his hands free. The boxes were warm, the contents, when she opened them, freshly baked in the pub's woodfired oven. A peace offering.

'I loved that man like a father,' Jason said simply. Without another word, he turned and walked back to his car.

A cold snap arrived, the first of the winter. It started with a frost so hard, it looked like snow on Trade Cottage's lawns. Cobwebs that had been invisible a week before now hung thick and silvery from every branch and window, as if strung from wet wool, while under the wych elm the pond formed a milky cataract that grew thicker every day. Then the real thing arrived – a snowfall deep enough to close schools, quilting the stone table, turning Kate's car into a giant pie topped with a thick white crust that the children soon broke into for snowballs. Trade Cottage's lawn turned out to be the perfect angle for tobogganing. They improvised sledges from sheets of cardboard wrapped in bin bags, and came in after three hours, wet but happy. Kate lit fires – Rosemary had been right, the one in the small sitting room smoked – and made hot drinks. The house was draughty, it was true, and not entirely watertight, but the Aga meant that the kitchen, at least, was welcoming.

She checked in on Rosemary daily. She, too, had heard nothing from Jamie, and for her part was perfectly happy about that. Kate offered to drive her to the shops if she needed anything – the roads were treacherous – but, rather to her surprise, the only trip Rosemary wanted to make was to the church, to visit Paul's grave.

In the churchyard, Kate helped her across the uneven ground – the snow here was already dotted with fresh molehills, the older gravestones leaning at random angles, like an advent calendar, glittery with frost – then stepped back to give her privacy. Paul had been buried next to their son, Andrew. There were some flowers on his grave, withered now by the snow, and Rosemary crouched down to tidy them up. She was talking to him, Kate saw, speaking out loud as if he could hear her. Telling him everything that had happened, perhaps.

After a while, she stood up, glanced at the smaller headstone next to Paul's, and came back to Kate.

'Perhaps things would be different if he hadn't died,' she said wistfully.

Kate started to say something about the grief still being raw, but Rosemary interrupted her.

'Not Paul. Andrew. One felt such a failure. And – well, I think I overcompensated. We both did. Trying to give Jamie everything Andrew would never have. It probably wasn't very good for him.'

'You're not to blame for what Jamie became,' Kate said gently.

'Blame? Possibly not. But responsible. As mothers, we always are.'

Kate dropped her off at The Old Tennis Court, then went on to Trade Cottage. As she parked – carefully: the compacted snow had refrozen and the ground was slippery – she noticed a duck flapping erratically by the frozen pond.

She suddenly realised it was the only one. The other ducks – around half a dozen – were all gone. But where? Their little island was covered in snow, and she could see what looked like webbed footprints . . .

*The ice.* The pond freezing over had made their island vulnerable to predators, she realised. Going closer, she saw feathers, a gruesomely bitten-off foot. A fox, doubtless itself starving in the snow, had killed them all.

The remaining duck was badly injured – one wing was almost ripped off, and its leg was bent at a peculiar angle. She took off her coat and threw it over the bird so she could pick it up. Then she hesitated. She could take it round to Rosemary, she supposed, and ask her to dispatch it.

Or she could do it herself.

Quickly, so she didn't have time to think about it, she got hold of its neck, twisted and pulled. The bird jerked and twitched. Then it was still.

Standing up, she threw it in the skip. It was horrible, and she felt mildly sick, but she also felt a surprising sense of achievement.

# SEVENTY-ONE

Matt called around six. He sounded worried.

'I'm at Waterloo – they're cancelling all the trains. Apparently, there's more snow coming.'

'Could you get to Basingstoke and get a taxi?'

'I doubt it, but even if I could, I'd never get back to London in the morning. And it's the mediation session tomorrow. Will you be all right if I go to a hotel?'

'Of course.' She hated it when he wasn't there at night, but it sounded like he had no choice. 'We'll be fine.'

She checked the local news. Sure enough, more bad weather was predicted to arrive later that evening. They were even talking about the possibility of thundersnow, a relatively rare phenomenon in the UK.

Already, high wind was making Trade Cottage sough and rock, like a ship straining against its anchor. She got the children to bed early with the promise of fresh snow and another school closure next day, then called Matt again.

He'd found a grotty hotel near Elephant and Castle. 'Everywhere else was full. But it's fine. I'll make it back tomorrow night, I promise.'

'Hope the mediation goes well.' They chatted some more before they rang off, Kate already pulling open the fridge and reaching for the open bottle of wine she knew was in there.

Then she froze.

In the fridge door, between the white wine and the grapefruit juice, was a bottle of Pol Roger.

# SEVENTY-TWO

She ran up to the children's rooms. Will was still reading, but Tilly's light was off. Flicking it on, she saw to her relief that she was there and all right.

'I need you to wake up, darling. I don't have time to explain now, but I need you and Will to go into Daddy's office and lock the door.' The attic room, directly above the children's bedrooms, was one of the few that had a lock.

Tilly started to protest, but Will, bless him, was already coming into her room. 'I'll take her. C'mon, Tills, we'll be fine,' he said, holding out his hand.

Kate dashed up to the next floor, to check the attic room was definitely empty, before going back downstairs. She wondered if she should arm herself with something – a kitchen knife, say. But it had always been drummed into them, back in London, that carrying a knife, even one you didn't intend to use, was what led to people getting stabbed.

Even so, she felt very exposed and vulnerable as she checked the downstairs rooms one by one. He could be hiding anywhere—

But he wasn't hiding. He was in the sitting room, standing with his back to her, looking out of the window. All you could see out there was black, flecked with occasional gobbets of snow that the wind was already flinging at the glass. But perhaps he was remembering what it had been like before, when he lived here.

He glimpsed her reflection in the glass and turned. For a moment, neither of them spoke.

'Saw you on the doorbell,' he said at last. 'Taking Mum to visit his grave. How dare you? How fucking dare you? That's my job.'

Of all the things she'd done, all the reasons to hate her, to focus on that seemed bizarre. 'She wanted to go, and the roads aren't safe. So of course I gave her a lift.'

'They won't bury *you* there,' he went on as if she hadn't spoken. 'Only proper locals get the graveyard. Our name still counts for something here. Despite your efforts to drag it through the mud. Emailing my schoolfriends. Spreading vile rumours about Dad.'

He took something from his pocket. It was a knife, she saw – the whittling knife Paul had given Will. It seemed a lifetime ago, now.

'This is mine.' He pulled it out of its sheaf to examine the blade. 'Dad had no right to give it to you. Just like this place.'

He seemed oddly calm – detached, even; the rage she'd sensed in him ever since his father's death strangely muted. Almost, she thought, as if the time for emotion was over, and this was now something else entirely.

'The tragedy is, all this could have been avoided,' he added. 'If you'd never invited them to spend Christmas here – if they'd never said they'd rather do that, than come to mine . . . I probably wouldn't have come back. So, you see, you've only yourself to blame.'

'You need to put that down and get out of my house,' she said firmly.

He snorted. 'Or what? You'll call the police?' He gestured outside the window. 'How fast do you think they'll get here in this? No, I'm afraid you're stuck with me. Quite literally.'

He held up the blade. 'The children go first. I've thought quite hard about that – whether it's worse for you to die knowing they're dead, or that I'm about to kill them. Tough call. But, in the end, I decided they go first.'

He was serious, she realised with a flash of horror. 'You must know you'd never get away with it.'

'You think?' He considered. 'Fresh snow covering my tracks, an alibi from the most prominent landowner in the area . . . I'd say I have a pretty good chance. And you've been getting death threats, haven't you? Anonymous notes in the post. That should keep the police busy for a while.'

'That was *you*,' she realised.

He nodded. 'Matt will definitely sell up after this, won't he? Can't see him living all alone in the house where his family was butchered. I'll probably get it for next to nothing. Nothing like the murder of some poor innocent kids and their mum to drive down the price.'

She couldn't help it – she glanced up at the ceiling, in the direction of the children. Her attention was only away from him for a second. But when she looked back, he'd vanished.

There was another door at the far end of the sitting room – once, in Trade Cottage's perplexing layout, the house's back door, although now it gave into the corridor. He must have gone through that. But to where?

She searched for him again, but it was like some terrible game of hide-and-seek, with him using his knowledge of the house to evade her. Drawing a blank, she went to the foot of the staircase. It didn't matter where he went, so long as he didn't go up there, to the children. So this was where she'd stay.

A sudden gust of icy air swept past her. He must have opened an outside door. But why? It seemed unlikely that he'd simply given up and gone away again. What was he playing at?

She went into the captain's study and, without turning on the lights, peered through the oriel window. The wych elm was thrashing in the wind, the last few leaves ripping from the bare branches, the shrubs tossing and straining from the ground as the storm intensified. Where the hell was he? And why?

Suddenly, he was there, right outside the window, grinning at her through the glass. He slid the ladder down from the scaffolding with one easy pull and scurried up –

The scaffolding. He'd realised he could use it to bypass the inside of the house completely. He'd see the children's bedrooms were empty, but it would only take him moments to climb to the next level, to the attic room where they were hiding –

She dashed to the open door. The wind, freighted with wet snow, hit her like icy surf breaking over her. She struggled to the ladder, then followed him up. The metal poles were freezing to the touch, the whole structure moaning and swaying precariously in the wind. As she climbed, she looked for something she could pull loose, to use as a weapon, but each pole was secured to the next with clips.

She reached the platform of wooden planks outside Trade Cottage's first floor. He wasn't there – he must have already gone up to the higher level. She took the next ladder more tentatively, in case he was waiting for her at the top.

He was standing at the attic room window, feverishly levering at it with his knife. Seeing her, he grinned wolfishly and pointed the blade in her direction, daring her to come and tackle him. When she paused, trying to work out what to do, he turned back to the window.

Inside, she heard Tilly scream. Desperately, she did the only thing she could – she put both hands against Trade Cottage's wall and pushed as hard as possible. For a moment, she thought nothing was happening, that the scaffolding wasn't going to give, but the savage wind was helping her and she felt movement underfoot. She wrapped her arms round the metal corner bar and got her feet against the wall, putting her back into it, trying to ignore the huge clots of icy snow pelting her face, and with a sudden wrench she felt the scaffolding peel away from the house, ripped off by the wind, the metal poles flying like matchsticks, the wooden planks collapsing under her feet. She saw his look of incredulity and shock, and then they were both falling, in a blur of wood and metal, a cascade of spars and planks and debris, and she mentally braced herself for the impact that was about to come.

# SEVENTY-THREE

Easter was late that year. The children still hadn't finished their spring term, but the first bluebells were already shimmering in the wood when Kate and Rosemary went down to look for wild garlic. She caught the heady, pheromonal reek of it as soon as they reached the trees. *Just follow your nose*, Rosemary had said to her, almost a year ago, but really, it was difficult to tell what direction it was coming from, so all-pervasive was the smell.

'This way.' Rosemary parted low branches with the agility of someone twenty years younger. You'd never have guessed she'd just turned eighty-four, Kate reflected as she followed.

They emerged into a small clearing. She recognised it as the same one Rosemary had brought her to when Kate came to measure for curtains, all those months ago. Back then, it had been bare earth, dusted with the skeletons of beech and hazel leaves. Now, it was a sea of vibrant green spear blades, with a few spiky white buds already thrusting up between them. This close, the garlicky smell was almost intoxicating. Deliberately, she inhaled, getting it deep into her lungs.

Copying Rosemary, she checked each leaf carefully before she added it to her trug, looking for blemishes or dirt. From deeper in the trees, a demonic head watched them warily. Then, unbothered, the muntjac pattered away, followed by its female and a tiny faun.

'This reminds me so much . . .' Rosemary looked around. 'I used to do this with Tess.'

'Yes, she mentioned it.' Kate glanced at her. 'She's very happy in Wales, I think. With her goats.'

'I know.'

There had been talk, in the weeks after Jamie's death, of Tessa coming back, to take care of her mother as she got older. But Rosemary would have none of it, and Kate had persuaded Tessa she was more than happy to keep a neighbourly eye out – and, indeed, to do more than that, when it eventually became necessary.

There was a companionable silence for a few minutes as they picked. Then Rosemary said, 'Did he really say that before he died? Jamie, I mean. In so many words?'

Something about the way she said it made Kate aware that this, rather than helping to pick wild garlic – which, in any case, scarcely required two people; their trugs were already almost full – might be the real reason they were here today, in this quiet, secretive spot.

'No,' she admitted. She'd told the police that Jamie had confessed to killing Martina, just before he clambered up the scaffolding. It had been one of several small fictions in the account she'd given them. Since she'd been lucky enough to land in a shrub, while he'd fallen on the lightwell to the cellar, breaking his back and dying almost instantly, she hadn't seen any reason to tell them she'd been outside too, let alone that she'd had a hand in the scaffolding's collapse.

But she didn't want Rosemary thinking Jamie had made some heroic, self-sacrificing false confession. He didn't deserve that.

'I only said that so they'd close their investigation,' she added. 'After all, if they'd decided it wasn't Jamie, and it couldn't have been Paul, because he didn't know exactly where Martina's body was hidden . . .'

'Yes,' Rosemary said, sighing. 'When you take away Paul and Jamie, there aren't many candidates left, are there?'

Kate didn't reply. Rosemary would tell her in her own time, or not at all.

After a few moments, the older woman said quietly, 'We would have had to sell Tray, you see. The shame – I think I could have weathered that. But she wanted so much money – enough for a nice house, and private school: all the things his other children had had, she said, or it wasn't fair. Paul refused to deal with it – he just blanked her, as if it wasn't happening. But she would have got a paternity test the moment it was born, and then everything would have come out.'

Rosemary gazed at the garlic with unseeing eyes. 'She came to the house one day, when she knew Paul wouldn't be there. She wanted to talk, she said, but really she wanted to crow. She hated Jamie by then, and I think she despised Paul, too. I met her outside, by the pond – I didn't want her in the house. I tried to reason with her – I even said we'd have the baby ourselves, that I'd bring it up at Tray as if it was our own. But of course that wasn't what she wanted. And then she said something derogatory about Trade Cottage, too – how it was an ugly old house anyway, and we'd be lucky to be shot of it – and I suppose I saw red. She turned her back on me at just the wrong moment and I . . . I hit her over the head with a stone.'

She paused. 'I never told Paul. Not in so many words. It was such an awful, monstrous thing to have done – I couldn't bear to tell him. He must have realised, when she just disappeared like that. But somehow it was easier never to speak of it.'

She looked at Kate. 'You're the only person I could ever say this to, but I really believe that, in some way, the house made me do it. Or is that completely mad of me?'

Kate shook her head. 'I've felt it too. Who knows? Maybe it's the bloodthirsty sea captain. Or maybe it's just because the house is so bloody lovely.'

'Perhaps.' Rosemary indicated the trugs. 'Shall we take these back up?'

# SEVENTY-FOUR

Later, when the pesto was made and she had Trade Cottage to herself again, Kate went around opening all the doors, letting the pale sunlight in. Taking a knife, she went outside and cut daffodils from the garden, and some magnolia blossoms, and a few crimson hellebores from the front of the house, where they'd miraculously survived the cascade of scaffolding.

She'd give a jar of pesto to Sally, she decided as she wandered, and another to Liv, and perhaps one to Jason. Relations with her neighbours were quietly mending, now she had Rosemary's seal of approval once more. Guy Pelham studiously ignored her when their paths crossed in the village, which she was perfectly happy about, but Gordon usually nodded; once, in the shop, he'd even muttered something about the children helping with lambing. There was still much she didn't know – she never did discover who those strange horseshoe nails belonged to, for example, or who had dumped the slurry on their drive, and suspected she never would – but that was all right: least said, soonest mended.

Coming inside, she got out vases and placed her little explosions of spring all around the house, brightening up the kitchen, the loo, the front hall. The very last vase she took through to the captain's study and placed on the desk, next to her laptop.

She was writing, now – or perhaps it was fairer to say, she was preparing to write. She had a document of half-ideas, jottings, notes for characters that might or might not coalesce into something. She had no idea yet what the plot would be, only that it would be set here, in Trade Cottage.

She touched a button and the laptop came to life. Sitting down in front of it, she took a breath, waiting for the house to come and whisper its secrets, and for the secrets to turn into a story; and in some strange way, it felt as if she and the house were one.

# AUTHOR'S NOTE

*'Houses are not like marriages . . . one cannot just walk out and leave them'*

– Daphne du Maurier

Two of my writing heroes, E. M. Forster and Daphne du Maurier, were both obsessed with houses. In Forster's case it was Rooks Nest, the house he'd lived in as a boy, which later became the template for Howards End. 'I took it to my heart,' he wrote soon after leaving, 'and hoped . . . that I should live and die there.' For du Maurier, it was Menabilly, the Cornish manor house she stumbled on, abandoned and almost derelict, while still a teenager, and which became, when she was stationed in Cairo with her husband during the war, the principal model for Manderley, as she dreamt *Rebecca* into life. That the success of *Rebecca* – and, in particular, Hitchcock's film version – made her wealthy enough to negotiate a twenty-year lease on the dilapidated property she had, at that point, barely stepped foot in, is one of fiction's extraordinary ironies.

Du Maurier's relationship with Menabilly was always an almost romantic one. In her autobiographical essay 'The House of Secrets' she describes how, after she saw it for the first time, 'the house possessed me from that day, even as a mistress holds her lover.' Her daughter Flavia noted her habit of occasionally kissing its stone walls: 'When she turned, her slightly flushed face had a look close to ecstasy.' Du Maurier herself wrote to a friend, 'I do believe I love Mena more than people', and compared having to leave it when her lease expired to the screaming of a pulled-up mandrake. I hope the ghosts of both writers will forgive me – Forster, for essentially stealing his premise, of a house spiritually bequeathed by one woman to another, and du Maurier, for pilfering these and many other instances of her attachment to her home. In particular, and in a spirit of acknowledging my debt, the last lines of *The Move* are a direct throwback to the last words of 'The House of Secrets': 'the secrets turn to stories, and in some strange and eerie fashion we are one, the house and I.'

Trade Cottage is not one house but many, a composite in a writer's head of several places I'm fond of. The speckled flint walls and secret cellar come from Tanners, the Hampshire farmhouse where I grew up; the bay window, wisteria-covered porch and panelled entrance hall from Peppard Cottage in Oxfordshire, which plays Howards End in the Merchant Ivory film of that name; the location, Smugglers Lane, from some particulars I found on Rightmove, which somehow kicked the whole project into being; the windows that open into another room from a house called Undertown in Cornwall, among others; the gardens and views from a neighbour; the pub and rural setting mostly from the village in which I live myself (my real neighbours are, of course, much friendlier than those in Pelham). I doubt such an architectural mash-up would ever get planning permission, but being able to create impossible dwellings is one of the pleasures of being a writer, and now that I come to move out of Trade Cottage myself, closing its eighteenth-century oak door behind me for the very last time, I find I'm already nostalgic for it.

In this, I'm not alone: in a 2017 survey, 62 per cent of respondents said they felt dread or nervousness at the prospect of moving from their homes, while a study in the same year by two neuroscientists found that homeowners love their houses as much as their pets or some family members. 'My house is not "just a thing." It is an extension of my physical body and my sense of self that reflects who I was, am, and want to be,' Dr Karen Lollar mused in a 2009 paper, a truth which may explain why houses have always been such a staple of psychological fiction.

My copy-editor has put a note in the margin of the manuscript at this point that says: *Remember to add individual thanks, here*. That reminds me that the first person I should thank is really her. Penny Price has copy-edited all seven of my psychological thrillers; if I sometimes look as if I can write without blunders, clunks, solecisms and howlers (but with commas, colons and, indeed, brackets) it's almost certainly down to her – having said which, of course, if any mistakes do remain, they're probably because I foolishly decided to ignore her advice on that occasion. I also want to thank the whole team at Quercus for their enthusiastic support and skilled brand-building over those seven books, most particularly Jon Butler, Kat Burdon and my wonderful editor, Stefanie Bierwerth. And, lastly but certainly not least, my thanks to my agent, Caradoc King, who this year announced his retirement after representing me for – unbelievably – the last twenty-nine years. Caradoc, you have steered me through bad times and good; I will always treasure in particular the memory of your wonderful, invigorating enthusiasm whenever I outlined a new idea or sent you a finished manuscript – thank you for that, but also for so much more than I can express with these few words.

I was wondering, as I came towards the end of the book, who I would dedicate *The Move* to. But I was also thinking about my own house, and how important it is to me. When we found it, many years ago, it was a near-derelict farmyard, with two small outbuildings that were partially collapsed, and a third knee-deep in cow muck but with potential for conversion. We synchronised building work with pregnancy, the idea being that our first child would be born here, a deadline that was frustratingly missed by just a few weeks. But it's where our second child was born, and where, just a few feet away, our third child died. It's where I wrote my first book, and indeed all the others too, and where I sit now, looking out over fields on a glorious spring day – as it happens, with the wild garlic just coming into leaf; tomorrow, my writing duties completed, I will go down to the wood and pick some to make pesto. It's where all our major family conversations have taken place; where we have loved, and sometimes argued, and cooked and eaten and drunk and grieved and danced. We have been, I recognise, incredibly lucky. So it seems appropriate to mark my gratitude, and dedicate this particular book, not to a person, but to a household god: the spirit of this place.

RAISING READERS

Books Build Bright Futures

Dear Reader,

We'd love your attention for one more page to tell you about the crisis in children's reading, and what we can all do.

Studies have shown that reading for fun is the **single biggest predictor of a child's future life chances** – more than family circumstance, parents' educational background or income. It improves academic results, mental health, wealth, communication skills, ambition and happiness.[1]

The number of children reading for fun is in rapid decline. Young people have a lot of competition for their time. In 2024, 1 in 10 children and young people in the UK aged 5 to 18 did not own a single book at home.[2]

Hachette works extensively with schools, libraries and literacy charities, but here are some ways we can all raise more readers:

- Reading to children for just 10 minutes a day makes a difference
- Don't give up if children aren't regular readers – there will be books for them!
- Visit bookshops and libraries to get recommendations
- Encourage them to listen to audiobooks
- Support school libraries
- Give books as gifts

There's a lot more information about how to encourage children to read on our website: **www.RaisingReaders.co.uk**

Thank you for reading.

hachette UK

[1] OECD, '21st-Century Readers: Developing Literacy Skills in a Digital World', 2021, https://www.oecd.org/en/publications/21st-century-readers_a83d84cb-en.html

[2] National Literacy Trust, 'Book Ownership in 2024', November 2024, https://literacytrust.org.uk/research-services/research-reports/book-ownership-in-2024